NINE LIVES

A JOURNEY THROUGH LIFE

by
Dan Fox

A Dolman Scott Book

Copyright Dan Fox/Ian Wilson 2010 ©

All rights reserved. No part of this publication may be reproduced, stored in a retrieval system, or transmitted in any form or by any means, electronic, mechanical, photocopy, recording or otherwise, without prior written permission of the copyright owner. Nor can it be circulated in any form of binding or cover other than that in which it is published and without similar condition including this condition being imposed on a subsequent purchaser.

British Library Cataloguing Publication Data.
A catalogue record for this book is available from the British Library

ISBN 978-1-905553-69-3

Published by
Dolman Scott

www.dolmanscott.com

To Vanessa Louise

Preface

Have you ever looked back?
Looked back on life?

Does it ever feel like the past must not be your own?
Cannot be your own?

As if parts must have been lived by someone else?
Someone different?

Like changing scenes in the journey of your life;
Different chapters; different lives.

And, just when you feel your life is finally under control, does all change?
The sudden arrival of some ugly presence, perhaps, or merely life continuing, not standing still?

In your darker moments, do you feel as if someone is throwing this at you, testing you?
That your life must be just part of some greater design, predetermined, beyond your control?

How far are our lives governed by the demands of the fates, by our karma?
Or are we all simply subject to the vagaries of luck?

Maybe, you see your life as a network of choices, proffered before you;
A web of opportunities, some to be taken to see where they may lead, others to be ignored.

A life of relationships with those who come into your life, for however long, good or bad;

Family, friends, lovers, relationships to be held, cherished for so long as possible, others to be let go.

Maybe, you see a life to be enjoyed;
A life to be lived.

This is my story so far;
A love story.

A story of feelings and emotions;
But, essentially, a book about life.

ARRIVING

Lights, bright lights, burning everywhere. Reds, greens, yellows and intense white, the decorative amidst the commercial, pretty fairy lights adorning the buildings mixed with huge neon signs promoting famous brands emblazoned high in the sky.

First impressions, a barrage to my senses, as I was ferried from the airport in the back of the limousine, newly arrived to the Territory of Hong Kong, to a land of excitement.

The lights of the Hilton came into view as the black car swung around the corner and swept up the driveway. Chinese lanterns hung from the canopy of the building, aglow with the burning amber of a thousand fireflies trapped inside, lighting the impressive glass entrance.

It was 1988 and this was a time when the Hilton still stood for the highest in luxury and their Hong Kong hotel was one of the finest; very opulent, with a polished marble entrance and huge pane glass doors.

Inside I could see a large ball of pink marble revolving in a plinth of water, the centrepiece of the lobby, a vast staircase behind sweeping upstairs. The walls were clad in a deep red wood inlaid with beautiful decorative veneers and the receptionists looked serene, all immaculately dressed in the long black traditional *cheongsam* Chinese dress.

The doorman in his bright red uniform with gold braiding marched over to open the car door but I did not get out; I sat there for a minute longer, taking in the moment. This is what life is about; this is what I had been working for. It was my dream. I had made it; *I had arrived!*

The next morning I awoke early; I had slept fitfully, excited and nervous at the prospect of this new life I was about to start. Opening the door quietly, I slipped out into the empty corridor to descend to the hotel's outdoor pool for a swim.

The air was already hot at six in the morning, like a cosy cloak, enveloping me in its warmth. I was completely oblivious of what was to come later when, by midday, the sun would be blazing and the air full with humidity.

I turned to float on my back, drifting awhile, my arms out wide, all quiet with my head half-submerged, the waters' calming touch at the sides of my face granting a welcome soft massage to my temples whilst muffling out any sounds of other life. Gazing upwards, the sky was a deep blue, framed on all sides by the shiny walls of glass of the neighbouring buildings reaching for the sky.

I floated some more, dreaming with eyes wide open, romantic notions of the traders and businessmen, the *taipans*, who had been here before me; the men who had built this place on a barren rock and created a world far from where they had come. A world I was about to join.

I knew I had not arrived here in quite the same way as they had done, fighting typhoons and pirates as they sailed across stormy seas in their old schooners, battling dysentery and scurvy as they raced to trade their goods to the new markets in the east, but this was still a long way from where I had started and to arrive here, I had also had my own struggles, my own battles to fight.

I showered quickly and put on my suit; a heavy British style which I would soon have to discard in the days to come as it became unbearable to wear in the heat, but when I first left England I had no money for such things as new lightweight suits and I was having to make do with what I had until the first pay cheque arrived.

I had been working in London these past couple of years for a relatively small multinational corporation and I had just taken a transfer to their Far East office. I had felt that I needed to make a change and hoped this move represented a chance for my work to become more exciting, more dynamic.

I was enthusiastic to get to work on this first day and to start my new life. I looked back to the rumpled sheets of the bed where I had just been. I could almost picture her; face down in the fluffy pillow, still sleeping, the curls of her long dark hair stretching over her neck to midway down her spine, the light sheets moving low to expose the small of her back.

She would have looked beautiful and it was the sharp sting of disappointment that she was not here with me that stopped me for a second, arresting my excitement for this new adventure.

In that moment, as I looked at the empty hotel bed, the memories of her flashed through my head, of how we had met, of how we had come to pass a wonderful summer together, but then, the memories were gone, just as she was also now gone from my life.

She, Louisa, was not here with me. No matter, I did not need her. I was about to start a new life of my own here and I turned to pull the door closed behind me.

LOUISA

He had first met her three years before back in London; he was not expecting it, he was not searching for it, he was completely unprepared.

It was in a bar, after work; he noticed her as soon as he walked in, sitting at the other end of their party's long table; the first glimpse of her grabbed him with a startling ferocity, bringing his breathing to an abrupt halt.

He had arrived late to meet up with some colleagues from work. He did not normally mix much socially with them; they were for the most part from a different world, a world to which he could not relate; a world in which he did not belong. He thought of them as phonies, hypocrites, from privileged homes and expensive private schools, they were largely spoilt and totally unaware of the harsh realities of real life for most people living in Britain at that time, unaware of the difficulties of the less fortunate families trying to stretch the pennies just to pay the rent, families who could not afford new shoes. They were blissfully oblivious to the squalor that existed for some of their young contemporaries, those who did not have the advantages of growing up in warm homes of perfect families; and they were protected from the aggressive atmosphere inside the inner cities and the broken new towns that would fill the night-time streets with meanness and violence.

Did he have a chip on his shoulder? Maybe. But what if he did, he could not care. He had worked hard, fought his way up to get to where he was, to escape from where he had come. What did they know? What had they experienced? They were not better than him.

No, they were not really his type of people, but the fates had determined that, begrudgingly, tonight he would go there to celebrate his friend John's birthday and so he had come for him.

Many of the people in their group he did not know; some he recognised vaguely from seeing them passing by in the office corridors, and many had brought friends that he surely had not met before. He was pleased to notice that this beautiful girl did not appear to be attached to any boy in particular.

Her legs were pushed up before her, feet resting next to her bottom on the front of the bench on which she sat so that her knees were just below her chin, cradled by her arms and brought to press against her chest. A gorgeous dark-haired girl, the fading light of summer's evening shone through the windows, washing her with a golden glow, painting her legs with a glorious bronze sheen, her long slender legs. The light seemingly danced for her, highlighting the differing bright colours within her brunette hair, picking out hues of copper-beech and red-chestnut as her hair swayed from side to side and across her face, her beautiful face.

Cheeks, smooth as the finest china, lips the colour of a pale dusty pink rose, the vision enhanced by the vibrant energy and vitality of a brilliant smile, she was as *Aphrodite.*

Such beauty, demanding your attention, but what was this feeling that accompanied the sight, something new, never felt before, a feeling so physical that his breath surely stopped, a desire, a longing? No, it was a want, a need, so strong that it hurt.

This emotion, thrust upon him, what was it? Love? Lust? This attraction, this desire, all at once both nature's gift and nature's burden and the uncertainty, arriving so suddenly, the incapacity any longer to determine perception from reality. Had she looked at him as he came in? Had she really smiled at him? Or was it just his imagination? Probably.

On this warm evening, she was wearing short denim shorts and a white vest, her eyes, deep pools of dark coffee-chocolate brown, , framed by that long hair.

With her smile and laughter as she chatted with her friends, she gave out an immediate impression of freedom but much like a wild horse, with that freedom there also seemed to be a signal of caution, an invisible warning sign to beware, not to come any closer. There was a barrier, something unapproachable about her, a wall, an aloofness to leave her well alone, the precaution of a young woman becoming used now to receiving the attentions of men, attentions unsolicited, attracted without conscious effort, often unwanted but sometimes enjoyed. She was still quite aware of this effect that her looks may cause, and it was this awareness that in turn could make her seem so dauntingly remote.

Innocent though she was of any action on her part to try and seek the attention of the men around her, aside from being born with the good fortune of a pretty face, when she did not observe a reaction she had come to realise it could occasionally cause her surprise and even perhaps a mild offense.

She looked up at him, briefly; she saw his gaze and, before returning to her conversation, gave him half a smile, surely real this time, not imagined. The effect was magical nd he was surely bewitched.

It is strange how we make decisions, instant decisions that can shape the rest of our lives, all maybe based on nothing more than an instinct, a feeling, an impression, an attraction.

His initial reaction was to start to make the excuses that you do when you look for a way out of something. She probably would not be interested. She probably had a boyfriend. The excuses to help you to take the easy way out, Not to try, not to fail. But he simply had to meet her; he had to talk to her. But how?

He was standing at the bar with his friend, John, talking about something that may have happened at work that day; he had long since lost track of the conversation, distracted as he had now become. How was he to meet her? How was he to talk to her?

He sidled sideways, manoeuvring himself closer, slowly edging around in a circle, trying not to be too obvious as he wanted to give himself a better view. Was she staring at him; was she letting him know she liked him? Or was that just the power of an overzealous imagination running away, misinterpreting signals that did not really exist? She pulled all her hair over to the right side of her face, turning her head up more to her left letting the long dark strands of hair fall down, seemingly smiling at him again; was it really true, was this really happening?

Flirtatious, the effect was devastating, leaving him, at once defenceless and, simultaneously, like a drug, craving for more. But unlike any drug, this was pure. He could feel his heart rate increasing.

So what did he do? He did as any boy, of course, he pretended to ignore her. And he found himself pulling up from where he was leaning on the bar, stretching himself to his full height, and starting to play-act. He started to talk louder to his friend, to show off, all performed unconsciously, part of his animal display programmed by nature.

She arose from her perch, coated in the golden light of the sun's brush, a masterpiece. She was coming towards him. His heart raced anew; he could feel the sweat starting on his forehead. Did she want to speak to him? What was he to do?

But no, she passed him by, going to the bar to order some drinks, holding onto the brass rail fixed to the edge of the cherry-wood bar as she asked for a refill to her spritzer. Of course she had not come over just to talk to him.

Think of something to say, quickly. Here's your chance; do not muck it up. Panic. His mind raced; offer to buy her a drink, tell her you like her hair, her shoes, anything. Speak!

But he froze. He remained silent and took another sip of his beer, somehow hoping, against all logic, that this simple action would be enough for her to swoon and fall madly in love with him.

All these thoughts were rushing through him, through his brain, his entire body, colliding, conflicting, these thoughts, all consuming, held him intransient for what seemed like an eternity as he struggled to do something. In reality it was only seconds, a small moment in all time in which to make a decision, a choice, to last a lifetime.

Beauty, it is such a distraction – and, for the holder, such a powerful weapon, a woman's power over men, rendering them defenceless, fools in the proximity of a face so exquisite, and so it was for Dan, left lost of all capacity for rational thought, unable to hear or to function normally, it was as if he was suspended under water, all sound suddenly deafened, watching the scene above detached from his own body, unable to help.

His mind came back to the present as she leaned back, still holding onto the rail, turning her head to the left, towards him, allowing her hair to fall down behind. She gave him a bright beautiful smile.

It was an inviting smile; she was making it easy for him. Still young in this world, she had quickly found the inherent natural feminine guile that existed within her armoury, and she knew that boys needed to be led as a horse to water, to drink from love's fountain.

Surely, now, he could say something.

'Hi, can I buy you that drink?'

'Why?' she frowned. 'Do I look like I can't afford it?'

'No, no,' he stammered, thrown by the confrontational response. 'Look, I was just trying to be polite.'

'What you really meant was you wanted to buy me a drink so that you could talk to me.'

'Yes, OK,' he laughed nervously but he was encouraged, she was giving him a second bite, helping him to try again.

'Do I look like I can be bought!' the abrupt response, it was not a question. Oh dear God he wished he had not tried, his body must have been trying to tie down his tongue for good reason, a defensive mechanism to try to protect him from this very thing and all he now wanted to do was to crawl into the nearest hole and hide for evermore.

'I'm sorry,' he stuttered over the words, whispering, contrite, 'I didn't mean to offend.'

She laughed, her eyes bright, full of mischief. 'Don't worry; I'm only teasing with you. Actually, I would have to reproach you if you did not care to speak to me – then, I would be quite offended.'

He smiled sheepishly, relief flooding through him. 'Can I start over? Hi, I'm Dan, what's your name?'

'Louisa,' she smiled; a big beautiful smile.

'Louisa, that's a pretty name.'

'Are you trying to insult me again?' She shot back abruptly.

'What? What did I say now?' He protested.

'Louisa, a pretty name,' she scolded sharply, 'I'm not stupid, I bet you would have said that whatever my name would have been.'

'Well,' he stammered again, 'at least I wasn't rude this time.'

'Oh, don't worry,' she laughed, enjoying his obvious discomfort, 'I was only teasing you again.' She looked at him through those eyes, deep dark wells, full of mischief. He could see she was going to be a challenge this one.

'OK, OK, I get it,' he said, 'I'll try harder to keep up. So, who are you here with?'

'Anna,' she replied, 'She's....'

'Oh, that's a nice name,' he cut in, laughing, pleased with his quick retort, 'I think I prefer it.'

She gave him a playful smack on his arm, 'Don't be so mean,' she chided, smiling; 'I'm not sure I want you playing my game.'

'Sorry,' he laughed, 'so how do you two know each other?'

'We share a flat and we were also at the same school together.'

'So, I bet she will have a few stories to tell about you.'

'There's nothing to tell,' Louisa smiled softly, lowering her head whilst simultaneously raising her eyes to look up at him in that sweet innocent way that only girls can do, gently twirling her hair around her finger.

'So what do you do?' Dan asked.

'I own an advertising company,' she replied.

'Really, I'm a professional dancer,' he laughed. He was not going to fall for that one.

'Well, I already know you work with that lot,' she laughed as she gestured a wave of her hand over towards the others sitting down at the long table.

What a lovely sparkle she had in her eyes. He was enjoying this and she seemed to be also.

'So?' he asked.

'OK, OK,' she replied, 'I work in an advertising agency.'

'And?' Dan pressed.

'I'm a PA there, for the chief exec.'

'Good place to work?'

'Yes, I guess so,' she hesitated; suddenly some vulnerability appeared, she obviously did not enjoy the job she was doing. 'It's a fun place,' she finished, without much conviction.

'Don't worry,' it was Dan's turn to reassure her, 'our place isn't that much fun to work at either.'

She smiled as if to say, 'Thank you.' And then, 'So what are you still doing there?' the vulnerability gone, the challenger was back.

'I don't really know,' he whispered softly, it was his turn now to sound unsure, and he smiled, 'Waiting for you, perhaps?' Half a statement but also half a question, it lacked confidence and was a poor recovery.

'Oh, that was pathetic,' she burst out laughing.

'Really?' He smiled, 'I thought it was quite good.'

She said nothing but looked up at him, a quizzical look on her face, as if to say, 'Are you sure?'

'Alright,' Dan grinned, 'you're right. It was pretty dreadful.' And they both laughed.

The others were by now sitting down in anticipation of the meal and Dan suddenly realised he and Louisa were all alone at the bar. He noticed her friend, Anna, giggling and whispering in a conspiratorial manner to her friend opposite, probably about Louisa and him. Somehow that felt good, almost reassuring that her old friend would be talking about them, saying something like, 'Look at Louisa, look who she' s talking to, who she's interested in.'

They went to take their seats for the meal and he could see that John had made it easy for him, taking places at the end of the table for himself and Dan, opposite Anna and the seat to where Louisa was now returning. She was gorgeous and he was captivated as they chatted throughout the rest of the evening. It was wonderful but while he tried so hard to outwardly appear cool, inside he was nervous still, frightened almost, the adrenaline coursing through his veins like he was on a wild uncontrolled ride. Dan could not believe how he felt; it had never been like this before.

He was probably trying too hard and, like an excitable puppy, his heart lifted every time she rewarded him with a flash of her smile. The evening ended all too soon and as they left the bar to the street outside, she asked, 'Where are you from?'

'You'll have to find out,' Dan really wanted to see her again. 'I'll give you a chance. I'd still like to buy you that drink,' he reminded her.

'OK, tomorrow night,' she said as she gave him her number and then, just like that, they both turned and parted on their separate ways; she left with her friend, Anna. Dan forced himself to act nonchalant and not hang around, but he could not stop himself sneaking a small look; he was pleased to see that she too was doing likewise, also looking back over her shoulder, watching him go.

'You seemed to be spending a lot of time talking to Dan,' teased Anna.

'Hmm, look at him walk,' sighed Louisa. 'He looks like he's prowling, like a big cat, a panther. It's sexy.' She giggled at how silly she knew she must sound.

'Looks like he's limping if you ask me,' Anna teased further.

'Oh, you're just jealous,' laughed Louisa, punching her friend playfully on the arm, then as she linked her arm and strode to the bus to take them back to their house she went on, 'So what do you know about him, what's he like? You have to tell me everything.'

'Actually, I don't know much about him at all,' replied Anna, 'aside from that many of the girls at work like him, of course.'

'Of course,' Louisa tried not rise to her friend's persistent teasing.

'He doesn't usually mix with us much. I was surprised to see him tonight. He's a bit of a mystery really.'

'A mystery man,' smiled Louisa, 'I'm beginning to like him more already.'

He woke early the next day, having not slept well, too excited, a mind full with thoughts of the night before.

He would not call her just yet; to call in the morning would be too early.

But soon the afternoon arrived, and now he really should call. First, a coffee and then he would call in half an hour. An hour passed; why was he so worried? The palms of his hands were clammy; Dan could not believe how nervous he had become. It was only a phone call.

He needed the guy he shared an office with to go out; he needed total silence. But his colleague was busy and it seemed he would never go. Eventually, he has to go to talk to their boss, Richard Knox, the head of their company, Knox International. This was his chance and he could not put it off any longer.

His pulse racing, his breathing quickened, fingers shaking involuntarily, he dialled the number. What had she done to him? What spell had she cast?

Louisa and Dan agreed to meet in a favourite bar of hers, close to where she lived. When he arrived, she was already there, along with Anna and some other of their friends, who he presumed had been invited to offer her some moral support, that and to size-up and pass judgement on him, her new interest. Dan saw her as soon as he walked in; she was sitting on the other side of the bar, wearing a loose, lacy white top and faded blue jeans, she was very cool, casual and relaxed. Although he hoped she had agonised for ages over what to wear and how she should look for him, Dan was also pleased that she was not someone who got too dressed up or put on too much make-up; hers was a natural beauty. Her hair this time was drawn back in the longest ponytail that reached far down her back, the dark colour contrasting against the white of her blouse, the hairstyle only serving to accentuate the features of her face. She looked up and flashed that glorious smile and his heart melted as she cast her spell anew.

Once again, they chatted excitedly and, once more, she was looking right at him, intently, deep into his eyes.

Later that night, as they left the bar, she let Dan walk her home.

They walked up the road together; separated by only a small distance, close enough to touch but neither of them so doing, a strange uneasy space standing between them, full of nervousness and the longer they walked, the more difficult it seemed to become to bridge the small space ever-growing now to become a canyon as the nervousness threatened to engulf them. Dan realised he must fight it, forcing himself to move closer to her.

Stretching his hand down to find hers, their fingers entwined for the first time. A new magic was ignited by their touch, coursing through their bodies, feeding on their happiness, overpowering anything that threatened to prevent its bloom.

She looked up at him and they both smiled, continuing their walk, still in silence but the silence now was loud with happiness as they both continued smiling to themselves until eventually they reached Louisa's house.

Here, outside her door, they shared a kiss for the first time.

He held both her hands out wide to her sides. Slightly nervous again, he looked into her eyes; she was staring at him, intensely, looking deep into his eyes, drawing him in, pleading with him, willing him to move closer. If ever there was an alluring gaze; an animal attraction, it pulled him in to that kiss. It was brief, and it was tender, but it was, oh, so magical; their first kiss; a kiss *ever-lasting.*

As he left her house, walking back down the road, Dan did not notice the pitch black darkness of the night; he did not worry that it was late and that he had over an hour to walk back to his home, and he did not notice the light drizzle of the rain starting now to fall upon him.

Dan was smiling, laughing and chuckling to himself like an imbecile, uncontrollably changing from a walk one moment to an excited run and jump the next, swimming through waves of peaks of ecstasy and troughs of despair. He felt like he was in heaven.

Louisa and Dan came to pass a wonderful first summer together, spending virtually all their spare time with each other. Life was varied and life was full; both just starting out on their lives, they did not have much money for extravagances, like expensive clothes or visiting nightclubs. Occasionally, they would party until late in their favourite bars of the West End, but more often, they would prefer the less fashionable and more down to earth atmosphere of a local pub, meeting in the evenings after work, and at weekends they would sometimes take a trip out of the City to the countryside where they would walk for hours, lost in their own company.

Dan enjoyed living in London; he loved the architecture, the feeling of history around every corner.

From the Palace of Westminster, where the Kings and Queens used to reign before being evicted by the birth of British democracy, the country's government taking residence in their place and remaining there still, to the monarch's modern day residence in such close proximity just a short stroll away down Birdcage Walk. A similar walk to the one that King Charles I took from St James' in January 1649 to be beheaded. It being a cold winter's day, the King had famously asked for an extra layer of clothing so he did not shiver from cold which could be mistaken for fear.

His execution took place on a scaffold outside the old banqueting hall in Whitehall, almost opposite what is now Downing Street where the Prime Minister, the British elected leader, now lives. That was the ultimate end of the governance of the nation by a King or Queen and instead the country was governed by an elected parliament. That these places are linked so closely in both their proximity and their history is a lovely irony in this large diverse metropolis.

From here it is but a brief journey down the beautiful tree lined Mall to Trafalgar Square where Nelson, the conqueror of the French and Spanish navies in 1805 at the battle from which the square takes its name, sits atop his tall column. And then, with the River Thames to the south and the famous West End theatre-land just to the north, this line of London's history continues onwards via the Strand to the ancient Law Courts of Justice and onto Fleet Street where the newspaper industry had lived until it moved in the 1980s to the old docklands in the East of London where the shipping traffic and sea trade on which this city had originally been built had become obsolete.

From this street, it is but a short walk up Ludgate Hill to the famous St Pauls Cathedral designed in 1673 by the architect, Sir Christopher Wren, and then just a few steps further to the financial centre, the Bank of England and the City Of London.

Black taxi cabs mingle with big red buses and the occasional posh Bentley of the businessman on his way to the next meeting, while courier cyclists nip in and out between all the traffic, their bags of letters and documents slung across their shoulders, caps pulled well down on their foreheads.

But what Dan loved most about London was its energy, that here was a place where things were happening. This city was vibrant, it was cosmopolitan, a patchwork of different cultures, different generations, different faiths, different beliefs. London was exciting; this was the place to be. This was where he finally felt he belonged.

Set amidst this busy metropolis, London was also home to the magnificent Great Parks, where he and Louisa could walk some more, feed the ducks and perhaps take a boat on the serpentine lake, so called because it snakes its way through Hyde Park into Kensington Gardens. They would drift along not needing to say very much to each other, just happy together.

In Green Park there were no flowers, just trees, hence its name and if the sun was shining, they would sit on the grass drinking coca-cola, staring up at the sky imagining shapes in the clouds; a white Arabian charger galloping along, followed by a dragon floating by as it morphed into a fluffy white poodle.

Or they would sit observing, people-watching, speculating on the lives of the people passing as the pigeons pecked at scraps on the grass.

There was the man in a suit sitting on a bench with his tie half undone, probably a business man who had just bet and lost on a new venture, now alternately sitting up and rocking forwards to put his head in his hands as he agonised how to tell his wife.

The prim lady rushed past, a schoolteacher perhaps, just returning from meeting her mystery lover in some tempestuous affair.

Across the park, the family with their two young children trudged on their way home, the youngest dawdling at the back, dragging a stick, not looking so happy as his father shouted to hurry him along, to catch the others up.

What was life like for all these people they observed, was it happy or maybe painful? You never really know what goes on behind closed doors, of any household, rich or poor. Who knows what pressures or demons exist in any relationships.

Louisa and Dan enjoyed each other's company, often walking for miles and miles, through woods, across fields and over streams.

He bought an old car just so they could escape from London some weekends, driving down late on a Friday night after work into the beautiful countryside where they would walk some more. As anyone who knows them will tell you, the South Downs of the Sussex coast are an area of incredible natural beauty; waves of green grass and white chalk roll along by the sea, the hills rise up and down, their peaks and troughs seeming to mimic the blue waves of the sea that they overlook.

They would pass hours walking up there, hand-in-hand, arm-in-arm, it was as if neither of them ever wanted to let go of the other.

Sometimes they would walk along the promenade of the seafront, occasionally with an ice cream, which Dan once pushed into Louisa's face in a way you can only do when you first meet someone, and her laughing in a way girls only do when they are just falling in love.

It was not just her looks that attracted him so, her sparkling eyes, her long legs and dark hair, it was also her company, her personality; he enjoyed spending time with her, she had a wonderful cutting sense of humour and she could be very wicked as he had experienced that first night they met in the bar with her mischievous nature but equally now, he had found she had a great vulnerability; behind that hard unapproachable façade was a shy girl, a little girl lacking in self-confidence, wanting to be loved and now, as she relaxed and trusted in him, he found a warmth beneath.

Sometimes their walks would last well into the evening, but the evenings of a warm English summer would last long before they became too dark to enjoy. They would sit high up on the hills looking out to sea as the sun dipped below the horizon and they would share their secrets, their feelings, their ambitions.

Dan would tell Louisa stories where the beautiful shy princess would eventually prevail over her wicked sisters, or where the poor pretty girl would meet her prince and they would travel the world together.

He would tell her how intelligent she really was, not to listen to those that put her down, and he would encourage her to be more confident, urge her to do what she truly wanted to do, and she would then throw these same sentiments back at him, challenging Dan to do what he really wanted to be doing.

Louisa had also felt the need to get away from her home town as early as she could and had also been drawn to the larger life of the City. He could understand this; he understood the need to leave only too well.

Dan would talk about his plans, his ambitions, of living and working in London. It was strange how he was drawn to it, but somehow he had always known that he would go there, that he would get away; away to the City, to the bright lights, to where the excitement was. He just did not really know why.

It was peculiar how they seemed to have such an affinity with each other, Dan and Louisa, an instant understanding; both of them wanting, and taking, their independence getting away from their family homes as soon as they could.

And now they had each other and that seemed like all they needed. They were blissfully happy, oblivious to others, consumed by their own world; a world together. It seemed like this was it; he was as happy as he could be.

Well, almost. For while his romance and happiness with Louisa was flourishing and all consuming, he was finding his work increasingly frustrating and unfulfilling.

Dan had been lucky enough to have been accepted on a select trainee programme by Knox International, a multinational corporation, relatively small by the standards of others with diverse interests in property, shipping and the media, and with offices across the globe, Knox was young and modern in its outlook. The places on their training programme were very sought after, with only a very few available, and so competition was very high and the acceptance process was rigid and tough, being conducted for a large part by the founder himself, Richard Knox, who at fifty-five years old was still a dynamic force, enjoying a hands-on approach.

These firms did not usually take people like him, people from where he came and so he was actually quite surprised when the offer arrived from Knox to join them. Maybe it was because he had been so brutally honest about his background during the selection process or maybe they saw something in him that he did not himself even know existed.

Dan had always been drawn to business, to be involved in exciting deals and this seemed like one way into that world, a world that was really so foreign and so far removed from his own, but still attracted him like a moth to a flame.

This job seemed to exist in a world well beyond the one that Dan lived within, so it was a strange choice to make for someone like himself, but once that choice had been made, he had to aim for the top, to try to be the best that he could be. As long as you always try your best and not sell yourself short, that is all you could ask of yourself, he would think; do not let the fear of failure stop you from trying, always give it your best shot, don't live your life in regret wondering what might have been.

As he grew older he sometimes wondered where his life may have gone if he had taken a different path, if he had not taken the chance of applying to this job which seemed to exist in a world well beyond the one that he lived within. What different opportunities would have been available; who knows where they would have led him.
But if he had not followed the path that he had, would he have ever met Louisa? Would Dan have missed that chance or would fate have reconvened and contrived to make another opportunity for their stars to cross?

Sometimes it could be an exciting and fast-moving world; they negotiated mergers, they dealt with multi-million pound banking finance and of course, they worked on large property deals, vast commercial developments, leases of shopping centres, and huge office blocks from New York to Paris.

There were meetings with investment banks, meetings with clients, negotiations with lawyers, often angry and heated. At times it was dramatic and varied, exciting as you met new people and creative as you helped to develop different ideas and new projects.

But, for some reason, Dan was no longer enjoying it; he was beginning to question whether this was what he wanted to be doing, whether he really did belong here, whether there should be more.

And so came one evening, it was early September, and they were sitting on the grass of the Downs, on top of the hills, high above the water. They were now missing the summer sun's warmth and, inwardly, they both knew an end was now coming upon them, the inevitable, unavoidable end to that first perfect summer, *their* summer.

Looking out to sea the sun was shining a golden band, a broad avenue coming across the sea towards them, silhouetting a small yacht becalmed in its path. This was perfect; Dan was so happy, and he wondered, was this how it should be? Why worry about working his way up in the corporate world. It would not matter what he did, as long as he was with her, would it?

The seagulls were floating high above him, effortlessly bobbing up and down as they rode the thermals rising from the cliff edge. Dan smiled inside as distant memories stirred, the gulls' rise and fall was somewhat rhythmical and he always found it reassuring; the future seemed so uncertain but sitting here now, he suddenly felt that all was going to turn out alright.

Louisa was dozing next to him, snuggled in close, nuzzling her head on his chest, resting peacefully. Dan stroked her beautiful long hair as he would come to love doing so many times over the following years, wishing this moment would never end, but knowing that it would, that it must.

'No, it wouldn't matter what I did, as long as I was with her,' he breathed, almost aloud.

But some emotion seized him, a foreboding; he knew a change was coming. The summer was at an end and he felt a shiver go through him; the chill touch of autumn, perhaps or maybe, the thought that as surely as summer turns to autumn and some leaves survive while others turn burnt orange or red before they die, so too did their romance have to find a way to evolve from their first summer or, if not, also wither and die. Could it survive and be evergreen?

Louisa felt it too, and on the drive home that evening, they sat there, together in body but strangely apart. A lonely space sat between them, a loneliness of words unspoken, truths they knew but neither dare speak of, two islands separated by a sea of reality.

A definite wind of change had entered their relationship; was it a natural transition of the seasons to autumn, or the harsh cold blast of winter?

When Dan left Louisa at her house later that night and went on his way, back home, all suddenly went quiet. Self-doubt sneaked its way into his mind; was their romance only a summer fling for her?

What had started a few weeks before as a chance meeting had grown into something far more, at least for him. But was it the same for Louisa? He had never felt like this before, so out of control. So in love? Was that what this was? If it was, then at times love can be exhilarating, empowering, freeing, granting you the feeling that you can do anything, that you can fly, just as when he had walked down Louisa's road after their first kiss. But now, this was debilitating, soul destroying, gut-wrenching, hurtful. Why was he so confused? What was this feeling? So much pleasure, so much pain, he had never felt like this before.

Soon it would be Christmas, their first Christmas together. For a present, Dan gave Louisa tickets to leave the next day for Paris. He did not have much money so they went by train and stayed in a small old hotel in the student area of *St Germain*. It was a cold Parisian winter, very cold. The wind blew and the wind chill was even colder, minus fifteen degrees. It was magical!

They walked on the *Rive Gauche*, the left bank of the river Seine. They walked through the corridors of the

Louvre, past the Mona Lisa and the works of so many of the great masters.

From there they crossed the wooden bridge of the *Pont des Arts* to visit the Cathedral of *Notre Dame* where they climbed up to the bell tower to look for the hunchback and his Esmeralda.

They took coffee in *Montmartre*, in view of the gleaming white dome of the *Sacre Coeur,* and walked along the Rue Saint-Honore where, with little money, they window shopped, their warm breath in the cold air momentarily misting up the glass fronts of the chic boutiques in which many famous designers had started their haute-couture careers in the rooms above.

They climbed the stairs of the *Eiffel* tower where Dan's bravery on the way up soon gave way to vertigo on the way down as the stone pavement far below came into view through the holes in the old iron steps.

They discovered a restaurant, *Le Petit St Benoit*, which has remained a favourite ever since. Rustic and lively, with good wholesome country fare that you would imagine to be served in the kitchens of many a farm throughout the French countryside, the wine arrives in carafes and the red and white squares of the gingham tablecloths are covered in white sheets of paper where, at the end of your meal, the chef calculates your surprisingly low bill freehand in pencil before you.

And like many young lovers, Dan and Louisa took a boat ride down the river Seine on the Bateaux Mouches, wrapped up in each other. It was so romantic. They were exhausted, cold and blissfully happy.

It was their last evening and, tomorrow, they would have to go back to their different apartments in London. They relaxed and drank some red wine, inexpensive but nice, in the quintessentially French cafe, *Le Bonaparte*, on

Place Saint Germain des Pres where the waiters, in their white shirts and black bow-ties and waistcoats, were so typically arrogant that Louisa wondered if that was also part of their obligatory uniform.

They took one last coffee, a strong espresso, to help them brave the cold once more and they walked to the gardens of the *Jardins des Tuileries*, originally commissioned by the French Queen, Catherine de Medicis in 1561 on the site of the tile kilns that helped build much of the Parisian skyline you still know today. The Plane trees of the gardens formed a perfect corridor from the *Musee du Louvre* to the *Place de la Concorde* from where the wide boulevard of the *Avenue des Champs-Elysee* extended to the *Arc de Triomphe* standing proudly on a slight rise in the distance.

In the *Jardins*, Dan faced his dislike for fairground rides as they went on the Ferris wheel, only then recently installed in the park. The people on the ground milling around the many market stalls gradually grew smaller and the deep orange lights of the sprawling city stretched out from all around them, almost as if they were at the epicentre of its large web.

The music of the fairground ride grew quieter, replaced by the rush of the wind; his right arm around her shoulders as she sheltered into him, against the cold, He pulled her closer, enjoying both the warmth and the feeling of being her protector. At the top, he felt a sudden urge, an impulse to burst out, 'Marry me!'

What was this feeling? An instinctive urge, so strong. The explosive rush of love's drug. Love, was that what this was? He struggled to stop himself.

Dan had always swore that he would be a confirmed bachelor to his dying day, but now, with Louisa, all had changed, all was different. Now he wanted to swear that he would never love anyone else, but Louisa and he had barely met just a few short months before. This was stupid. Could there even be such a thing as love at first sight?

Surely, it can only start with a physical attraction, a lust. How can you immediately know this is the love of your life before you know anything about them, about their personality, their character, their compassion?

Or is it possible? Can you learn all of these things from a smile, from a fleeting glance?

And if the start was just an animal attraction, could that ever evolve into something more? Into what we call love?

Or was he just caught in a mirage, a fiction of his own creation, imagining a love that did not really exist? Surely it is just a word, created by man.

How did he even know if love was real?

What he did know that this was impulsive, rash; so it must be wrong, he reasoned. It was illogical, irrational. So Dan fought the feeling and he suppressed it.

But still, he did feel like in some way he knew her from before, that they were connected, as if she was the person he had been waiting for, the person he somehow already knew, destined to meet at some point when the fates designed their paths to cross.

HONG KONG

But she was not here, it was not meant to be. I did not need her; I was better off on my own. So, I took one last look at the white sheets of the hotel bed, the vivid image of her from a few moments before now gone just as the flash of those memories past had also now disappeared, and I turned to leave the room; to leave the past behind – to leave the past and embrace the future.

I marched through the lobby of the Hilton; I was in no particular hurry but it was with the fuel of adrenaline and enthusiasm that I strode out into my new world, to my new beginning.

It was but a short walk from the hotel to my new offices in Jardine House. I crossed Ice House Street, passed the Mandarin Oriental hotel and went up an escalator to a walkway that would take me to my building.

It was the end of the 1980s and Margaret Thatcher's Britain was just entering a recession, in the times of the highest interest rates people could remember, and it was becoming increasingly difficult for me to meet the ever-rising bills.

My work was challenging and I was excelling; however, for some reason that I could not quite identify, I was becoming increasingly restless and disillusioned; it was not what I wanted it to be; it just was not *'me'*. I knew I wanted something more. I wanted more control over my life. I wanted more excitement.

So when Richard Knox offered me the chance to join their Far East office, I jumped at it. Richard had a specific project for me; it seemed exciting and it would pay well, with a driver to take me wherever I wanted to go, and a huge apartment with a harbour view being made ready for me.

So, that is how I came to be in the back of the limousine that evening, sweeping up the drive of the Hilton in Hong Kong, and that is how I came to feel I had made it on that first night. Now, I felt, I had finally arrived. Now, my life was finally made.

It was still early, as I wanted to ensure I had lots of time to find my bearings before the day started and although there were some people rushing this way and that, heads down, marching quickly as if there was no time to lose, all in Hong Kong being done at a fast pace, I would learn that this was still the calm before the storm when the Central Business District would later explode into a flood of people, coming at you without relent.

I entered through the building's main glass door and, despite the early hour, the blast of air conditioning that greeted me was very welcome.

I took the elevator to the eighteenth floor, to the offices of Knox Shipping (Far East) Ltd.

I was not surprised to find that the glass doors were locked but I could see that the cleaners were already there to make the offices ready before the working day began and, so, I pressed on the doorbell.

A small, smartly dressed local Chinese man came round to answer the door.

'Hello, hello,' he said. 'So, you must be Dan. Welcome, I'm Michael Tang.'

'Oh, hello,' I replied, a little surprised. I knew that Michael was the Managing Director in charge of the Hong Kong office and I was surprised to see him in so early.

I recognised him from his photo in the company's prospectus but I was surprised by how much shorter he was than me, a good six inches below my six feet and also, so slightly built. He was probably around ten years older than me, in his late thirties but immaculately turned out, his thick black hair combed neatly to one side, not a hair out of place. Very well dressed, his suit had the look of being very expensive and I could not help but notice the bright yellow-gold watch sitting proudly on his wrist, wanting to be noticed.

'I thought I would come in early to greet you and make sure everything was ready for you,' said Michael, 'although, I didn't expect you quite this early. You'll soon learn that Hong Kong is a place where people work late and socialise even later, so it is not often a place for the early bird. Come, I'll show you to your office.'

We walked down the corridor together, side by side, as Michael pointed out various things for me and mentioned the names of the people who occupied the different rooms that we passed.

At the end of the first corridor we came to a large corner office, with huge floor to ceiling windows. They were round, big enough for a man to stand inside; you could stretch from one side to the other like Da Vinci's Vetruvian man. The room was full of light and was nothing like any office I had been in before. High up, it had a dominant view of the waters of Hong Kong harbour below and the busy traffic tirelessly going about their business.

'That over there is our own container terminal,' said Michael as he pointed across to the other side of the harbour where many large ships lay at anchor in the bay, waiting while others were in port on the southern tip of the Kowloon peninsular, loading and unloading their cargoes of brightly coloured containers.

'Quite a view isn't it?' he paused before continuing. 'Richard said that your project was very important so I thought it best that you had good surroundings. What are you here to do, set up a similar terminal in China isn't it? I'll take you around ours so you can see how we work here.'

'That's right,' I said, immediately now on my guard, I purposely kept my reply brief. I knew I had to be careful not to upset Michael who Richard had warned me may have his feathers ruffled a little by my being here. 'That would be great to see; only when you've got some spare time of course.'

'You'll have to excuse me, I've just got a few things to do but we'll catch up later. My office is similar to yours, on the corner down the end of this corridor,' the last few words were said over his shoulder as he turned away to leave the room, leaving me alone with my thoughts.

As I watched him go, I thought about what Richard had told me when he had first mentioned the possibility of this opportunity for me, just a few weeks ago now.

He wanted me to come to Hong Kong to develop a special new project for him, to set up a new container shipping terminal in China, the great new frontier, he was convinced that it would be a land of untold new potential and opportunity for the Knox business and they had to be there and take that opportunity now.

For some reason, Richard seemed to have a lot of trust in me; it was true that I was making a name in the firm as someone with initiative who could get things done, and I had come to be chosen by Richard to work with him on some of his most important projects.

He told me that, at first, he expected Michael would probably be a little put out that he was not heading up the project himself but that he figured once Michael realised that I was not interfering with his operations, he would probably see no harm in it. Probably, Maybe.

That is what Richard thought *could* happen, and that is what Richard had assured Dan *would* happen; but he had not told Dan how likely he thought that may be, or how difficult, or how long it may take for Michael to accept. Richard hoped that Michael would not make things tough for Dan once he was out there. Richard hoped that Michael would not put any obstacles in Dan's way, but he could not be sure of it.

Michael was indeed a little jealous of Dan. He knew he was out here working on a special project reporting back directly to the owner, Richard, in London; a project looking at setting up a new operation in China, the great new market for business. Why could he not have overseen that, he thought? Would it not have made more sense for it to come under his Far Eastern operation, a local with knowledge of dealing with the mainlanders, rather than this fresh-faced kid with little experience who he would probably have to nursemaid?

Deep down though he knew it would have been too much for his office to have handled as well. China had the potential to be so big that it could have taken over all of their time and as his business already covered Singapore as well as Hong Kong, he knew it probably was right for this to be seen as a different operation.

Still, it would have been nice to have been consulted, to have been asked his opinion. For the past twenty years, Michael viewed that he had been fighting the battles at the forefront of the Far East, making so much money and running such a successful business for Knox that helped keep Richard back in the London office in his lavish lifestyle.

But what support or appreciation did he get from them? Little or none to speak of, however, he thought, he probably should not complain too much; at least Richard trusted him enough to leave him alone to manage his office how he wanted, at least that was something.

The last thing he needed now was someone getting in the way, interfering, upsetting the way he ran things, poking their nose in, so Michael hoped that Dan's business would be kept separate and not get in the way of his.

That was why he had come in early today, to tidy up his office and make sure he was there when Dan arrived. Richard must think highly of this young man if he had put his trust in him for this vital project. So, he would have to keep an eye on him, make sure he did not start to tread on his toes, to get in his way or, worse, win Richard's ear and takeover everything he had worked so hard to set up.

At the end of that first day in my new office, Michael had arranged for me to go on the firm's junk with a few of my other new colleagues.

I had imagined a junk to be an old Chinese wooden boat with big red sails like I had read about in old romantic novels and seen from a thousand tourist postcards, but the junks now used by many of the large corporations and investment banks were, in fact, smaller motorised versions, designed for pleasure trips like this or lazy weekends anchored in one of Hong Kong's many bays.

Queen's Pier, the main jetty in the harbour for pleasure boats, was just a short walk from the Knox offices and I was amazed at how busy the harbour was in the evening. There must have been twenty or more of these junks bobbing around. The waters of the harbour were very choppy as the waterway was so busy and the junks had shallow bottoms meaning that they rocked heavily from side to side and heaved up and down.

The boat boys driving the junks would wait and take it in turns to come in alongside the jetty to pick up their cargo of passengers once all the guests in the party had arrived. Like much in Hong Kong, it was a disorganised chaos that somehow worked.

As the junk moved off that evening, becoming more stable as it gathered momentum, I became quiet, watching the activity in the port fade behind us. Jardine House stood proud overlooking the pier; it was an iconic building, the large round windows covering its entire height now resembling portholes in some tall ship; the same windows, impossibly large when inside, gradually becoming smaller and smaller now as the boat moved further away, until they became just a cluster of brightly lit pinholes in the sky.

We were going for dinner in one of the fish restaurants of Lamma Island. It was a place that I would come to visit many times over the ensuing years. And it did not matter how many times we would come to make this trip, I would never cease to wonder at the activity and variety of the work going on in the harbour. We would pass the Star Ferries linking across Kowloon on the mainland to the island of Hong Kong, then past large container ships at anchor, resting before taking on another load of toys and shoes, televisions and stereos, to ship across rough seas to the shops of Europe or America, all part of the seemingly endless trade from east to west on which the life of this rock was founded.

We passed cargo ships carrying food from China to Hong Kong's supermarkets, and little fishing boats returning with the day's catch for tomorrow's street markets and even amongst this busy mix would be tiny sampans hustling and bustling about, driven by old Chinese men and often old ladies, impervious to the large ships and large swells around them.

It was a hardy, industrious environment, everyone trying to get on with their own business, determined and undeterred by others around them.

The evening air was warm and still clammy at the beginning of September, and there was a smell in the harbour. It was not a smell I had experienced before, a smell like nothing else. It was difficult to describe, but impossible to ignore. For sure, the harbour was not the cleanest water to swim in, but it was not a smell of sewage, and it was not a smell of fuel. It was a smell of everything. It was a smell of Hong Kong.

Michael came over and offered me a can, white with an emblem in green and gold; it was Tsing Tao, the local Chinese beer. 'So, what do you think of the place so far?'

'Incredible,' I replied, 'you can almost feel the industry, feel the buzz.'

'Too true, but be careful, it can become infectious,' he smiled. 'When were you born?'

'January 1965'

'Oh, so you are a Dragon,' he exclaimed. 'Congratulations,' and he raised his can in salute.

'Really, what does that mean?' I asked; I had not heard of this before.

'In the Chinese zodiac you were born in the year of the Dragon; you just got in on the tail before the Chinese New Year changed, we follow the lunar year you know. And the Dragon is the most powerful and prestigious of all China's mythical creatures,' he continued, 'and this is also a year of the Dragon; perhaps Hong Kong will be kind to you.'

'How so?' I laughed, but, actually, feeling quite pleased, reassured, at this thought.

'Who knows,' smiled Michael, 'it will be up to you to make the most of what she offers to you.'

I turned again to look back out over the harbour. Our junk was making good speed; the harbour had now receded well behind us and the windows of all the tall office buildings became fairy lights hanging prettily in the sky as people continued to work throughout the night. It was a beautiful sight, buzzing with life and excitement.

I felt encouraged and allowed myself a small smile. Maybe, just maybe, I had now, finally, found somewhere I belonged.

At the back of the junk, many of my new colleagues were chattering excitedly, making a loud buzz, like electricity. It felt good. With them was Michael's wife, Connie, she was speaking to some of her girlfriends. One in particular, a pretty Eurasian girl caught my eye. Michael noticed the subject of my gaze, 'Connie insisted on bringing some of her friends to meet you,' he laughed, 'let me introduce you.'

I turned my head to face him, raising an eyebrow quizzically. 'Really,' I replied, 'well we mustn't disappoint them then, should we.' Perhaps Michael was right; maybe Hong Kong would be good to me.

Like London, Hong Kong too was vibrant and exciting. But where London was a cosmopolitan mix, Hong Kong was an eruption, the resulting earthquake from a collision of continents, a collision of cultures. It was all at once ugly, dirty, threatening, lively and sexy.

It was a place of extremes with extravagant shopping malls at the foot of the high rise office buildings, housing many of the world's most expensive boutiques, every famous designer wanting to have an address here, contrasting with the street markets bustling just around the next corner.

The fine apartment blocks and luxury hotels, with their marble lobbies, co-existed side-by-side with old ramshackle housing containing three generations or more within.

I was fascinated and explored all over the Territory.

I took the trams that went across the entire width of the Island from east to west for the impossibly small amount of two Hong Kong Dollars, about twenty British pence or thirty American cents.

I would visit the markets in the Wanchai district with the raw meat hanging up in the sweaty air as men chopped and hacked at carcasses before washing the blood away down the streets into the drains.

Fish came past in tanks on backs of lorries carrying them to restaurants, the water sloshing about and spilling over as the lorries accelerated hard and braked harder, and dead chickens were whisked from markets to restaurants in impossibly large baskets on the fronts of bicycles pedalled by old men in vests that used to be white.

The proprietor of a famous snake shop in the Wanchai market area would give a show at the weekend to a crowd of locals, taking out the much valued gallstone of a live snake with his teeth, the show ending with him biting the head off the snake, still alive, it's body wriggling in his hand outstretched in triumph, all part of his street theatre. He saw me, the only *gweilo*, white ghost, amongst the crowd and offered, in Cantonese, what seemed to be an invitation which I politely declined and took as my exit.

In the evenings, you could hear the 'click-clack' of the mahjong tablets coming from rooms above the street, possibly just a friendly game between grandparents and children or, maybe, a fierce contest with large sums at stake.

I never ceased to enjoy taking the green and white Star Ferry across the harbour to Tsim Tsa Tsui, the southernmost tip of Kowloon. With the passengers sitting on old wooden benches that had backrests which could swing to and fro so they could always face forwards in the direction that the boat was travelling, the Star Ferries would tirelessly carry thousands of passengers across the harbour without interruption all day. It was a vital artery in the territory's many varied links, still providing an essential and much-needed service as it had been doing since its first operations in 1880.

The giant dark oily ropes would creak as the crew wrapped them tight around the gigantic cleats to bring the bobbing boat closer to the jetty, eventually under enough control to keep the rise and fall sufficiently low to allow the hundreds of passengers to disembark via the old gangplank.

Here, Kowloon was actually part of the mainland of China. This was where the large cruise ships would dock at Harbour City when in town, right in the centre of everything. And from there it was a short walk to the many electrical, camera and clothes shops along the tourist trap of Nathan Road.

The Peak tram was another favourite mode of transport for locals and tourists alike, carrying its first passengers way back in 1888, a funicular tram built into the cliff face to ferry passengers from the Central district up the impossibly steep slope to the famous Peak where the wealthy had traditionally first built their homes to take advantage of the cooling breeze before the days of air-conditioning.

From here, the Territory appeared visually spectacular, unusual skyscrapers reaching for the sky; the architecture never ceased to fascinate me. I would often say how I could not stop walking along with my head bent back, constantly admiring, amazed at the magnificent glass structures, buildings which were for the most part made with the use of bamboo scaffolding. Yes scaffolding, for some of the tallest buildings in the world were made from bamboo poles fixed together with twine on which the Chinese workers would climb in their black plimsolls with no safety harnesses.

But here it was not enough for a building to be tall and glass or to be in a style in keeping with its surroundings. No, here it was the opposite, almost as if each new building had to be totally different to the previous, a statement by its owner. The resulting mix was a complete kaleidoscope of styles and an ever changing skyline.

I would sit in the back of a taxi going down Garden Road past the white colonial governor's residence, dwarfed by the tall Bank of China building with its 'chopsticks' on top, two gleaming white aerials. For what was a communist state, this was an incredible building, a three sided tall glass structure that from the right angle could look like just a single flat sheet of glass.

At the time it was built it was the tallest building in Hong Kong, looking down on the neighbouring Hongkong and Shanghai Banking Corporation's head office.

The HSBC building itself was a truly incredible feat of engineering, its glass floors suspended above the pavements so that pedestrians could walk underneath and take a vast escalator to enter up into the belly of the building, inside the main banking hall, and here was always a hive of activity; a great demonstration in efficiency, architecture and engineering that combined to actually work superbly together.

The HSBC building had only been constructed a few years before the Bank of China's tower and it was to be their worldwide headquarters, intended as a testament to their financial prowess. However, secretly the directors were now jealous of their Chinese neighbours' newer, taller glass tower dominating the landscape.

Outside the HSBC building, the emblems of the bank, two large brass lions, guarded the building at different angles, it was said, a result of the demands of *fung shui* to ensure they were in line with the dragon's back that ran along the Island's earth beneath the foundations on which the bank was built and so to best defend the bank against the evil spirits that would otherwise steal away its treasures.

Fung Shui played a great part in the local culture, even the offices of Knox Shipping had to have been checked and blessed by a local master, with a large tank of goldfish stationed strategically in one of the corner offices in order to bring luck and most importantly, as the senior director, Michael's office had to have a door at an angle to deflect the money safely down to the accounts department and keep it away from any evil forces.

My apartment was in one of the many residential blocks that seemingly grew out of the hillside looking down onto Central below; the boats moving in the harbour beyond, ensuring my view was constantly changing, always alive, the ships plying their trade subconsciously inspiring me with their industry.

I never shut the curtains so as not to miss any of the show, waking to the new light of sunrise, watching the golden glow of sunset, for the scene later to change again to the twinkling lights in the night, the lights of boats in the harbour and of the aeroplanes coming in to land at Kai Tak.

Kai Tak, with its runway jutting out into the harbour from Kowloon on the opposite side to me, was for years the main airport for the whole Territory but would sadly come to be replaced. Landing there was an experience in itself;

banking right at the very last minute, you could see people hanging out their washing at the back of their apartments, close enough to see the show they were watching on television, seemingly suspended as the aircraft slowly turned in its final descent.

The work with Knox was exciting, and the social life outside of the office, lively. Life here was great. My luxury home was paid for by the company, I was given membership of the prestigious Royal Hong Kong Yacht Club and invited to an endless stream of parties.

I was also pleased that my relationship with Michael did not seem as difficult as it could have been. I was an outsider coming into his world but not under his control or authority and I could understand how he could easily have become upset and made life difficult for me.

At first Michael had indeed been a little defensive, just as Richard had explained he would be. It was human nature to be a little put out, jealous even when someone new is imposed upon you by your boss of many years from overseas. I was fast learning about human emotions and dealing with people to put them at ease, so I had gone out of my way to explain that my role there to set up the China terminal was only a temporary one until we found offices in Shanghai. I went out of my way to ensure Michael felt no threat from me, and Michael, on the whole, had seemingly gone out of his way to welcome me and I now felt very comfortable in his company. We were fast becoming friends and I valued the advice he gave me on my dealings in mainland China.

Often, after working late at the office, the two of us would chat over a beer in one of the many bars of Lan Kwai Fong before heading home. Michael would share with me some of the issues that may be troubling him in his Far

Eastern operation and would always be ready to offer me advice should I need any help with my project.

Michael had a wide circle of friends and he introduced me to many important people, influential people, business leaders, *taipans* and to his closest friends.

He and his wife would often invite me over to their house for dinner with other friends or to their club, the American club where they often socialised, the club being in the Aberdeen marina where they moored their super new white motor yacht, a gleaming white floating gin palace. It was amazing the amount of money that Michael and his friends seemed to have at their disposal. The consumption in their toys was conspicuous and even at times seemed somewhat distasteful, super-yachts, fast cars, designer clothes, Swiss watches. It was almost as if each was trying to outdo the other. And of course, there was expensive jewellery for their wives, ever ready to show off their most recent prize, they were also part of some unspoken competition.

For Michael, it was indeed a competition and it was very real. It had not always been like that for him as, unlike his friends, he was not from a wealthy family, but after he had been introduced to Connie he had to find a way to have her; she, so beautiful, so sophisticated; beyond him really, beyond his dreams, him being a small, simple boy, from a deprived background in the Mongkok district. She came from a world well beyond the one that he had lived within; that was why he worked so hard, always trying to please her, trying to buy her precious things, trying to keep her loving him.

Much like Dan, Michael's position with Knox also existed in a world well beyond the one in which Michael had lived. Originally, he came from a poor family, living in a small crowded flat. He had shared a bedroom with his elder sister, a younger brother and their other sister who was still just a toddler and seemed to need lots of attention; he had learnt to grow up quick.

Money was tight; his father worked on the docks as a stevedore, loading and unloading container ships of their cargoes, occupying a very lowly position in a kingdom that his son would later come to rule, but nobody would have envisaged such a day back then and indeed, Michael had tried to leave this past behind.

His mother was a cleaner, taking any job, no matter how dirty, wherever she could to make sure her children went to school with smart, clean uniforms. Money was always scarce for the family but they were happy and proud.

Michael's childhood however was more difficult; short and weak with thick glasses like bottle-bottoms, at school he was teased and bullied, mercilessly, and so he would withdraw further into his own shell becoming even quieter, feeling even more an outsider.

But he was clever and excelled in his school work, so he saw his opportunity with the possibility of a scholarship to George Washington school, the most exclusive in Hong Kong; each year, it would take one boy from a disadvantaged background, a boy less privileged than its other pupils, the sons of *taipans* and judges, who would surely go on to become the same.

So he applied himself, working hard, studying late into the night by torchlight under the covers so as not to disturb his sleeping siblings in their cramped bunk beds. This was his chance, to escape and enter a different world where he could start afresh and be someone new, a better world away from the bullying, away from his unambitious family, away from Mongkok.

He would never go back, but it was ironic that with the view from his office window of the Knox container port, which was next to Mongkok, his ambition gave him a daily reminder of his roots, of where he came from, the embarrassment he still felt, that he wore as a scar, a reminder that he was still trying to be accepted.

With its mostly clammy humidity, rising pollution, the people constantly hacking their coughs, and raw meat being transported unhygienically on trolleys through dirty streets, to some, Hong Kong seemed like the ugliest place on earth.

To others, it was still the most exciting, and to those willing to seize it, the place of opportunity.

I was enjoying being here; but it was not all just fun and games, there was also a lot of work to be done.

The China project was a huge undertaking for me. It was a vast project to take on, the opening of a new business in China. To construct a new container terminal and all that would entail, building issues, construction contractors and architects, financial, bankers and investment firms, commercial matters ,customers and strategic partners, administration, licences and permits, people, good staff and advisers and, of course, the language and cultural barriers but I felt that I had to make it work. I could not fail; Richard had shown such trust in me; he had placed his faith in me; that meant everything to me and I could not let him down. The pressure was really on me; I had put the pressure on myself; I had to make it a success.

I was happy building this new project, creating something from nothing, building something completely new, being the architect of the strategy, visualising it and then implementing that vision with all the elements such a project required, it was in itself a complex puzzle; I enjoyed the challenge of it. It seemed very natural, like what I was meant to do; no training could have prepared you for it, you had to just get on with it and find your own way.

We followed our plan to open the shipping terminal business in China; previously foreigners and foreign businesses could not own a company in China. The closest you could get was to have a share in a joint venture which only lasted for ten years or so, a sort of short term partnership, if you will, during which time the foreigners trained the Chinese who then took over what had been built once the initial term was up. But as many of these original joint ventures were now coming to an end and so the next step in their business relationships was being renegotiated, China was beginning to permit more permanent joint venture operations and even some wholly foreign owned enterprises as these became a necessity to continue to attract high levels of foreign investment.

I had insisted that our China company should be wholly owned by us, and on the basis of all the business and employment we would bring and how we would help China to develop, attracting other western companies to follow, the Chinese authorities agreed.

Our operation, my operation, grew into the first of its kind in China and soon became the centre of one of the busiest container terminals in the world.

The date was now in the first part of the 1990s and London had been in free-fall, still fighting recession. Those in England who still had jobs kept their heads down while many others spent demoralising days sending out yet more *curriculum vitae*, ringing round and chasing frustrating leads for possible employment that would inevitably lead nowhere.

But in the Far East, China was not just awakening as the western media thought; it was *already* wide awake and accelerating forwards. The manufacturing companies that had previously put the 'made in Hong Kong' labels in your training shoes or on your toys were now investing heavily in factories on the mainland and most products were now instead reading 'made in China'.

As western consumption grew, so did the demand for more competitive prices, and so grew the worldwide search for cheaper labour, more production, bigger factories. This was a search that increasingly ended in the Far East and in China, in particular. At first, the demand was based upon price but as investment continued to grow, the Chinese factories invested in technology, in the latest machinery, increasing their global appeal through quality, which gave their new revolution as the world's production facility great longevity and with the rise of more factories, so the number of containers shipped through our terminal and on our ships, increased dramatically.

We worked hard and then we worked harder, with many long hours and interminable meetings. Sometimes we were faced with seemingly insurmountable obstacles, problems that at times meant I could see no way through to the finish line. But we would regroup and, with a determination to succeed, we would take things back to basics, always keeping it simple, and we would eventually find a way, find a solution.

So our business grew, and we did become successful, and, with our success, so the fickle society life wanted me.

It was not really my world, strangers suddenly appearing to be your friends. It could at times seem very false. Were any of these people really my friends or did they just want to know me because they saw the success; would they have liked me in a life away from this Territory? But I knew this was, largely, how business was still done here and I was having fun; it was hard work but lots of fun.

The work was booming, and the pace was fast. We were doing deals, high profile deals. It was exciting, and it was glamorous. I attended extravagant, glitzy parties; I was having the time of my life.

As we became more successful, my life became ever more lively. I enjoyed all that was best in life. I ate in the best restaurants like Petrus; I drank in the new bars like Felix at the top of the famous Peninsular hotel, and I shopped in the designer boutiques like Prada and Cartier.
It was a 24/7 place. It was intense; it never stopped. I was intense; I never stopped. I was consumed by driving the business forwards, it was what I did; what I had to do to make our project work. Success is not easy, no-one gives it to you; you have to put in the effort, the 'sweat' to achieve. I had to make it work. Outwardly people who met me, friends, acquaintances, they all thought I was calm and cool, unflappable but inside was a constant struggle, a battle always raging. I was anxious, I was worried. Would it last?

As the new China operation continued to succeed, so the business became even more consuming. I often found myself in the office at weekends, working weeks on end with no day off to rest. The life all became a blur, one big challenge that I had to work on constantly. I had to work on it to make it as good as I possibly could. I could not stop thinking about it.

I became oblivious to spending any time on anything else as I continued to push unabated. I knew no other way. I wanted to see my project fulfilled, I wanted to create my vision and I was driven to make it work, I was driven to make sure it could not fail.

As for relationships, I had no time for them, what was the point; they would surely only end in disappointment, just as the one with Louisa had.

Connie was constantly trying to pair me off with yet another of her friends and always despaired when I would see them only the once, at most twice, before moving on. I think she came to see it as her mission to find me the one that I would fall for but of course that just made it more fun for me not to do so. The truth was that the social scene in Hong Kong was fast and full. It was wild, with so many young people just wanting to have a good time; it was much like Sodom and Gomorrah with no shortage of willing female company to satisfy the urges of the flesh.

'Don't forget we're going out tomorrow, and I promise there's no blind dates arranged by Connie. Just the guys, and perhaps some nice girls we might meet on the way,' Michael laughed, a twinkle of mischief in his eye, much like a naughty schoolboy.

'How could I forget,' I said taking a swig of beer. It was Friday evening and we were having a quick drink at the end of another hard week in one of our favourite haunts, the Captain's Bar of the Mandarin Oriental hotel.

It had been an unusual week, I had been in Shanghai for much of it meeting construction companies and negotiating with the authorities for possible sites for our new terminal, but in my absence, one of our ships, the Knox Princess had been hijacked by pirates and this had fast become the talk of the office.

'So what do you think of this hijack then?' I asked as I ordered us another two beers.

'It's a bit strange really,' answered Michael slowly.

'How so?'

'Well its nothing new to have attacks in the South China Seas, they've been happening for years, but what's different is that in the past the pirates have mostly just taken small amounts of cash or valuables that the crew or sailors on yachts might be carrying. Even the yacht race from Hong Kong to Manila is accompanied by a Royal Navy frigate to help protect the fleet as the risks are so high.'

'Really?' I asked, surprised.

'Yes, there are so many hundreds of islands, north of Indonesia, around Malaysia, in the Straits of Malacca and near the Philippines, pirates can easily attack. They hide at night, silently come up behind the huge cargo vessel in their small highly-powered boats, throw a grappling hook and climb aboard, armed to the teeth with automatic weapons. The crew don't even know it's happening before it's too late. Then, once they've got what they came for, they're gone again, disappeared as quickly as they came, consumed by the night.' He paused, possibly for theatrical effect, clearly now enjoying telling the story, before continuing with a touch of gravity in his voice this time, 'But, the concern now is that these guys are different.'

'Oh, how is that?'

'Well, previously, the pirates would usually leave sealed containers alone, but now they're targeting the containers and they seem to be quite good at finding the valuable ones without slowing down their escape.'

'Interesting,' I said.

'Anyway, drink up,' he said finishing his glass. 'I'm off home now.'

I looked around the bar; a pretty, dark haired girl standing alone at the bar had just caught my eye. 'I think I might stay here a little longer before setting off.'

'Ha ha,' he laughed, 'OK, it's alright for you. I'll see you tomorrow at the track.'

'Yeah, for sure, looking forward to it,' I replied and, as he left, I motioned with my glass to the pretty girl by way of offer for her to join me for a drink.

HER WALL

I awoke wearily; my mouth was dry. That was not unusual after a hard night partying. As I came out of my sleep, I thought it was her; a shock of dark hair lying beside me. They were always like her; they all resembled her in some way; I seemed to only choose ones that looked a little like her, all similar in her image, but ultimately, they were not her – they may look like her but they were nothing like her for she had been quite unlike anybody else. I never had interest in any conversation with them; I never had anything in common with them; there was never any connection; they were not her.

I swung my legs out of the bed, quiet so as not to wake her, not because I cared particularly about her, whoever she was, I could not even remember the name of this one. No, I wanted to be alone.

I went to make myself some coffee and shuffled out onto the balcony to light a cigarette. The smoke circled upwards, thick white at the bottom of its spiral, gradually fading until it had apparently become nothing, completely dispensed into the air, invisible to view even though the individual particles were surely still present, merely just dispersed and diluted now, less concentrated and enveloped by the greater volume of air.

I watched the boats at work in the harbour, the huge cargo ships at anchor wallowing like colourful whales beached in the shallows, smaller launches zipping between them mingled with the ever-present wooden sampans.

My thoughts turned to her; what would she be doing now?

*****

Born in a small village in Devon, Louisa was the youngest of three girls, with two elder sisters who would tease her mercilessly, constantly putting her down, telling her how stupid and how different she was, they being all blonde to her dark hair, they would tell her she was not part of their family. That she had been left by gypsies one night, unwanted. So she had grown up with no confidence.

Her parents' house backed onto fields, typical English countryside with green fields lined by hedgerows, and next door was a small stable where she had spent most of her time, not just the weekends but also mucking out in the evenings after school when she really probably should have been doing her homework. Her parents used to joke that the horses were her real family.

Louisa craved her independence, maybe because of the relationship with her sisters she wanted to prove herself, or maybe she just wanted to get away, to have her own space and not be in their shadow, not always be their little sister. So as soon as Louisa was eighteen she left home and moved to London.

She lost touch with her interest, as many teenagers do when they find the social world of partying and pubs and clubs, and when she moved away from home to London, there was no time for horses so they were soon pushed back, deep into her head and, eventually, almost forgotten.

She had started with various tedious temp jobs, filing or answering phones, sometimes typing but she tried to avoid those assignments if she could as her accuracy was not particularly good when she found things become a little tedious and she could no longer be bothered to pay attention anymore. Eventually, she managed to find herself a role as a PA for an executive at an advertising agency where she had initially gone to answer the phones for a week. It had seemed like a more fun office to be in than some of the others she had visited recently so she tried that little bit harder to make a good impression in the hope that she would be asked to stay.

But although she enjoyed the excitement of her new life in London, there was something missing for her.

She enjoyed the socialising with her friends from work, but they were not her real friends. She only saw them because they were the people who she just happened to meet because they were there, in the same office as her at that time; they had not met because of any common interests, she had not particularly chosen them to be her friends.

As for the work, she did it because it paid the bills and it enabled her to be here, living her own life, giving her the independence she wanted so much.

She had fun at work; she enjoyed most of her days, but she did not particularly enjoy what she did; she was going through the motions. She had no eye for detail. It was not that she was not that clever; it was just that she did not particularly care enough to make the extra effort to be as good as she could be. She found her job quite easy, it did not particularly challenge her and she did not push herself; she did just enough, just what she had to do.

But she did have the ability to make others like her, if she so chose to allow them, for those that she did not were unable to comprehend how any of their friends could like such a cold, harsh person.

She was not at all ambitious. She did not care at all for titles or for recognition. But she did want to enjoy her life; she did have a romantic notion of her somehow enjoying her days, free from the constraints or requirements of others, but doing what, she had no specific idea.

Now she had met Dan. Oh Dan, how wonderful it seemed to have met someone who seemed to understand her so well but why did this bring so many other emotions? It was such happiness, but also such confusion.

It was a strange feeling, she reflected. Strange how both she and Dan were so fiercely independent, how they had both left their homes as soon as they could and now, suddenly, all that had changed. Suddenly, they could both only think of being together, prepared to throw themselves into becoming dependent on one another. It made no sense but they had no choice in it. That must be love, was it?

But after years of independence, how could she trust that she could open herself up to him, trust to leave herself open to him, and if what she felt for Dan was so special, why did it feel like there was still something missing for her? Did not love conquer all and overcome any other misgivings?

It was ironic that it would be on a rare trip without him, on a visit home to Devon that she happened to bump into the lady who ran the small stables next-door to her parents' house. She had always liked Louisa; after all she had virtually grown up in her yard with the amount of time she had spent with her horses. So she was always interested to learn from Louisa's mother of any news about what she was doing now. She thought it a shame that Louisa had stopped riding; she knew that this love of horses and the love of the outdoors would not have just disappeared.

On this occasion it just so happened that Louisa's parents' neighbour had her old friends from her days in the showjumping ring over from Ireland, the McGowans, and from this chance meeting came the opportunity for Louisa to go and work at their famous yard in Greenclover; an opportunity sown and fertilised by Louisa's caring neighbour. It would be her dream job. She had loved horses for as long as she could remember, truly all her life so she was really excited at the thought to be given the opportunity to go and work at the Greenclover stables. The stables were well known in horsey circles and very successful and Louisa knew she was lucky to have been offered the job, *but*......

But the yard was in Ireland, just outside Dublin. But, *what* a chance; *what* an opportunity!

The stables had twenty-five horses, which is quite large by most standards and they were run by a homely Irish family, the McGowans, who were very welcoming to her. The countryside there was truly beautiful, wild and natural, close to both the sea and to the raw countryside inland.

Part of her job would be to help exercise the horses and so she would ride across the open green fields, across the heather, sometimes with others from the stable on a hack together jumping ditches and hedges and sometimes she would be all alone. What an opportunity!

They had shown her some pictures of the stables and some of the horses; her favourite was a dark chestnut brown called Apollo. She loved a horse's majesty, his beauty, his loyalty and she could imagine looking into his deep, dark eyes. She imagined riding him until dusk fell in the evening, taking him down to the beach to gallop on the wet sands of the shallows beside the frothing sea, the wind blowing his dark mane wildly as they flew along, joined together, almost as one.

Instantly, she knew this was the job for her; no, not just a job, *the life* for her. This was where she wanted to be, not stuck inside some office in London.

But what of Dan? It had all happened so quickly; so unexpectedly.

She thought how Dan seemed to be acting on impulse. 'If it feels right,' he would say, 'then, why not do it?'

She wanted to be more cautious, surely that was the more sensible thing. How did she know he was being genuine; how did she know if it would last?

What a wonderful life she could have there. Was this feeling for Dan worth sacrificing all that for? What were these feelings for him, even? She had never experienced anything like this before. Sometimes, for no obvious reason, she would cry herself to sleep, which just made her feel stupid. She had always been so strong before, so independent, but this thing, this thing they called love, she could not control it and if it was the right thing to do, why did she feel like this? Why did she feel so bad about it?

'Why stay?' she would reason with herself. 'Maybe Dan does not even really feel the same way about you and then where will you be? Or maybe he will just leave you for someone else anyway and just think all that you would have given up, all that you would have lost.' She cried some more.

There was so much she did not even know about him. No, she was better off leaving. It was safer to go, more sensible. It was definitely the best thing to do. So why then, why would this horrible feeling not go away? This sickness, this hurt. For love does not disappear just because you reasoned it should do so; love does not reason. Is this what love is? Louisa asked herself; how did she even know if love was real?

'You're both too young to try to settle down,' her flatmate Anna would try to help, 'and he looks fickle to me.'

'Fickle?'

'Yes, like he'd leave you for the next pretty thing that crosses his path.'

She knew her friend was probably right, that they had met too young, that even if he did not leave her for another girl, something else would come along for him, some great job opportunity, that he would just go and leave her without a second thought.

Because of her elder sisters' teasing she had grown with little confidence and over the years she had built up her defences, intentionally seeming cold and carefree, uncaring what anyone who met her may think. It was little wonder she preferred the company of the horses next door to her home; they did not tease her.

Born from this lack of self confidence came the impression given to those who did not know her of someone aloof and uncaring but, really, it was just her mechanism for self-preservation. It was all just part of her facade, an act, her wall, the one she had built to protect her from just this very thing, to protect her from ever being hurt.

She had never had a really close relationship before, never allowing herself to fall that far. For it was not arrogance that gave out the warnings Dan had sensed in the bar on the first night they had met, rather the opposite, it was her wall, built for her protection, saving her from harm, from rejection but now, here, when she needed it, the barrier did not help. None of it helped. She still wanted to be with him. She still wanted him. With Dan, she could not help it. True love did not recognise her artificial walls.

She did not know how it could have happened but he had somehow got behind her defences. Dan had somehow entered into her fortress, scaled her wall. She could not stop it; she had no choice. So what should she do? What was there to do - nothing but to run.

The decision was made, she had to leave; she would only regret it otherwise, it was the sensible thing to do. She could not trust; she could not allow herself to be left open to any harm by anyone. She could not take that chance.

So Dan had agreed. How could he not; after all the encouragement he had given her to do what she really wanted, to build her confidence, how could he stop her now? How could he do anything else, after continually saying they should seize life's opportunities that came their way, how could he now do anything but encourage her to take such a once in a lifetime opportunity? How could he?

They both put a brave face on it; Ireland was not so far away, just a train and ferry ride or, if they could afford it, a short flight across the Irish Sea.

At first there were a few phone calls but Dan sensed a new coolness from her, the excitement and warmth evaporated and her enthusiasm for his visits disappeared with each new weak excuse and different reason why she would not be available, the unreturned calls making a man soon give up trying – you can only take so much.

So then..... then she was gone.

*****

I squinted my eyes as I took another long drag on the cigarette, now almost down to the final butt end. From my terrace I could see one of the large ships making its way out of port, guided by two tugs. Life stands still for no man and continues with or without you, like it or not.

'C'est la vie,' I breathed. 'Our paths crossed too early,' I whispered to the final puff of white smoke as it too disappeared into the air. I turned my back on the scene to return inside and slid the glass door to the balcony shut on such thoughts.

That night I would be off to the horse track with Michael and his three best friends. He had introduced me to them many times and often we would gamble and drink whiskey into the small hours. Together the four of them would chatter excitedly whenever they were together, laughing loudly; it was infectious and I enjoyed their company.

There was Vincent Kao who ran his own business, a very successful company making compact disc players, radios and other electronic machines. He now had a factory just over the border in China, in Guangdong province, all set up with money given to him by his father.

Edward Kwok worked for one of the Territory's largest property developers. Good apartments were always in short supply in this small slice of land so the clamour for new apartments was always intense and speculation would send prices soaring even before they were finished. Vincent always seemed to have the inside knowledge on what new development was occurring and to be able to secure opportunities early.

Larry Chung, the son of an extraordinarily wealthy businessman, was now running the family business. He was the quietest of the group, did not drink so much, never lost control. In some ways I felt sorry for him as he always seemed lost somehow amongst his friends' louder more colourful behaviour.

I smiled at the thought of the evening ahead; I knew we were going to the race track to see the horses but they also said they had something special arranged and I was looking forward to it.

The four friends were on good form that night, very animated and loud, they were all in a mood to have a good time, even Larry was less quiet than usual, each excited, perhaps, at the prospect of an evening out without their wives.

They had taken an exclusive box at the Happy Valley race track, built by the Hong Kong Jockey Club for horse racing it was an amazing temple to gambling. They loved to gamble in Hong Kong but the horses were the only legalised form; this did not stop the locals from finding anything to gamble on, mah-jong games, or anything they could find, but it meant that betting on the horses was incredibly popular – the Jockey Club even had ATM style hole-in-the-wall machines dedicated to betting stationed at various places around the Territory to help satisfy this thirst.

The scene on a Saturday night was something to behold. The white-bright floodlights picking out the animated faces of thousands in the crowd., the brightly coloured silks of their chosen champions, the excited commentary over the PA system like a freight train accelerating to the crescendo of the finish, the excited, ever-hopeful disciples shouting, screaming, as they urged their chosen ones over the line first, and, inevitably, the white squares of unwanted betting slips fluttering down, discarded into the air after each race, a beautiful scene contrasting with the lost hopes and dreams of what the tickets could have been for their owners.

The evening was going well and Vincent and Edward were particularly pleased with themselves having won quite a sizeable amount of Hong Kong dollars between them.

'So, where did you guys all meet?' I asked as I took a sip from the brown bottle of Carlsberg beer and leaned back in my chair.

'We were all at school together,' Michael replied.

'Yes, the most exclusive school in the Territory,' cut in Vincent laughing, he was always the most excited of the four. 'Michael was there on a scholarship, he was the clever one; we all used to copy his homework.'

I caught the look on Michael's face as he gave a half smile, looking a bit sheepish. Was that a humble look at his friend's protestations of his brilliance, or embarrassment at the memory that he was not there at the school like them, at the expense of wealthy parents.

'Yes, he was going to be a brilliant doctor or something, going to find the cure for cancer, weren't you?' continued Edward. 'That was before we introduced him to Connie;

then he was hooked, smitten and decided to become a tycoon instead.'

'It's true, we ruined him,' laughed Vincent, raising his glass in Michael's direction.

Michael gave another sheepish smile. I suddenly felt sorry for him, living in the shadows of his wealthy friends, constantly trying to keep up, trying to impress, ceaselessly climbing a steep oily slope that could never have any end.

'What new trinket is she demanding now?' Vincent continued and we all laughed.

'*Siu Bo Shek,*' teased Edward in a mock high pitched voice.

'What? What's that?' I asked.

'It's Cantonese for Little Gem,' said Edward, 'it's his pet name for her,' and they laughed some more.

'I know, I know,' Michael shook his head in a resigned fashion. 'But you can't talk, it's just as bad for all of you.' The four friends laughed some more at the thoughts of the presents their wives now expected but, inside, each knew it was different for Michael, for each of the others came from so much money they did not really have to work to meet their wives' expectations, whereas Michael, he was having to make his money to keep Connie satisfied, to keep her from leaving him for someone else, for someone better.

'Apart from young Danny here,' said Larry quietly contributing now to the conversation. 'Look at him, no wife, no ties, you seem to have a good thing going here, as much skirt as you want.'

I smiled and nodded my beer in his direction before taking another sip.

'Yes, seems a bit unfair somehow,' laughed Vincent.

'What I don't understand,' cut in Michael, 'is how you seem immune to the girls.'

I raised an eyebrow, not sure I understood what he meant.

'I mean,' he continued, 'you never seem to fall in love with any of the girls. You're never remotely interested in seeing them again or doing anything with them, being with them?'

I shrugged and smiled, 'I think, my friend, that you are confusing sex with love.'

'Have you always been like that?' Michael asked. 'Was there ever anyone special?'

My smile faded a little and I looked down as I started to pick at the label on the beer bottle. 'Perhaps, I thought there could have been someone once, but I was wrong, she's gone now.'

'Oh really,' laughed Michael excitedly, 'so you're not so impervious after all.'

'No, no,' I tried to join in the laughter. 'It was nothing. She wasn't the one,' I tailed off, perhaps unconvincingly. 'Anyway, don't you think you guys should concentrate on your own problems and how you're going to keep all your demanding wives satisfied? Don't worry about me, I'm free.'

We all laughed some more, but inside something was nagging at me, not letting me rest. It was the truth - that I had let her go - that I had let her escape.

At that moment Larry's phone rang. He answered it in Cantonese and spoke just a few words followed by a smile across his face.

'Wang?' asked Vincent, 'Is everything OK?'

Larry nodded.

'Fantastic!' Vincent exclaimed.

'Good news?' I asked. All four of them seemed very happy.

61

'Excellent,' replied Larry calmly, always the least excitable of the group. 'You see we have a little syndicate going and we've just done rather well. So it seems my friend that we also have nothing to worry about, we will have more than enough to keep our little *tai tais* happy.'

'Syndicate? What sort?' I asked. 'Betting on the horses?'

'Something like that,' smiled Edward. 'Hey maybe you could join in.'

'Not until he's married,' laughed Vincent.

'Yes, he won't know he needs the extra money until then,' said Michael and they all laughed.

'Come on, time to go to the club,' declared Edward. 'We can celebrate some more there.'

Nightclubs in Hong Kong were usually one of two types, either a traditional disco style bar, overly crowded and full of young expats, or the girlie bars of Wanchai where girls in brightly coloured leotards would dance on a stage in the middle of a bar which encircled around them, at which the punters would sit sipping beer watching the show.

But the friends' club was like nothing I had ever been to before, a club for members only, there were three different bars, each with a different theme; there were private cubicles with comfy seats upholstered in leather of dark burgundy and private rooms for each group to party away from the main bars if they preferred.

The girl hostesses were gorgeous and tended to our every need. Michael and his friends seemed to be very popular and to be receiving a lot of attention, Larry in particular.

We were sat in the jungle bar, the four friends had gone on to drinking whiskey as was customary in the Far East when they had something to celebrate, and the bigger the win, the more expensive the whiskey. I was still drinking bottled beer.

'He seems very popular here,' I said to Michael as I pointed over to where Larry was sitting with a pretty little hostess sitting on his lap, 'is he the member here?'

'Who, Larry?' Michael asked turning to look over his shoulder in the direction my bottle was pointing, then laughing 'He should be, his dad owns the place.'

I laughed with him.

At that point, another man came across to the booth where the other three were sat with their girls. Vincent and Edward in particular seemed happy to see him; they both shook his hand vigorously and clapped him on the back. He was a big man, broad and rough looking with a big dark moustache and a cut on his left cheek; he looked much like a Mexican bandito from an old western movie. He did not seem like the others somehow, although they were pleased to see him and had greeted him warmly, he was obviously deferential, respectful to them.

'Who's that?' I asked.

'That's Wang,' replied Michael. 'He works for Larry.'

'So he's the guy who called earlier at the track, bringing all the winnings I guess for you lucky bastards in your syndicate.'

'Something like that,' smiled Michael.

At that point they were joined by a tall dark girl, stunning in a tight black dress that clung to her every curve. With her long black hair falling down her back she was very exotic; she certainly caught my attention.

Edward started to walk her over towards us, 'Dan, this is Lara. We've told her all about you and how badly you treat all your girlfriends and she still wants to meet you,' he laughed.

'Well, I'm charmed,' I said, looking her directly in the eye. 'Do you work here at the club, for Larry?'

'No' she laughed, throwing back her hair, 'I'm his banker.'

'Really,' I laughed, surprised. 'You're certainly the most attractive banker I've ever seen, actually, you could be the most attractive person I have ever seen,' I finished, surprised at my own seriousness.

'Well thank you,' she answered coyly.

'Can I buy you a drink?' I asked, intrigued by this mix of beauty and brains.

'Not now,' she replied, 'I've got to go but here's my card, call me. I'd love to go out.'

'Well,' I breathed as she turned and left towards the stairs heading for the exit, 'that was quite a surprise; a very pleasant surprise.'

'Lara?' said Michael. 'She is quite something isn't she.'

'You can say that again, and a banker as well,' I continued, my breath still somewhat taken away and not yet fully returned.

'Yes, evidently a very good one, Larry trusts her with many of his dealings; she doesn't normally socialise with us unless she happens to be doing some business with him, so she must like you. Are you going to take her out then?'

'Maybe,' I smiled at my friend, 'just maybe. Perhaps I'm the real winner tonight then, rather than your syndicate.'

'Maybe Lara will be the one to help you get over her,' laughed Michael and then, getting serious, 'So, tell me, who was she?'

'Who was who?'

'The girl you mentioned before, at the track, your only love.'

'Whoever said anything about being in love?' I tried to laugh it off but not very convincingly.

Michael raised his eyebrows at me, 'Come on!' he urged.

'OK, OK,' and so, with the drink getting the better of me, my defences down, I told him about Louisa. I told him of that wonderful summer we had spent with each other, I told him how much time we had spent together, how it felt like we understood each other, how we had always known each other, and I told him how she had to go away, she had to, I could not have prevented her doing that, to have got in the way of her dream life. I had not told anyone any of this before, perhaps it was the beer, but once I started I could not stop.

'Wow,' breathed Michael 'I had no idea. So you sacrificed yourself for her, you never told her how you felt. You must have really liked her, loved her and it sounds to me like you're still hung up on her.'

I scowled ruefully. 'You're a good friend Michael but no, you're wrong; there are plenty more where she came from. I just haven't bothered trying to look again yet. The bitch means nothing to me, she's gone.'

Michael seemed taken aback by the power and the bitterness of these words, but then Michael did not know what I had just recently heard.

'No, she's not who I thought she was, who she might be,' I thought, 'or could have been!' I whispered to myself, pulling at the label on my bottle of beer.

A PROPOSAL

It was six o'clock in the evening in Ireland; the skies were full of low thick clouds in differing shades of grey, darkness was arriving fast and the clouds were moving at a pace, all combining to create the feeling that the sky was closing in, descending upon the field from where Louisa was now returning with Apollo.

As she reached the wooden gate, she heard a voice call out to her. It was Frank, the McGowans' son. A gentle breeze caught the ends of her hair, blowing its wavy curls to one side, the lighter shades of chestnut catching in the evening sunlight. To Frank she had never looked more beautiful.

'What are you doing out so late, Louisa?' he asked. 'I've told you before you can finish at five.'

'I know,' she smiled, 'but I've also told you, I enjoy Apollo's company.'

'More than mine, I suppose,' he replied, hoping she might reply in the negative.

'Of course,' she giggled, 'he's my special man.'

'Uh,' he grunted, disappointed, even though he really knew better than to expect anything more from her. 'So are we still on for this evening?'

'Maybe,' she smiled, never making it easy for him.

'I've booked a table at the Westbury in town; it's hard to get in you know, I had to book this a month ago.'

She smiled, he had told her all this before but she knew he was trying to make sure she was not going to make her excuses and cry off.

'We'd better be going soon, don't want to be late,' he continued, 'shall I collect you in an hour?'

'Yes, OK, that would be perfect, I've just got to brush him down and put him away then I'll get ready.' She saw the anxious look on his face, 'Don't worry, I won't be late.'

He gave a nervous smile as she turned to lead Apollo into his stable.

Poor Frank, he was the McGowan's only son, tall and dark and now increasingly taking over the running of Greenclover as his parents grew older, he should have been quite a catch for some girl, but he was not the brightest and Louisa found him easy to tease. Louisa and Frank had been dating for a couple of months now. About seven years older than her, he was an ordinary looking man, neither particularly unattractive nor extraordinarily handsome. He was somewhat shy and his personality was not exactly charismatic; he was more likely to shrink into the shadows of a room rather than light it up on his entrance.

As she rubbed Apollo down, Louisa did think how he was not him, how he was not Dan. She knew in another life he may not have been the person she would have chosen to be with, however, he was dependable and she was looking forward to going out to the City tonight.

Indeed, later, all dressed up and out from the farm, she was quite excited, if a little uncomfortable in the posh surroundings of the formal restaurant. They were shown to their table and flutes of bubbling champagne were soon offered before them.

'Cheers,' toasted Frank, raising his glass to her.

'Cheers,' she tilted her glass in reply.

'What are we drinking to?' she asked, taking a sip anyway, the effervescent nectar tasting good as it danced and fizzed on her tongue.

Frank's face suddenly appeared to take on a somewhat serious expression as he frowned and, after a pause he said, 'To you. I'm so happy you came here Louisa. You know I asked you earlier why do you work so late?'

'Yes, of course, but you know I love it; it's not work really is it?' she declared, replying quickly, the words jumping from her in her excitement.

He paused again, as if a little unsure of himself. 'You do love it here don't you?'

'Yes,' she replied, hesitating, a little surprised at the change in tone of his voice, softer now.

'Well, why not make it more permanent?'

'I didn't know it wasn't. Why boss do you know something I don't, are you planning to fire me at any moment?' She laughed and then continued, more seriously. 'My life is here; this *is* my life now. '

'Well,' he faltered, 'I just meant that perhaps you wanted to put down some roots.'

'In what way?' she spoke haltingly, unsure of what he was trying to get at.

'Well, I mean, why not marry me?'

'Oh Frank,' she said, more in a manner of pity than excitement, 'this is all very sudden.'

'But I know its right Louisa, I'm sure of it, and you do love it here at Greenclover, it's your life now, you just said so yourself,' he urged, desperation entering his voice.

'Yes, but.....'

'But what?'

'But Frank, it's such a big step. Let me think about it.'

That night, through a thousand tears, she kept thinking about the proposal, but the tears were not those of happiness. She knew she should be so happy but she could not persuade herself to be so.

No, the tears were not of happiness; she knew the tears were of him, of Dan; he who was so many miles away now, enjoying himself. She had heard he was very successful and involved in an exciting and colourful world. She knew that was what he wanted and this here, in the country with her beloved horses, this was what she wanted, and she came to realise the tears were now of a past that had surely gone, tears of goodbye.

The next morning, by the side of the stables, she saw Frank. He looked nervous of her, shy even, as if he did not really know her, as if he did not really want to talk to her, unsure whether he wanted to hear what she might have to say.

'Don't go,' Louisa called out to him. 'It's good news. I would like to accept your proposal. I would be honoured to be your wife and live here in your beautiful world.'

Frank whooped for joy and picked her up by the waist, lifting her high into the air and twirling her around before giving her a big kiss, full on the lips.

'Come, let's go tell Mum and Dad,' he cried, his voice an octave higher than usual, 'they'll be so thrilled.'

Of course, Mrs McGowan was indeed so happy, talking at a hundred miles an hour. She was so happy, not just for her only son, and not because they genuinely liked Louisa, no, Mrs McGowan was so happy because now, finally, she had a wedding to plan. The words spat out like bullets as she talked so excitedly about plans for a summer wedding. They would use the big barn for the reception; there were so many guests to invite, cousins, aunts, uncles, old friends, she really must go off and find her address book, there was so much to do.

Mr McGowan was less excitable, he did not care for such fuss but he knew there was no use trying to stop his wife when she was in this mood, and he gave Louisa a reassuring smile as if to say 'Don't mind her, dear.'

*****

I heard she was to marry, and the knife cut deeper, the knife that was ever-present, the knife that was Louisa, constantly felt in varying degrees, with good days and bad days. Now it cut deeper and twisted sharply, intensified with an additional pain, its tip now enhanced with the poison of jealousy that penetrated into me and made its evil rush through my veins. Where before there had been the dull throb of something lost, now there was also the sharp sting that what I craved was now lost to another. At least I now knew one thing. At least I was now positive there could be no such thing as love.

PIRATES

It was midnight; Captain Svenson was taking a final drag on his cigarette before he would return inside to the wheelhouse. Standing outside here high up on the bridge of the Knox Star, the night was very still, the only breeze being the apparent wind generated by the ship's slow movement. All was quiet, the only sound coming from the muffled thud of the ship's diesel engines mixed with the wash of the waters as the boat made its way through, it was a soothing sound.

The Captain smiled, he enjoyed moments like this; it was why he went to sea, the peace, the tranquillity, the freedom, and at these times he allowed his mind to drift to thoughts of his family, far away in Sweden, his wife of so many years would be trying to get their young son to bed. He loved them and was missing them now after what had been a few months shift plying his trade ferrying cargoes from east to west, but the sea was his mistress and it was a curse he and his wife had come to live with. 'Not long now, Freya,' he whispered under his breath to the dark night.

They were entering the Malacca straits and all around them was dark. He did not hear them, there was no sound, no warning. The next thing he knew was the feel of cold metal to his head, hard round steel like the size of a large thumb being pressed forcibly to his temple.

'Do not make a sound and do as I say and you will not get hurt,' the voice said, his English heavily accented; he sounded Chinese.

The Captain twisted slowly to look around as much as he dared against the constraint of the fearful pressure from the pistol to his head. Suddenly, where just before there had been no-one, he was now accompanied in his quiet sanctuary by at least four men, all armed to the teeth with automatic weapons.

'Take what you want,' breathed Svenson, 'just don't hurt my men.'

'Give them the order then, not to resist,' urged the Chinese man menacingly, 'it's futile in any case.'

'Ok, OK, that's not going to be a problem,' he tried to sound calm as he reached for the tannoy to give the command to his crew over the address system. Down below he could see more of the pirates, all dressed in black and all armed, scurrying about to the commands of their leader who had now left the Captain guarded by just one of his men who eyed Svenson up and down nervously, ready to shoot at the first signs of resistance. But the Captain was not going to give him any bother, he knew the drill, they were all instructed not to risk any resistance for some faceless organisation's cargo, it would all be dealt with by insurance, just preserve the safety of his men, the crew's safety was paramount.

Svenson, actually, was quite intrigued with how efficient the pirates were. They each seemed to understand their role and obeyed the orders without the slightest question. They seemed to know exactly what they were doing and knew the layout of the ship so well, as if the raid had been rehearsed and practised many times before; it was all done with such precision, almost military-like in organisation; the Captain was impressed.

Soon they were gone, lost again to the night.

I was in Shanghai when the call came through of the attack from my secretary in Hong Kong.

'What was taken?' I asked.

I knew the reply before I received it.

On the flight back to Hong Kong, I was trying to work out all the pieces to the puzzle. I had learnt that, indeed, just as Michael had told me in the Captain's bar a few months earlier, it was not uncommon for attacks in the South China Seas, but, although they had been happening for years, previously the attackers had mostly been searching for small amounts of cash or valuables but now the pirates were targeting containers full of valuable goods and, somehow, they seemed to be becoming increasingly good at identifying their target.

There were so many hundreds of islands in these Straits, it was too easy for the pirates to attack, undercover of the dark cloak of night. Noiselessly they would come up behind the huge cargo ship in their fast, manoeuvrable boats and camouflaged by the vast size of the vessel that was their target, its crew, defenceless, did not stand a chance, not even knowing the attack was happening before the pirates were already upon them.

The next day I was back at my desk in the Knox office; however, I could not settle, something was troubling me, although I could not quite put my finger on it.

From my big round window high up in the Jardine building I could see the harbour and I could see the ships moored up in the channel waiting to be unloaded before going on their way to the next destination.

Richard had designed the offices so that they overlooked the Knox terminal where their ships would unload and take on the next cargo, and I would regularly get up and pace over to the window looking down at the ant-sized workers beavering away on the dockside. The pacing and watching, observing, helped me to think.

Down below me today the Knox Princess ship was in dock, a container ship, one of the largest of its kind, the random patterns of red and green rectangles, the containers, slowly being removed one by one. This was the same ship that had been raided those few months previously and it belonged to our Singaporean subsidiary.

'The Knox Princess,' I thought, suddenly reminded of something I had seen somewhere before and I laughed to myself, a half smile emerging across my face at the irony of it. That is it; that must be it.

A gust of breeze caught the flag on the ship's stern, a Panamanian flag lifted and fluttered, gently, from side to side.

I paused a moment and caught my breath.

'What if,' I whispered quietly. 'That's brilliant, absolutely brilliant,' and I picked up the phone. I quickly explained what was needed to the person at the other end of the line. 'andI need the answer today, as soon as possible,' I ended. 'Wait, don't call me here at the office, call me on my mobile,' I added, abruptly.

AMBITION - PRIDE - HONOUR

'Oh hi Dan, I wasn't expecting you,' Michael opened the front door to his apartment. 'We're not having dinner until tomorrow are we? Connie's out.'

'I know but there's just something I wanted to talk to you about. Can I come in?'

'Yes, of course, come on in. Go through to the terrace, I'll put the coffee on.' Unusually for Michael he was in jeans and tee-shirt, not his usual immaculate self as he would be if expecting visitors. 'What is it that couldn't wait until the morning; something private you didn't want to talk about in the office?' he called to me from the kitchen as I made my way through to the terrace.

'Something like that,' I replied.

'You haven't got some girl into trouble have you? It's not Lara is it? I told you she would ruin you?'

'No, no, nothing like that. It's probably nothing really, just something I wanted to run by you. Something you can help with perhaps.'

'OK. Well of course I will if I can. Hang on, let me just pour this. You like yours strong don't you?'

'Yes please, strong and black. Are you having Chinese tea?' Old friends now we knew each others tastes and idiosyncrasies well.

'Yes, freshens the palate you know,' he smiled handing me my cup.

'Hmm,' I paused to take in the aroma of the freshly brewed coffee before tasting a first sip. 'That's good thanks; how's the boat?' I asked, looking towards a photo of his white motor-cruiser hanging proudly on the wall behind him.

'Good, good thanks,' he replied a little hesitantly, still unsure why his friend had dropped by unexpectedly and wondering what it was that he wanted to talk about.

'Maybe I should get something like that, to play with at the weekend, smaller of course, seeing as I don't have any family.'

'Yes, good idea; then we could motor off to the New Territories together,' Michael relaxed a little at the talk about boats.

'Maybe,' I replied, 'so how much does something like that cost? Must be way beyond my means?'

'Yes, it's not cheap,' he laughed.

'How much then?' I smiled.

'I can't remember,' he replied. 'It was a little while ago now.'

'Really, I would have thought when you spend that much money you'd remember it to the last cent, it's like buying a house isn't it? Go on,' I urged, 'what, it must have been about a couple of million Hong Kong dollars, perhaps just a little more?'

Michael caught himself, suddenly slightly cautious, he replied slowly, 'Yes something like that, I guess.' In fact, it had been almost exactly that amount, two point one million dollars in fact, but how could his friend have known? Perhaps it was just a lucky guess or maybe he was more serious about buying a boat than he had let on and had already done some research? Perhaps that was why he was here. 'Why not get a ski boat then and we could tow it and do some water-skiing together.'

'Maybe,' I replied, without much commitment.

There was a pause as I took another sip of my coffee.

'How could you afford that?' I smiled ruefully, and, as I looked around the room, 'How can you afford any of it, Michael? The luxury apartment, the cars, the jewellery, the clothes? Any of it?'

'Are you worried about me my friend?' he laughed nervously.

I turned to look directly at him, 'I'm very worried for you,' I said softly.

'Well, don't be,' he smiled. 'Look, your concern, it's nice. But honestly, any concerns you have, they are misguided; everything's fine, it's all under control.'

'But is it? Really?'

'Yes, yes no problem,' he laughed.

'Hmm, well that's a relief.' As I finished my coffee, Michael's eyes did not leave mine. I put the cup down and made as if to get up to go.

'So, if your mind's now at rest, I'll see you in the office in the morning,' he gestured with an outstretched arm towards the door.

'Oh but there was one thing I did want to ask you about.'

'What was that?'

'You can probably clear it up for me. That little syndicate you have with Larry and the others, doing well is it?'

'Yes,' he replied hesitantly, unsure of himself again. 'We have our good days and our bad ones. Luckily they're mostly good.'

'What is it you gamble on again? Horses wasn't it?'

'Yes, mainly. We get some good tips.' Where was this going thought Michael, what was Dan up to?

'Hmm,' I let it hang there for a few moments, I could see him struggling to understand. 'Yes I thought so. But that night at the track together, what I can't figure out is why did that guy who works for Larry, what's his name again?'

'Mr Wang,' breathed Michael, certain that Dan already knew this answer.

'Yes, that's it, Mr Wang. Well if you guys won big on the horses, and we were at the track, why did he have to phone you from somewhere else with the news of the winnings, and why did he have to come over a few hours later with the money?'

'Oh Dan,' laughed Michael, 'so naive. Not all gambling is done at the track you know. Much better odds and bigger bets can be done through betting elsewhere and Mr Wang can make those sorts of bets for us.'

'I see, I had no idea but,' I left a pause, 'did you know that a ship of ours, the Knox Princess was hijacked the night before we went to the track?'

'Yes,' this single word was said very slowly, Michael was defensive.

'Well, I read the report. Just out of interest you understand, it's not really my thing but,' I paused again, 'what I don't understand, is how come Mr Wang came to be on that ship that night?'

Silence. I could feel my heart rate increase rapidly. It had been one thing before I came here this evening, calculating what I would do but now, in the moment, as I turned the contemplation into reality, the adrenaline rapidly began to kick in; my pulse raced.

Michael rocked forwards, clasping his two hands together in front of him as he first looked down at the ground then, after a long pause, slowly turned his head, looking up at me. 'This is not a social visit, is it?'

'No, it is not.'

Michael's eyes narrowed, he suddenly seemed dangerously cold. He whispered, 'So, how do you know about that?'

I tried to keep calm, 'Well, I probably would have thought nothing about it; however, I remembered that in the report it said that the pirates were Chinese, which in itself was probably nothing special, but on that hijack something went wrong as they were leaving and the first mate said in the report that he managed to slash the pirate leader with a hook as he was leaving, a Chinese man with a thick black moustache, who looked almost Mexican.'

I looked at him. Michael's face was impassive.

'So when I recalled seeing Mr Wang in the club that night with a cut face, it got me thinking. As you know, I could not understand why it was that the pirates all of a sudden knew which containers were the valuable ones to go for. So I thought what if what if they had someone on the inside, someone who had access to the ship's manifests, who knew what cargoes were inside which containers.'

'Then the hijack last night of the Knox Star,' I looked at him, 'Michael, you're the only one I told,' I paused to let it sink in. 'About the container of arms and ammunition. I told you in the Captain's Bar, remember and I conveniently left the ship's manifest out in the office showing the container they were in. I knew that if it was you, the prize would be too good to resist. Only, really that container was just full of heavy machine parts that the pirates couldn't move and that's how they were listed to everyone else. Your guys went straight to it, they may as well have come round to the offices and fingered you themselves.'

'Well, well, what to do Dan? We've got a good thing going now. It pays very well. It needn't stop, you could join us.'

I gave a half laugh, 'I'm sorry, I couldn't.' I had replied instantly, before any devil of temptation could even begin to stir within me, it was an instinctive reply. I am not sure why, it was not even a conscious decision it just was not

79

me, I was not driven by money. I just had to do the right thing.

'If I had not seen him, Mr Wang, you know, I would never have known. But once I knew, I had to find out.'

'So, aren't you the clever little detective,' snarled Michael, getting angry now, the anger of an animal cornered, getting ready to fight its way out. 'You think you're so very clever, coming over here, poking your nose into my business.'

I paused, trying to remain calm, trying to suppress my fear and maintain my resolve for what I knew must be done 'And there's more isn't there?'

'What, what do you mean?'

'Michael, I know about *Siu Bo Shek*. I know about the Knox Princess and *Siu Bo Shek*.'

'What?' Michael froze.

'The rent you've been paying to Connie's company for our boat,' I said softly. 'Yes, we've checked the register, and I've just had it confirmed that the ship we think we own was apparently sold and registered by the buyer, your wife's company, two years ago. But of course, Knox never received any money from you for the sale because they never knew about it and now we have to rent it back from you. Only you got your little friend at our accounting firm to keep it on the books as if it was still owned by us, hoping no-one would notice. Unfortunately for you, your new company had to register its ownership in Panama; I saw it flying a different flag in port.'

When I saw that flag flutter in the breeze that afternoon, I already knew what was in the accounts, I knew that they showed our Singaporean subsidiary owned the Knox Princess but I was also sure that all their ships were registered in Hong Kong and if so, they should all be flying the Hong Kong ensign, and I now remembered that the accounts also showed that they were paying a lot of money to rent a ship. Why would that be? So, the call I made was to our lawyers to get them to check the shipping register of title to see who did actually now own the boat and where it was, in fact, registered.

'So,' he said slowly, the anger that he had shown now replaced by uncertainty, 'What happens now, what are you going to do?'

'Well,' I paused, 'I guess you'll have to pay it back, the money Knox is owed for the ship, all of it.'

'But I don't have it anymore, I've spent it,' his voice was barely a whisper.

I looked around, 'I suppose they'll sell everything.'

'No, no, please,' he was crying now, sobbing, 'you could join us. Please, please Dan, don't take everything away, don't take it all away from me, Dan, please.'

'I don't think so.'

'But Dan, there's so much money to be made, more than enough to go around,' he pleaded. 'Think of the life you can have. What about Lara? With so much money, she's sure to be yours.'

'Lara,' I laughed, 'she means nothing to me.'

'What?' He was surprised. 'But she's so beautiful, surely you couldn't resist her. Even Larry had second thoughts about letting her go to you. He could make her be yours.'

'Larry?' It was my turn to be surprised, taken off guard, 'What's he got to do with her?' I paused, Michael could see me struggling to piece it all together.

'Yes, that's right. Lara works for Larry, she was his mistress but he decided you should have her, he thought it would be useful to have you on-side, I guess just for a day like this. He was sure you would not be able to resist her charms.'

'Well, he was wrong, wasn't he. I told you, women mean nothing to me,' I replied tersely. 'So, is Larry your leader then? He makes the decisions?'

'Yes, his father's the Dragon Head, a triad leader, he's very powerful. Please Dan, please join us.'

'Sorry it's too late. It's out of my hands now.'

'Why? What have you done?'

'I expect the police will come soon. I thought it best while Connie was out,' I said softly. 'So did he arrange Connie for you? Work out you could not resist her, was she just one of Larry's workers?'

'Oh Connie, Dan, please, Connie will leave me, I love her Dan, I had to do it. It was the only way she would have me; I had to improve. Please Dan, please don't turn me in. She'll leave me, I'll have nothing. I love her.'

'That's not love,' I sneered some more.

'How did you become such an unfeeling bastard? So hard, so cold-hearted?' the tears rolled down his cheeks.

I shrugged, impassionate, all respect for my old friend now lost. 'Anyway, there's no such thing as love,' I breathed softly.

'You don't know what it's like,' he snivelled. 'You don't know what it's like to come from nothing. To have to fight for everything, not to have it all handed to you easily like all my friends. I'll lose everything. You don't know what it's like. You don't know what it's like not to fit in, wanting to be accepted, longing to belong.'

'Don't I?' I threw back tersely as I turned to leave.

'If only he knew,' I thought.

As I stepped out of his apartment building, I stopped to look up at the night sky, breathing a heavy sigh, a wave of mixed emotions flooded over me, relief that it was over, sadness for the nastiness in this world and my friend's corruption;

before entering his home this night, I had still hoped he may somehow not be involved, that I was somehow mistaken.

The night was very clear, despite the storm brewing over the horizon. The stars were bright, hanging against the dark backdrop. I could see the constellation of Orion's Belt; and I remembered her pointing it out one night during that glorious summer of ours. All those stars, usually they made me feel very small, insignificant amongst the vastness of space and the infinite past and future of time but, strangely, I know not why, I would also take strength in such thoughts and tonight, I took some comfort that somewhere, amongst all the craziness of this world, perhaps, just perhaps, she could be looking at the same piece of sky as I.

Michael looked around the room. Now he was left on his own it suddenly seemed very quiet, abnormally so, as if he had lost his sense of hearing, submerged as he was in his self-pity.

What was he to do?

He picked up his phone, to call Larry, he would know what to do, he always had an answer, calm amongst any storm that had ever come their way. As the phone rang, Michael's heart missed a beat with each unanswered tone, desperation rising within him. Eventually, Larry's soft voice came on the other end of the line. Michael explained everything to him, about Dan's visit and how he knew it all. 'What shall we do?' ended Michael.

'We?' asked Larry. 'It's your problem, deal with it.'

'But..... but, Larry, please. Help me, we're friends. I need you.'

'What do you expect from me? We helped you, we gave you everything. We found Connie for you, hell, we even got you that job, just so you could be useful to us, have you not even worked that out yet?' sneered Larry down the phone.

'Don't forget, I gave it all to you and I can take it away, everything. So you make sure you tell the police nothing, nothing, you understand!' Larry finished violently and then, the line went dead.

So, Michael was all alone once more. What could he do? He was about to lose everything, the apartment, the boat, he would go to prison, he was sure of that. He had lost his job and as for Connie, in that instant he knew the reality of their relationship.

He went outside, through the sliding glass doors to sit on the terrace. Their apartment was high up, the penthouse overlooking the south side of the Territory. The night was full with the clammy humidity of an impending storm, thunder was echoing around the hills in the distance and dark clouds were now rolling in from the South China Sea, like the riders of retribution. The sound rising up from the street was a mixture of traffic, voices and music, a chatter, a symphony of the life below, providing a soft background to this sad scene.

It had not always been like this. At first, when he had started with Knox, he had been eager, keen to impress Richard, but that was many years ago now, before he had come to want more, before ambition had blinded him with her promises of infinite treasures, of a better life, and before he came to resent the work he did to make the money he made for others. But maybe that was human nature, so easy to forget that others gave you the opportunity in the first place to make a better life for yourself. It had been before he had met Connie. He was not stupid, he knew a girl like that was beyond him; he knew Larry and the others had only introduced her to him because they wanted something from him.

The night reminded him of a time years before, starting out, the poor disadvantaged kid, making-good in his first small apartment in the Mid-levels district, much more upmarket than where he originated from.

He was sitting up late alone and again; the noise from the street below was rising up to his window. The rhythm of the traffic, it did not stop, providing the backdrop, the beat as he struggled with himself, trying to decide what to do.

The decision was whether to help his friends or refuse, knowing full well they would turn their backs on him, that he would forever be an outcast. But, here was an opportunity, to take it, to help them, would lead to acceptance, finally, he would be one of them; finally, he would belong.

In truth, his decision had already been made and he was now just trying to justify it to himself.

Temptation was being put in his path and he had to decide which way to go. He felt the pressure; what a decision to make. To take the easy path, of riches, of power, of important friends, of opportunities laid before him, or to choose the hard road, the difficult but more righteous path, obstacles set before him, certain to be an outcast for evermore.

His old school friends were in the triads. There was nothing particularly surprising about that. Probably half his old school friends were involved with the triads in some way or another. And he was sure many powerful local businessmen had some form of triad help so he reasoned, it all depended on how good your connections were.

But Larry was different; Larry's father was a triad leader, very powerful, dangerous to resist and very influential to have on your side. All they needed was his help. It started with shipping illegal goods, drugs and other items to be listed as more mundane products and cleared through customs. Over the years the favours came to extend to drugs and arms and more recently to give the details of any valuable cargo that Knox might carry. That was all, they would do the rest. He would not be involved at all.

How could this have happened he thought to himself. He had not set out to be dishonest, he used to think of himself as a good person; he could still remember the innocent child of so many years ago, intelligent with dreams of helping people, of making a difference. But once the claws of greed had sunk themselves well within him he was caught in the web and drawn deep within by Larry and his friends.

Larry, quiet on the outside but hard within, ice-hearted; Michael knew Larry could be a violent man, he had seen what he could do to those who got in his way. What would he do once the police had come for Michael? Would he send help, an expensive lawyer perhaps, Michael hoped so or would he seek to arrange his silence, even if Michael gave it, just to be sure?

Michael should have known that Larry would not have helped him and now, thinking of Larry, Michael was reminded of the bullies from his childhood and instinctively his gaze turned towards the north, where his old home in Mongkok would be in the distance and he thought of his parents out there somewhere and his brother and sisters who he had left behind, and for what? Michael had been embarrassed by them and of where he came from, now he wished they were here with him, now he was ashamed of himself. Waves of emotion engulfed him as he contemplated the disgrace he would have to face and he felt, oh, such shame; how could he ever face them again, or Connie, how could he ever face anyone again? He had never felt so alone, so small, just like the little child he had been so many years ago, the little boy he had tried to escape from being.

What should he do? His mind was racing, with a throttle red-lining, out of control, chaotic, in an emotional turmoil. The walls were closing in on him as, once again, he felt the pressure, to make a decision, to make the right decision. He did not have much time, Dan had said that he had informed the police, that they would be on their way. He was surprised they had not arrived already.

Out to sea the sky was dark as ink but to his right, over the land, the sky was just a half-dark, as the black of night was interrupted by the glow of the lights from the buildings lining the streets, much like the half-light of a dawn as the sun warms the darkness even before it rises above the horizon, all of this added to the drama of what he knew he had to do.

Once again, the decision was made.

The police found him, sitting on the balcony. They had to break the door down to get in. A plastic bag was over his head, its opening closed tight, stuck with thick carpet tape wrapped around his neck. His head slumped forwards on the teak outdoor table he had pulled his chair close under, presumably to help hinder any chance he may have to escape as he struggled with what he had done to himself, gasping for the last remnants of air to sustain his life just a little while longer.

Suicide, what could drive someone to do such a thing to themselves, the ultimate sanction? Guilt, pride, face, an ancient concept of honour, just as with defeated Japanese samurai who would be permitted to take their own lives to ensure their honour was upheld.

The police did wonder if, perhaps, it might not be suicide. They knew Michael had been involved with the triads and they wondered if one of his gang had got to him before they could arrest him, perhaps to stop him talking too much about their activities.

But I knew that was not it; I knew it had suddenly all become too much for him to bear and he would not be able to live through the embarrassment, the loss of face; he could not live through Connie watching him lose everything he had worked towards. He knew he could never again face those from his family who really loved him, his father, his mother, his brothers and sisters, those who he had dismissed from his life; he could not face them again to see what he had become, to see the result of the prostitution of their values, the prostitution of his soul. Realising now that the greed had infected him, corrupted him, he was now as a samurai, trying to regain some honour.

Perversely, somehow, this made me feel a little better, giving me more faith in human nature. For if he took his own life, I reasoned, it proved he was not really a bad person at his core; if he had been truly evil, he would have no remorse, no embarrassment over what he had done. No, Michael had just been corrupted, badly influenced by others, just as we can all be influenced in our choices to one extent or another, the temptation had been too much for him.

However, later that same evening, I would reflect on the expression Michael kept using, of losing 'everything' but after the material possessions were gone, I could not help thinking, what of these who loved him or who he loved, Connie, his family, surely he still had them? Or did he think he had now lost all of them as well?

And it made me think, 'Who did I have to love? Who did I have to love me?'

The evening was still young in London when the phone rang and Richard Knox was in his Mayfair apartment, pouring his first glass of whiskey.

'Wow, well done,' he whistled down the line, struggling to come to terms with all that I had just told him. 'I had no idea, well done indeed. There was something that told me I could not quite trust Michael with everything, that's why I sent you to set up the China project; I didn't want him in charge of the whole thing out there, but still, I had no idea he was so dishonest.'

'I know,' I replied, 'I thought he was a good friend but, well, I guess maybe we never really know that much about the others around us.'

'True,' he spoke into the mouthpiece, 'but I wouldn't be too harsh, we don't really know the pressures he may have been under, the power of the temptations before him.'

Richard heard the silence from my end and he could sense the turmoil in my head, the feelings of guilt that my actions had played a part in Michael's ending. Before I went to see him that night, once I had my suspicions confirmed, I had struggled with what I had to do, with what I had just done. I had still felt drawn by Michael's friendship. I knew it was not my fault that this had happened. It was not my fault that Michael had decided to steal, to thieve from the hand that fed him. It gave me no pleasure doing what I had done to expose Michael's scams; I was just doing what was right. It was Michael's own fault that I was in this position, I had reasoned and still reasoned now. But I still felt bad.

I would have far preferred a simple life, not to have been drawn into this. It would have been easy for me to have left it not to have confronted Michael. Hell, it would have been easy to have joined them. But, I knew the easy route was not an option for me; I knew this was the right thing to do.

There had been no going back; it was the only thing I could do.

Richard realised my doubts, saying softly, 'You did the right thing you know.'

'I know, I know; but......,' another pause, 'but it's still difficult.'

'I'm sure,' he said, 'but now I need you to run it for me; the whole shooting match; all of Asia, China included.'

'I don't know,' I replied.

'You can name your price.'

'Yes, but, I'm not sure that's what I really want.'

Back in his apartment, Richard replaced the receiver and lifted his crystal tumbler up to the light and stared at its bottom, the dark yellowy-brown liquid seemingly mixed into the thick glass.

He thought some more about what Dan had just told him; he had seen a lot in his near-sixty years on this planet but life never ceased to amaze him.

And he thought about Dan. He was certainly driven but, and it was a big *'But'*, by what?

It was not by ambition and it was not by greed.

Driven to do what was right, maybe?

Or driven to prove himself? It was almost as if he had a big chip on his shoulder but then he did not seem resentful of anything in particular. However, he certainly seemed driven to prove himself somehow but why, for what reason? Whatever it was, Richard hoped it would not consume him.

Michael on the other hand, he reflected, had become consumed by temptation, enveloped by greed.

Dan was right, we never do really know that much about the others around us but Richard knew one thing, good people are hard to find, not just in business but also in life, as friends. So, if you are lucky enough to come across them, good people, honourable, principled, honest people, they are special and you should want to keep them close; you should want them in your life.

PARIS

She was sitting on a bench enjoying the quiet of the early morning, the warmth of the spring sunshine on her cheek felt good, it was a feeling she had not experienced for some time after the long winter in Ireland that often seemed to start where autumn should be. The sun had now risen above the roofs of the Parisian skyline, but yet still at this early hour was more orange than yellow, the day just beginning, a slight mist rising from the earth before her as the dew evaporated.

She was sitting once more in the *Jardin des Tuileries* beside the Louvre, watching the pigeons peck at crumbs on the grass, the occasional jogger, and inevitably, even at this time, a few couples, young and old, walked along, arm-in-arm in Paris, the City of love.

A sharp pain stabbed inside, regret; had it been the right thing to leave him, to follow her life in Ireland, to leave Dan? Her life there was wonderful, riding horses in the wilds of the hills outside Dublin, the hospitality and the warmth of the Irish people. Yes, it had been everything she had imagined it would be but there was still something missing, something preventing her life from being complete. Him.

She had met others, of course she had, but they never matched up to him; she did not have the same affinity with any of them; there was not the same connection; they were not her soul mate; they were not him.

Of course, there was Frank and the beauty of Greenclover. She thought again of Apollo and she smiled. He was indeed her favourite; she loved looking into his deep dark eyes, speaking into them, looking for answers perhaps.

Yes, she did have a wonderful life, she was very lucky really. Had the sacrifice been worth it? She could not answer that.

Through the early mist she saw a dark shadow coming towards her. It was a dream she had had many times before but always a dream from which she would awake, never real. It was a sensation she sometimes felt in crowded places where the mind could easily become confused and play tricks, but it was always a mistake, always ending in disappointment. Her heart would stop, miss a beat before reality resumed and life could go on. The stranger, mistaken for something familiar, would continue on, a stranger still.

Only this time the dream continued; she did not wake up; this time the stranger continued toward her, his features becoming ever more familiar, the gait of his walk, the shape of his shoulders, the profile of his face. She looked closer; it could not be, could it? Could it really be him coming towards her, getting ever closer now?

This time it was not a dream, it was real; this time it was not a mistake, it was not a stranger. This time it was him. Her heart had stopped, not daring to beat, feeling as if it could not ever start again, her breath caught, frozen in a moment in time. Until now, here he was before her, standing tall above her, smiling that broad happy smile. What was happening? How could it possibly be so?

'Hello,' I said.
'What?' Louisa stammered. 'What are you doing here?'
'Perhaps its fate,' I replied softly.
She looked up at me, strangely as if to say, 'What do you mean?'

I thought about the last time we were here in this very same place, so long ago, so much had changed yet also so much still the same.

'Actually, it's not a coincidence Louisa. I've come to get you, to make our own destiny.'

Her heart skipped again, could it be true?

'I had to find you; I have to tell you something, tell you how I feel,' I whispered, the nerves not letting my voice work properly. 'Do you remember the last time we were here?'

She nodded silently.

'We rode on the Ferris wheel. It was here, right next to this bench where you are sitting. You know I was so happy, I had this strange urge.'

She looked up at me quizzically.

'It was an urge to shout from the rooftops, to shout how much I loved you and..... and to ask you to marry me.'

'What?' she asked, the colour now spreading across her cheeks as her eyes became moist with the beginnings of tears preparing to burst, daring not to speak for fear this moment may be lost, another dream from which she would awake, without him again.

'But I suppressed it, I stopped myself. I thought it stupid; we had only just met. But you know, I've regretted it every day since, not a day has gone by when I have not thought about how different might life have been if I had told you, told you how I felt.' I paused, the tears on her reddened cheeks encouraging me to continue. 'I miss you; I want you to be in my life. I love you. So, if there's a chance you could love me, Louisa, follow your heart. You don't always have to do what seems the most sensible. As long as we love each other, we will find a way, a way to be together, to enjoy our lives, a life together. I know that now.'

I paused some more, 'I had to tell you this; I could not carry on living my life any longer without telling you. But of course, if it's not the same for you, if you don't love me, well then.....'

As I tailed off she looked up at me through sore eyes as she flung her arms around my neck. 'Oh Dan, I've missed you so, so much; I love you.'

I did not speak, there was no need.

A shaft of sunlight burst out of the clouds in the distance, casting shadows through the plane trees, washing one side of her face in its still early golden glow. The light, like a beacon, was shining directly onto us, picking us out in its spotlight.

And then, as if on cue, out of the sun's beam they appeared like small jet fighters with noiseless engines, the only sound that of the air rushing as they dived swiftly past us, a swarm of birds, swallows, swooping up, diving down low, turning this way, then that, as they fed on the wing, giving us their own private display, seemingly endorsing our union, celebrating us finding each other again.

I pulled her close and, wiping away the wetness from her cheeks with the side of my thumb, I kissed her gently on the forehead before drawing her in to cuddle into my chest.

'It hasn't changed,' she whispered; perhaps she meant the gardens; perhaps she meant Paris; but I think she meant our love.

So, there we sat on that bench, in the same spot where the Ferris wheel had been those many years before and, we kissed again.

'So how did you find me?' she asked between sniffles, drying her eyes.

'Well, I had thought you were getting married.....'

'I couldn't,' she cut in, 'it's you. It's always been you.'

I smiled, 'Yes, your old friend Anna told me, she was out in Hong Kong working on something for Knox. And knowing how badly I felt when I heard you were getting married, when I thought I had lost you forever, I had to find you, to see if there was a chance that you might still want me. I called your mum and when she told me you were coming here, to Paris, for your birthday,' I paused as I looked at her, 'I hoped with all my heart that this was where you would come. That it meant as much to you as it does to me.'

She smiled, 'But what now? You live so far away. I hear you've become very successful.'

'I'm leaving. If you'll have me; I can make it work,' I replied and then, the instinctive burst, the same one I had experienced here all those years before, a burst of emotion that this time I did not suppress, '*Marry me!*'

Earlier, on my journey from Hong Kong to try to find her, to try somehow to win her back, conflicting thoughts were raging in my head, arguing about the wisdom of my impetuousness.

Self-doubt made his evil way inside and nagged at me, telling me how foolish I was and demanding to know why had I not just stayed at home.

What if she did not really want to see me?

But then, almost nineteen hours from the Far East after the door had slammed shut to my apartment, there I was stood in Paris, in the early morning mist of the *Jardins*. I could not believe what my eyes were telling me, for there she was, here before me, sat on the bench.

Oh, could the fates really favour me so, could fortune really shine on me in my plan, that she should be here, that the dream could become real. Could it possibly be so? Was this slice of fortune, created by my actions, an opportunity to be seized or was it just a chance coincidence, a cruel trick of the fates played for their own amusement to relish in my stupidity at thinking I could win her back or was it our destiny, unavoidable, pre-determined that we would meet again, that we would be together?

Now the moment was upon me, it had arrived, this moment that I had been playing over in my head a hundred times and more, rehearsing in so many different ways, now it was reality.

I thought about turning away, of not approaching her; maybe for fear of rejection, perhaps worried how silly I would feel to find my mind may have contrived to build some fantasy between us which did not really exist.

What to do? To take this leap into the unknown, to risk ridicule; to risk rejection?

Why had I done this? Why had I put myself into this position? Would it not have been easier to have just stayed at home, to have avoided the possibility of failure?

But I knew the other option, to do nothing, to not try to seize this opportunity, to not take the chance to follow this new path; that was actually the greater risk, and I knew that this was no option at all. So, I decided to jump and, as I did, as I took that final step and spoke those first words to her, all the self-doubt immediately evaporated, swept aside by an instant realisation that I had done the right thing, no matter what the future may hold for, in that moment I knew, no matter what her answer may be, that I had done the right thing, to follow my heart and all the resentment, the bitterness; and the pain I had been carrying washed away as I resolved to take control, as I took the choice to give myself a chance.

We have so many choices we have to make in our lives, choices that ultimately shape our own destiny. How easy it is to choose not to do something but then, what might we otherwise miss. Sometimes we have to choose not to be afraid to fail. To be prepared for that possibility, yes, but still try our hardest to avoid it, for not to try at all, that would be the biggest failure. So, even if my declarations of love for Louisa had not been reciprocated, I would have been happier, at least, in the knowledge I had tried and I had told her how I felt, rather than continuing to live my life every day in regret, wondering whether it might be possible that a life between us could exist. But now, I smiled inside at how different life would be, for at least having taken the choice to try to win her back.

You can sit and wait, hoping that fortune will be kind to you or you can try to influence her, seize the moment, to make things happen, to create your own destiny.

Of course he had not known her past, how she had persuaded herself not to return his calls when she first left, how she had forced herself to concoct the excuses not to let him come over to see her, crying herself to sleep at night.

He could not have known that even as she was saying her goodbyes to him, forcing herself to be sensible, it would have only taken one word from him, if he had just said some little thing to ask her not to go, she would have relented; how her heart had been bursting for him to try to stop her, she was ready to fling her arms around him and stay, for she realised back then, in that very moment of leaving, that was what she really wanted – but he did not.

He did not know the turmoil and heartache that Louisa had been battling with over the intervening years, a struggle that became ever more intense as the planned day of her wedding came nearer and nearer, her thoughts increasingly turning to him to Dan, a thousand miles away.

Louisa's melancholy had not, however, escaped Mr McGowan, unusually distracted and lost in thoughts elsewhere, she did not seem to him to be the same lively girl they first knew, a mood lost to his wife and those others around him, imperceptible through their veil of excitement at the coming day. And, so, as the day came closer with her mind more distant, he became resigned to having to do something about it.

'Louisa,' shouted Mr McGowan across the yard, 'will you be giving me a hand with Apollo over in the field now. And bring his tack along with you.'

She immediately put down the buckles she had been cleaning and went over towards where Apollo's tack was hanging, walking quickly to try to catch up with Mr McGowan who had already turned and was striding away, purposefully, towards the field where her favourite horse was grazing. She knew he was a busy man and she did not want to keep her employer waiting.

Sometimes he could be quite gruff, not because he was a nasty person but, rather, because he was always working, such is the nature of a yard; he often did not have time to waste and so had developed a habit of being pointed, short, sharp, economical with his words, which could come over sometimes as being quite abrupt. But essentially, he was a kindly man with a ruddy complexion weathered from a lifetime working outside on top of typical red Irish genes, not ideally suited to a life spent outdoors.

When she reached the fence to the field, Mr McGowan was already leaning on the top rail of the wooden fence.

'He's a lovely horse isn't he?' said Mr McGowan.

'Yes,' replied Louisa a little unsure of herself. This seemed somewhat strange, Mr McGowan did not usually talk much to her.

'Will you be worrying about the wedding; having any second thoughts, Louisa?' He had decided he could only be direct about what he had to say, it was his only way, but, still, he used a lower tone, trying not to appear unkind.

'I don't know, maybe. I mean, a little, I guess,' she mumbled, tailing off, surprised to receive such a question from him; this seemed even stranger.

'Not much you haven't.' he laughed; a soft laugh, a kindly one. He continued. 'Listen, Louisa, you've got to be sure.' Words so significant, breathed so softly, 'But if it's true, if it's right, you will know it; there will be no doubt.'

He paused awhile, a significant silence shared by the two of them, before he continued as gently as he could be, 'You are young. You cannot make decisions about your life based on your job or your friendship with the horses even. Never take the safe option, Louisa; don't ever settle for second best. You have to follow your heart, always. I love this yard, it has given me so much enjoyment, but I love Mrs McGowan more and if I had to give it all up tomorrow for her, I would, without hesitation.' Following another brief silence he continued, 'Frank's not the one, is he? Lord knows he's besotted with you, and his mother's going to kill me but.....but it wouldn't be right, would it?'

That question the question, already asked inside her a hundred times or more, now heard outside, now real, no longer able to be ignored. Emotional tears were released in answer and she whispered, 'Thank you, thank you so much,' she sobbed, the confusion and pain flowing from within, to be replaced by relief, a great weight taken from her shoulders, realising how right he was, knowing now she could never marry Frank, it was not what her heart really wanted and, with the relief, a new hope sparked, for something lost that now, maybe, would not be forever gone.

That night, back on the porch of her small cottage she had stared up at the sky. It was clear and dark save for the bright white pinpricks of the stars. She could make out Orion's Belt, it was the only constellation she knew and she recalled pointing it out to Dan many years before. Louisa closed her eyes, imagining herself enveloped in the night's dark cloak, allowing her mind to float free in space, as she was carried among the stars. A calmness flowed through her, washing over her head and rippling down her spine to the ends of her toes; she felt the bright energy of the stars' lives; she felt strangely connected, almost as if someone faraway was watching her, and she made a wish, she wished for him to come and find her.

THE DREAM

'Quick, hurry up,' Louisa's sister Jade burst into the room, 'we're going to be late.'

Looking at herself in the mirror on the dresser as Mrs McGowan adjusted the ring of flowers nestled amongst her dark wavy hair, Louisa smiled, 'Don't worry, he'll wait.'

Kate smiled back at her younger sister, calming down immediately and after a pause, 'Are you sure you want to do this?' she asked softly.

'I've never been so sure of anything in my life,' replied Louisa, as much to her reflection as to her sister standing now over her left shoulder.

'It is time,' said Mrs McGowan with a warm smile of encouragement. She had been initially annoyed with her husband for his involvement in Louisa's decision not to marry her boy, but she had come around to forgiving him when she saw how happy Louisa was on finding again her true love and, indeed, Mrs McGowan loved her husband the more for the old softie he really was. Now here she was with a wedding to host as she had wished for in any case, even if it was not for her Frank. He had been sent to America on the pretence of inspecting some new horses for the yard, and his time would just have to wait.

Louisa was pleased for Mrs McGowan's presence, a welcome protection from the over-excited storm that was her own family downstairs filling the McGowan's house with nervous excitement, panicking, fussing, and worrying needlessly. She took one last look at herself in the mirror and smiled inside, confident with the knowledge that they were following the right path, and rose to leave.

The hum of excitable chatter was reaching a fast pace, fever-pitch, frenzy, machine-gun repetition as Kate rushed down the stairs, 'She's coming, she's coming. Come into the hallway.'

'Quick where's the camera?' her other sister, Lucy, the eldest, asked excitedly to no-one in particular as she reached for her handbag.

Suddenly, a hush fell, an exquisite heavenly silence. Lucy stopped her fussing and turned to see. Her mother's eyes were moist with tears just starting. Her father, a jovial man, was smiling broadly. At the top of the stairs, the subject of their admiration was standing, a vision, serene as she started to descend towards them, floating on a sea of lace.

Her mother started to reach out but stopped herself coming forwards, knowing her youngest daughter would not appreciate the fuss or the tears on her dress.

Her father offered out his arm as he asked with an encouraging smile, 'Are you ready?'

'Absolutely,' she replied.

'Is my tie straight?' I asked to my best man, John to my right the one without whose birthday party in the bar all those years before I would not have met her, unless the fates would have somehow contrived another opportunity, another crossing of our paths; would they have done so? Were we bound to meet, destined to do so, our stars crossed inextricably, or was that the one sole opportunity that we had to catch a future together?

A murmur started from the back and I turned to look as she entered the small church, walking up the aisle with her father. With the sun's rays flooding through the arched door, the effect was magical, her simple white dress and veil seeming to catch the light in their lacy web.

As she came to stand next to me, I walked forwards and, lifting her veil, I looked deep into her dark brown eyes and whispered, 'I love you so much,' before leaning forwards to give her a brief tender kiss. I then took her hand and turned to face the priest at the front of the church.

I knew it was not protocol but it was how I felt at that moment and, no longer, did I want to not follow my feelings.

We had not wanted a large ceremony and so we were being married in the small village church close to the fields that backed onto the house and stables of Greenclover. It being Ireland, the ceremony was a Catholic one, even though I had not been raised in the faith.

Personally, I had not in my young life thought much about religion and faith but I was now increasingly coming to ask myself questions, to wonder if there was some almighty creator, to wonder how far our lives, our destinies are predetermined, questions with answers I could not possibly know but what I did now know was that I had come to believe in love.

As we knelt on the steps before the altar, Louisa's head was tilted down as the minister spoke the words, her eyes looking up towards me. There was a connection between us, strong, almost telepathic as we looked into each other, deep inside, our private moment oblivious to those sat behind us in the congregation, our unspoken speech saying more between us than words ever could.

The ceremony complete, we turned to walk down the aisle, Louisa holding tightly to my right arm, we came through the cool shade of the arch over the entrance and into the sunshine, out into a bright new world, as husband and wife.

As we stepped out of the church, I could see her stop and take a small gasp, unbelieving at what she saw. The impossible prettiness of the honeysuckle growing over the old walls of flint that surrounded the quaint little chapel and there before us, completing the scene, at the end of the narrow cobbled path, waited an open carriage adorned with white roses, her favourite flower and standing before it was Apollo with the same corsage as mine in the shoulder of his leather harness. Proudly he stood, looking back over his shoulder towards her as we appeared out from the arched entrance. Louisa was certain he was enjoying being part of her day, approving of her union.

'For you,' I whispered, smiling, happy just to bring her a little joy.

Mr McGowan, sat atop the in the driver's seat, raised his top hat in welcome as one of the stable lads opened the carriage door; Louisa's sister Jade, one of her maids, helping her gather her long dress as she stepped up into the carriage.

The reception was to be a small relaxed affair back in the warm homely atmosphere of Greenclover. Here, the nervous excitement of before was now replaced by the warm buzz of happiness as everyone relaxed and shared in our joy.

The day was basked in glorious sunshine and everyone spilled out into the gardens, drinking champagne before we went into a marquee newly-erected for the occasion. Little girls sat on the grass in their pretty dresses with coloured bows, while young boys pulled at their stiff collars trying to loosen the ties that their mothers would not let them take off yet. The McGowans' young nephews, twins, both with shocks of fire-red hair, ran around the garden making life miserable for the two girls that they liked, as ever has been the way for boys down the ages to demonstrate their first interest in a pretty girl, always rendered incapable by the power of their superior female company.

The dinner was happy, relaxed and noisy as old friends caught up and new friends were made. When the meal was finished, I rose tapping my glass with a spoon; a hush fell as I turned to her to say:

'Louisa,'

'You, you are my new day rising;
You are my energy;
The sun that starts my day;
I know not by what design we were brought together;
Whether it was written in the stars that we would surely meet;
Or just a moment of luck in an unordered universe.
But now that I have witnessed your beauty;
And known the radiance of your smile;
Now that I have felt the warmth of your humour;
And experienced the wonder of your soul;
Now that I have found you;
I will never, ever let you go;
For now I know what love surely is;
For You, You are me;
And I , I am You;
So take my hand, come with me;
And let us share in whatever our lives may be.'

As I offered out my hand to her, a band of locals from the village started to play and we shared our first dance as husband and wife, waltzing slowly, rising up and down as we circled around the dance floor.

The scene was from a dream, viewed through the misty, soft focus of Louisa's happiness, with the volume somehow turned down, her senses buffered by an overwhelming emotion of a new calm serenity, an impregnable fortress of peace. As she surveyed the field outside the marquee, she saw people standing, sitting, talking, laughing and, in the corner of the lawn under the oak tree, there was John trying his hand at chatting up Louisa's pretty cousin. It was a scene of people relaxed and happy, entranced by the spell of the magic cast by an occasion of pure joy.

'Oh, Louisa,' exclaimed her mother once more, arms open wide as she came up to her daughter to hug her once more, kissing her again upon the cheek, 'Oh, I'm so happy for you. What a wonderful day and you look so beautiful. You are happy to have found him again aren't you?'

Looking over at her new husband on the other side of the lawn, engrossed in conversation with his old boss, Richard Knox, she smiled, 'Yes, he's the one mummy, I just know it, he's the only one.'

'I'm so pleased that you found him again, you look so good together, so truly happy,' sighed her mother. 'It's a shame Dan's parents weren't still here to see this.'

'Yes,' Louisa agreed softly, a touch of sadness suddenly spreading through her. His parents had both died while he was still young, well before she had met him. It was the same sadness she always felt whenever she thought about his past and of how he would never talk about it.

The only child of elderly parents, she supposed being orphaned when he was young must have been what gave him the drive to succeed, why he could seem to be so resentful over certain things, over those from more privileged backgrounds but maybe it was also what made him so different, so appealing.

She watched him, she knew it must be emotional for him, that under the surface there must be a hurt, raw, painful and she wanted to know more, she wanted to help. But he would not let her in and so now she had stopped trying. It was a small chink in the circle of their relationship, a little hole that made her feel they were not quite complete.

'Congratulations my boy,' Richard had said, shaking my hand heartily. 'What are you planning on doing next?'

'Oh, I'm not sure yet,' I replied. 'I've got a lot to do here, a lot of work to do at the house. It's a great life here, simple, quiet, relaxed, much better than the stress and dirt of Hong Kong.'

'Ha,' he laughed, 'I don't believe it. So you're sure you're not coming back?'

'Certainly,' I said, 'stop asking. I'm never going back to live out there.'

'OK, OK. I hear you. But I could have something else for you, closer to home, if you're interested?'

'Stop trying,' it was my turn to laugh now. 'I'm happy here.'

'Hmm,' he paused, thoughtful, 'but I know you Dan, how long before you get bored here?'

'Look at her, she's so happy,' I replied. 'As long as Louisa's happy, that's the only important thing; that will be enough.'

'And you?'

'Can't you see? I have everything I could possible want.'

It was true, I was now as happy as I could be, that she would be with someone like me, that she should have chosen me.

PARADISE

I lifted the blind over the plane's small oval window and bright sunshine flooded into the cabin. We were beginning our descent after a long overnight journey from Europe and what a wonderful sight welcomed us below, a crystal clear azure blue sea, without a ripple in sight save for the wake of the odd little fishing boat speeding along.

This was our honeymoon, the start of our new life together; we had decided to go somewhere exotic, to see the sights and sounds of different cultures and to feel the warmth of the sun on our backs so we had elected to come to Thailand, with its fantastic scenery; and wonderful friendly people, the land of smiles.

We had thought about spending a few days in the Thai capital of Bangkok, a city full of incredible sights, ornate palaces and temples, decorated intricately with bright blues, reds, greens and gold, always a lot of gold and many, many Buddhas of all different sizes along with a nightlife legendary for its excitement and fast pace.

However, we had instead opted to spend all our time on the quiet holiday island of Phuket, tranquil and peaceful with its beautiful sandy beaches.

The plane finished its approach and we were soon disembarking onto the tarmac just outside the small old terminal building. The heat was intense; I looked at Louisa who had already donned her large round dark glasses and was smiling broadly; I grasped her hand, this felt wonderful.

We were soon checking into our hotel, it was vast and airy, large wooden beams held up high ceilings, a cooling breeze gently running through. The rooms were situated on either side of a large open atrium with the soothing sound of running water in the pools there from which tall plants grew with shiny dark green leaves of all different shapes and sizes.

The high ceilings continued in our spacious room, together with tall windows stretching from the floor overlooking the bay beyond, allowing light to flood in, giving the impression we were already standing outside. Pink marble steps in the bathroom led down into a large sunken bath and the dark wood of the king-size bed contrasted against the fresh crisp white sheets.

The sandy beach was long and wide, in a bay surrounded on both sides by tall cliffs clad in differing shades of green of the local vegetation. As we walked along the beach, hand-in-hand, we searched for pretty shells and Louisa started to string together ones with holes in.

The local fishing boats, narrow and long, were powered by engines with small propellers at the end of slender shafts that the driver dipped in and out of the water behind him to steer his way. The young children all seemed very happy in this immense playground, smiling as they swam, splashing in the shallows and climbing the trees. They were mostly the sons of local fishermen or of the farmers who worked in the fields neighbouring the hotel, some with mothers and elder sisters and brothers who worked on the resort complex. The tourism was a welcome addition to their way of life.

The occasional elephant would walk on the beach with its trainer, stealing bananas it could find if the stallholder was not vigilant.

In the evenings we visited restaurants set on stilts in a lagoon, serving fish freshly caught that day from the Andaman Sea lapping around us. There were ever-smiling waitresses wishing to please, a band playing and dancers dressed in traditional colourful costumes incorporating, inevitably, much gold, acted out local folk-stories of gods and monsters from histories past.

I arose early on our last day, wanting to walk the beach alone while all was peaceful, before the chatter of the invading tourists spoilt the calm. A blood-red sun broke the horizon to herald a new dawn, a new day. It felt like something more to me, a new beginning, the start of a new act in my life.

In the distance, a lone fishing boat pushed out to try his luck for the day's catch. I sat on the sand to contemplate how beautiful the world could be and how lucky my life was. All was still, the sea just lapping gently at my feet, tiny crabs scuttled across the sand before me, burrowing into the sand to escape my giant's tread. This, surely, felt like paradise.

I returned to the room to find Louisa just as I had left her, sleeping peacefully on her side, her long dark hair falling down her back set against the whiteness of the pillow. She looked just as I had imagined she would have done all those years before in Hong Kong when she was not with me.

Now.....now, all was perfect.

I heard a buzz at first, the mixed sound of many different excited people, all saying something different but all stirred by the same thing. I looked up from my book; Louisa was dozing face down next to me under the shade of the palm tree on a patch of grass just above the beach. I was not sure what to make of it at first; it suddenly looked as if the sea was disappearing, retreating out away from us and now you could clearly see rocks and sand that just moments before were not visible, hidden under the sea.

'Louisa.'

'What is it,' she murmured quietly, slightly irritable that I would be disturbing her.

'That's strange.'

'What is?'

'I don't know, take a look. The sea's moving back. Look,' I urged.

As she slowly sat up, a grumpy tired expression on her face the differing reactions of the various people around us were surprising to watch. Some were walking towards where the sea was going, calling to their family and friends who were out there staring at the receding waters, others were sat like us, watching and others were running, running towards us, running past us, running away from the sea.

'Run,' shouted a little boy, barefoot as he ran past. I looked at him quizzically and his elder brother, who I recognised as the barman at the pool came running up, fast, to take his young brother by the hand He shouted to me, 'You must run.'

'From what?' I asked.

'From the sea,' he implored, 'it's a tsunami.'

'A what?' I asked, not understanding.

'A big wave, you must run, you must get to higher ground, quickly!' he urged.

I half wondered whether he was telling the truth or over reacting. Big waves, what did he mean. I had heard of tidal waves but they were just things of legend, were they not?

'Dan,' said Louisa, pointing back out to sea, 'Look!'

'Yes, I see it,' I replied coldly. The sea now looked like it had stopped going away and now it looked as if it had somehow risen higher to become a large high wall of water, suspended, it could surely not remain there, instinct decreed that it must return. 'We'd better go. Quick!'

By now, more people were running past us, screaming and shouting. I could feel the panic begin to rise as the sudden danger of our situation hit home.

'Run,' I shouted as I grabbed Louisa's hand, 'Run!'

'Where to?' she cried.

I was not sure, I did not know. 'Head for the entrance,' I shouted.

Behind us a strange noise gave chase, a noise before unheard, a thunderous roar, a cataclysmic noise of devastation, a sound that was escalating, ominously becoming louder, building, building into an inevitable crescendo yet to come.

The sound behind us changed. I looked behind to see that the water had now reached the top of the beach to engulf the grass where we had just been sitting, impossible that it could have covered so much ground so fast. As it hit the incline and met with obstacles, the air was filled with the shrill machine-gun like cracks of trees uprooted and snapped like twigs as they succumbed to the water's almighty force mixed also with the lowest noise of thunder as the wall of sound now came crashing down. It was the sound of destruction.

The entrance to the hotel now appeared to be so far ahead of us; I looked behind again, the water was almost upon us, I was not sure we were going to make it.

What to do? What could we do? Was this going to be our fate, to end here, to end so soon!

A little girl, no more than five or six, stood before me, barefoot, just in her pink flowery swimsuit with wet hair, not moving, not running, frozen looking out to what we were running from standing, sobbing, crying, with no words.

On the terrace above us, a lady, desperate, one arm outstretched to the girl beyond her reach on the path below, the other hand clasped to her forehead, her face contorted in anguish, sobbing, crying, 'My baby, please, my baby.'

What to do? We surely had no time to stop but something would not let me pass, let me do nothing.

To my left was a low white wall - perhaps? I grabbed the girl under her arms and lifted her up, running across the grass to the wall I jumped onto it and swung the child high to her mother's outstretched arms. I had to release Louisa's hand to do this, shouting, 'Follow me,' it was the only chance.

I looked back over my shoulder once more to see the wave of destruction advancing towards us, unrelenting, growing in its terrifying enormity. Louisa had indeed followed just behind me, not wanting to leave my side. From the top of the wall I reached down and pulled her up beside me to see her trembling silent face, not screaming, not crying, a face silent with fear.

As, as I did so, I turned to see the advancing, muddy-green wall, could it really be water? It seemed above me, we were not high enough. Almost upon us now, the sound was deafening, like being in the middle of a thunderstorm in the very epicentre of the chamber where the gods met in judgement, to scream, to deliver their wrath.

I jumped high and just managed to grab the tiles of the terrace of the floor above, somehow I managed to pull myself up and as I turned to see her hand outstretched up towards me, I saw in her eyes the panic take her in its all consuming grip, a look of blind terror.

The water crashed down, it engulfed her, she was gone.

'No!' I screamed, as a searing pain went through my right side, red hot my arm was pulled from me, twisted. I was turned onto my back, my head feeling the hard smack of stone as I slid against a terracotta pillar of the terrace, pulled by an enormous weight at the end of my arm, somehow still attached to my body, an excruciating weight which my body would not allow to let go.

I looked down, there at the end of my arm, the cause of the pain, amongst the raging torrent was a head - Louisa, there she was; miraculously, our hands had locked just as the wave hit.

I looked at her, surrounded now by fierce white waves of water disrupted, trying to pull her down and our eyes locked, the look on her face had changed, a glare, of fear, yes, but within a plea, a silent cry louder to me than even the wave itself a plea to, 'Pull me up, save me, do not drop me.'

This hurt, this hurt so much. I had nothing left, I had no strength.

I saw the angry waters below her, swirling, like a vicious whirlpool, trying to grab her ankles and carry her away.

I looked down and closed my eyes and screamed, a primeval cry, from where it came I do not know but with it I pulled, I pulled in a way I could not imagine and with it, she started to come back, gradually, her feet now clear of the water. I threw my other arm down and grabbed her some more and up she came, back to me, until she was there, with me now lying on top of me, both exhausted, spent. I grabbed her wet body, tightly, I was never going to let her go, and as I lay there, all suddenly seemed calm and quiet, my body concentrating the senses to focus only on calculating its immediate needs. I became acutely aware of my chest heaving up and down, taking in every new breath, I was conscious that my body was feasting itself on what it had almost lost, that it was savouring life.

Slowly, I was again aware of the terrible crescendo reverberating all around, the thunderous echo stuck within the walls, unable to find an escape. I peered over the terrace to see once more the horror just below. The water was like a raging river rushing past, the hotel now its ravine, flowing so fast, with such force, like a deathly stampede of galloping white horses – it was shocking that something so beautiful when calm could become so terrible.

Eventually, the waters appeared to lose some of their ferocity, settling to become as a gentle stream, innocent almost in its nature but for the milky colour from the sand of the beach churned within it and the mess it still carried, the logs of splintered trees, tables, chairs, all clues to the hideous crime the river had just committed.

On the terrace across from us, they slowly came, the lucky ones, soon joined by others from rooms around and above, those who had escaped the waters' wrath either, like us, by virtue of a mad dash for survival, or simply by the good fortune of being in their rooms when the wave hit.

It seemed as like the end of the world, ourselves the only survivors, strangers coming together, some quiet, others chattering excitedly, a group all alone, unable to comprehend any normal life existing beyond our circle all in shock at the violence of nature, ourselves becoming insignificant miniatures in its face.

The mother with the daughter in the pink costume, brightness amongst so much dark, was stood beside us now holding her little girl tight to her chest, kissing her hard on the top of the dark hair on her head, 'Oh, thank you, thank you so much,' she cried, still sobbing big tears, a mixture of distress, shock, relief and joy, her daughter quiet now, expressionless, recovering in the comfort of her mother's bosom, back to her natural sanctuary where all was well.

'Papa,' called the young girl, smiling now, looking towards the end of the corridor. Around from the corner of the stairwell limped a man sporting a thick moustache, his black hair full of water, flattened down against his head from where dark blood was flowing freely; olive skinned like the rest of his family, their appearance was of an exotic hereditary, from the lands of the Pharaohs or the Persians, Arabic, far away from the horror in this land they had heard was an ocean paradise.

'Saska,' he called and, seeing his family safe, he slumped against the wall and slid down to lie prostrate on the ground, spent, exhausted from his desperate attempts to try to reach his child but knowing she was now in the arms of her mother, the beyond human effort that drove him to move in spite his broken leg now left him and a happy wave of unconsciousness washed over him as his body allowed itself to shut down to protect him from the pain of his injuries. We rushed to his side and with the help of others who now came, we gave him what aide we could to revive him and to try to halt the flow of blood with white towels from the rooms that soon became red with the blood of a battlefield.

His name was Mohammed and it transpired that his family were just leaving the room when the wave arrived, their daughter running ahead, full of excitement to see whether the elephant had yet arrived upon the beach. From the terrace above he had heard the roar and seeing his little girl stuck, he rushed to the stairs to try to reach her in time, knowing it would be too late but still going just the same.

As he came out of the stairwell he saw the miraculous sight, of the man grabbing his child and lifting her to the safety of her mother. He turned to go back but the wave was soon upon him, throwing him like a rag doll against the hard walls, tumbling him as if inside a washing machine, over and over, around and around, his lungs filled with water, death was surely upon him but he fought to survive, he had to survive, his family needed him.

Eventually, the waters would come to recede and we started to take our first, uneasy, steps down, tentative, unsure about leaving the safety of our high sanctuary, worried another wave may hit but emboldened in part by the comfort and company of others, the apparent feeling of safety of the group and driven by the need to find some normality, to find life.

Outside again, we found yet more people wailing, crying, looking for their loved ones and we saw the bodies of those not so fortunate. All around there was confusion, shouting, screaming, crying.

How were we to get out? Or should we wait?

In a field near to us, an old rice farmer on a tractor that had somehow survived was waving, beckoning to us, ceasing his own evacuation to help us as well.

There was no time to lose, we made our decision.

'Come on,' I urged; and, with Mohammed slumped across my shoulders, we ran as best we could to where the old man was now hitching a rusty trailer to his battered old machine. He gave us a toothy smile, contrasting against his dark brown face, weathered and wrinkled from a lifetime working in the harsh sun. His was a friendly smile; he did not speak any English but he did not have to; words did not need to be spoken, of our gratitude, of his noble gesture, one that did not consider races, faiths or any divide between the poor working the land and the wealthy visitors in the hotel next door. As for the tourists that travelled to far flung destinations in search of serenity and calm, to be close to nature, well now that nature had given a demonstration of what it could be capable of, paradise shattered by just a minor hiccup from within its earth.

Here, in this part of Thailand, the Christian and Muslim religions had superimposed themselves upon ancient rituals and customs, giving rise to a unique blend of strong beliefs based on experiences of the land and of the elements mixed together with the ancient stories of their ancestors and old tales from the foreign people, Christian missionaries from the north and Muslim migrants from India. However alien the resulting faith may seem to us, its basis was an humanitarian one, as all religions should be, only here they had not forgotten, their actions proved this, that they did not put themselves first, above others, all were equal.

We helped his family, his old wife and two daughters, who must have been about the same age as ourselves, to jump into the trailer and we slowly moved off. We sat in silence on the only possessions they brought, chickens in wicker cages, their lifeblood and we all stared back at the sea, wondering at what it had just done and would now bring to their farm. What would be their fortune? What would be their fate?

Amongst the carnage, amongst the fear, the old farmer was calm, relaxed and happy. At first I could not understand why? He was at risk of losing all that he had, all that he worked for, the future for he and his family was now so uncertain. He did not cry in anguish, he did not despair. I supposed he had already settled that this was karma; his family were safe and whatever else would be would be. Perhaps he had already decided he could not change his destiny, that you cannot control it that you cannot change fate?

The family stopped a few miles down the road at a bigger village inland where, thankfully, we were now safe and many other people were gathering from other villages and resorts along the coast, all with differing stories to tell of near misses, of heroism, of loss, of devastation and of sadness.

Here we found a room to rest and, we were told, in a few days we would be able to catch a flight home, 'If you are lucky.'

Lucky! It already felt like we had been granted more luck than we perhaps deserved. Amongst hundreds and thousands who perished, who had lost loved ones, we had somehow survived, we had both survived. Our share of fortune was surely already full.

Time, it is a strange element, how timing affects everything.

The events you get caught up in or miss what otherwise may have been in store for you, merely by virtue of being in a place a day, a week, an hour, a minute before. The experiences you have, the inspirations we receive, the opportunities we miss, the opportunities we take. The chance meetings with people we would not otherwise meet if we had passed by but a few hours or days later, interesting people, people to befriend, people to avoid, people to love.

STARTING AGAIN – THE NEXT ACT

So, eventually, we were returned to Ireland and, at long last, able to truly start our life together. It was the best feeling in the world, it felt so right. It felt like, finally, I had found what was missing, finally, I felt that my life was complete.

We moved into a fabulous house in the countryside of County Wicklow, just outside of Dublin. Richard had been very generous to me when I left and with the money I had made whilst in the Far East, I would not have to worry about working for some time and I was able to buy Louisa her dream home, our home.

It was a large old farmhouse, secluded and private, perched high in the hills of the beautiful Irish countryside. As anyone who knows them will tell you, the green Irish hills of County Wicklow, just a short drive from Dublin's city centre are stunning in their beauty, wild and windswept, a creation of nature, rolls of green stretching along seemingly without end where we would walk, endlessly, clutching tight, perhaps to shield against the harsh wind or, perhaps, now we had found each other again, it was that neither wanted to let go, ever.

We would jump over streams and brooks, the sound of their flow contrasting against the silence of the wood, save for the whisper of the tall trees gossiping together when a breeze blew amongst their high leaves as they swayed back and forth. The light danced across the tops of the ripples as they flowed downstream, still in the shallows where you could see the different coloured pebbles, the water becoming white where the stream ran faster against the rocks in the deep on the outside of a bend.

Occasionally, we would venture out to party until late in Dublin's bars that lined the River Liffey, they being so close but gradually, the importance and lure of the nightlife diminished, becoming less attractive to us both as our life together evolved. Mostly at night, we were content just sitting in our large living room, perhaps watching an old film, happy in our own company, sharing a bottle or two of wine on our large warm sofa.

Louisa was relaxed, truly happy, enjoying our life together, working still at Greenclover and riding her beloved horses. She would take each day as it came, unworried now by what the future may bring, determined to enjoy whatever it may be.

The village local to our house was gorgeous, quintessentially Irish and full of character, a small bakery serving warm bread, freshly baked, an old style grocer, stocked with fruit and vegetables just picked from farms nearby, tomatoes so plump it was impossible to prevent the juices running down my chin as I ate them on the walk home and a bar built from local stone blocks overlooking a square where everybody went about their business, old women arguing animatedly, young children playing and old men watching, silently; they had seen it all before.

Our house was simply stunning, made from the stone bricks of the local hills light grey in colour with random seams of white, blues and black running through them and the roof clad with old slate tiles.

The living room was vast with high wooden beamed ceilings leading into an old style country kitchen with a large *aga* oven where Louisa would enjoy spending hours cooking a new creation, swearing that everything tasted better cooked this way. Perhaps she was right or maybe the fresh ingredients were the reason or, maybe, it was purely subliminal, psychosomatic, our love, our happiness acting as a placebo for all our tastes, of the food, of our entertainment, of our life.

The kitchen spilled out through glazed double doors onto a wide terrace overlooking a smooth green lawn, bordered with shrubs and scented roses climbing all over, the white waves of their petals bursting out amongst the dark green leaves, hiding the harsh barbs of their thorns beneath.

In the spring, brightly coloured flowers of hidden bulbs would push their way through the soil from their hibernation in the dark earth below, searching out the warmth of the sun to celebrate winter's passing. First the bright yellows and occasional whites of daffodils, followed by reds and other bright colours of tulips and dahlias.

The views from our position here, high above the coast, followed a broad panorama stretching from where the sun rose over the Irish Sea in the east, all the way to where it later would eventually set, falling below the green hills in the west.

The house though was a major project for me, it was old and needed a lot of work to bring it back to former glories, with some modernisation along the way but that in itself was part of the attraction to me. So, while Louisa would be working at Greenclover, I would be busy decorating the house. I had the living room to paint, we had a garage built. We created new bathrooms, installing a whirlpool bath so big that you could almost swim in it and using only the finest stones and marbles. There were meetings with architects; and meetings with builders. Secretly, I was renovating the old stables for her

but the project was not just my own, it was a shared love, weekends spent together searching through local markets for interesting furniture, curtains to be decided on and new light fittings to find.

I would like to take a walk down by the sea and in the ports on the coast, ambling through with no particular purpose, watching the craggy old fishermen with faces full of character, weathered by a lifetime on the sea, as they went through the day's catch or mended their nets as they hung out to dry; it was as a life from an era since past; my dawdling like this infuriated Louisa; yet another port to walk around, for no particular reason, with no particular purpose. But she did share my liking for people-watching, much as we had enjoyed together those years before in the parks of London.

We were truly happy, we enjoyed being together, we were, once again, very much in love; everybody would comment upon how close we were, like best friends, but more, so much more, soulmates, if ever there could be such, inseparable, difficult to imagine one without the other and better together than alone. We had become as one. *I had it all!*

Sitting out on the terrace one evening in my wicker chair, enjoying a strong coffee, I reflected on the life I had left behind in Hong Kong, the success, the wealth, and I knew I had made the right choice, that life is not all about money or titles or corner offices with harbour views. I had given that all up, given it all up to enjoy my life. This now seemed so clear, so natural; for Louisa and I to be together, being with her was the most important thing; it just seemed so right.

Hong Kong with its fast life, its opulent dining, wild socialising and partying, the extravagant lifestyle, it had become empty, one junk trip had become like any other. It was false, I did not belong there anymore. I knew that time had expired, that chapter of my life had finished and I had moved on *onto another life!*

It was as if my senses had come alive again after the barrage they had been subjected to in the unrelenting pace and the dirty, polluted atmosphere of Hong Kong. But here, now, in our new home, a strange feeling felt within. I had done it; once again, I felt I had arrived! I remember thinking that was it *I had won!*

Louisa, arriving on the terrace behind me, gently placed her hand on my shoulder before leaning down to give me a tender kiss on the cheek; sensing something, reading my thoughts even, she whispered, 'You look happy.'

I leaned back to look her in the eyes, 'You know what, I believe I am.'

CIRCLE OF LIFE

It had been a wonderful holiday, a Christmas spent alone in New York, walking arm-in-arm through the streets of Manhattan, happily enjoying each other's company and we had both returned in good spirits, refreshed and ready to start the New Year.

But on the morning of the first day back, the phone rang as Louisa was preparing herself, getting ready to leave for work. It was her father; that was strange, we had only spoken to her parents but the day before to wish them, 'Happy New Year,' before we flew out from John F Kennedy airport and he would know it would be a mad rush getting ready the first day back. An early morning call was news, either so good that it could not wait or very bad. He was calling to tell us that her grandmother had died.

We travelled back to England and arrived at Louisa's parents' house. It was quiet, sombre, as you might expect. But whilst the occasion was sad, it was not full of grief, for Louisa's grandmother had been in her eighties and had lived a good life. No, it was more an atmosphere of quiet reflection as Louisa's family each, perhaps, took time to consider their own mortality.

I remember well talking to her grandfather, in a quiet moment when no-one else was around. Not a religious man; he was, however, an incredibly honourable man, kind and always helpful to those less fortunate than he. A pillar of the community, helping with good causes and fundraising for charity, you would expect he would be very devoutly religious. But no, he was the opposite, a devout atheist, if there could ever be such. But, when we spoke on that cold winter's morning, he wanted.....no, he needed to describe how he had held Louisa's grandmother on the edge of the bed as she suddenly passed away.

'I can't hold on any longer,' she had said. He took these words to mean she was slipping off the bed, so he went to help her and as he held her close, he felt a rush, a *woosh* as, in his words, 'her life went out of her,' he came to realise that her words meant she knew it was her life that was slipping away.

This was something he was adamant he had felt, something he had most certainly experienced. He had always said he was a devout 'non-believer' and he said he had no 'faith' because he did not believe in a god. But he had loved his family: his wife, his children, his parents, so he did believe in something, he did believe in love and after this experience with the rush, he did wonder whether he believed in something more but he knew not what.

After attending the funeral the next day, we had to rush immediately to the airport to take the flight to return to our home in Ireland. With this unexpected trip following straight on from our American holiday, we had now not been at home properly for some weeks so, after we landed, still in a melancholy and somewhat reflective mood, we called in at the local store for Louisa to buy some much needed provisions.

I was busy unloading the car when Louisa came up to me. I assumed the tears in her eyes were for the sadness of her grandmother, now lost to her.

She put her arms around me; and as I gave a hug in comfort, she whispered that she had some news. She was pregnant, we were expecting our first child.

I wondered, is that what is meant by the circle of life? Whether or not, the phone call she made to tell her grandfather the news was a good one.

So our first child was born in a hurricane.

Unusual for Ireland, the announcement of the imminent arrival of a hurricane was met with a mix of stoic dark humour and disbelief such that life carried on much as normal in quiet anticipation to see what the gods may bring.

But, as Louisa went into labour, the fates did indeed contrive to bring a hurricane to pay a visit to the Emerald Isle. All the advice on the radio and television stations suddenly was not to go outdoors, to stay inside the safety of your home. But our baby was not going to wait for the hurricane to go away and we had to get to hospital, knowing our chances were better if we did battle with the elements rather than rely on my own attempts at delivery which would surely be inept at best. So, we bundled Louisa into our little car and headed down to the nearest hospital on the outskirts of Dublin.

At first we saw signs outside shops swinging to-and-fro, trees bent over blowing wildly in the wind, then we came across debris strewn across the road, leaves and small branches but still nothing too alarming. The rain was lashing down now and the wind howled, buffeting our small car, apparently banging on the doors trying to come inside. I feared that some large rocks would fall down the hillside next to the road as we descended, perhaps landing on us.

Then, as we came round the final bend we encountered a large tree that had just fallen across the road, blocking our path. I braked hard and the car skidded to a halt on the wet tarmac. Louisa looked at me, silent, her expression showed she was not impressed before her face then contorted as the pain of another contraction grabbed her and saved me from a verbal assault.

I got out and looked at the tree; it was obviously too big to move but I still tried to lift its slimy wet trunk anyway. No movement, it would not budge, but we had to get to the hospital, the baby was also not going to wait for the road to clear. We had to get through.

I went to the root-end of the tree and saw that it had been uprooted, pulled completely from the ground, no longer attached to the muddy bank. Rushing, back to the car, I got in quickly and pulled it onto the other side of the road so that the front of the car was now pushing up against the very top of the tree, the end furthest away from the bank. The trunk met our car just above the bumper, all we could see were the branches of the tree sticking up above the bonnet and into our windscreen. I put the car into first gear, revved high and slipped the clutch gently.

There was a crunch, followed by splitting sounds as wood fought against metal. We pushed against the trunk and slowly it began to move; gradually the tree turned.

Was there room enough to squeeze through? Maybe. We had to try, we had no option. I could not deliver the baby here. I revved the engine higher, the branches responding in kind with high-pitched screeching as they scratched down the side of the car like a team of vandals on a Saturday night.

And then.....then we were free.

Louisa becoming pregnant had not been a conscious decision and looking back, I really had not planned very much during the pregnancy. I had no idea of what lay in store for us, or for me! I had carried on life much as before, living from one day to the other, carefree, concentrating on our renovations to the house and enjoying our new life together. Other than envisioning being a parent as simply comprising playing football with my son in the garden, I had really not given the birth much thought at all.

We had not even bought any baby gear, like cots and prams, for fear of putting a jinx on the birth. And we had agreed upon an older more traditional role for the father at the birth. A role of no use at all once the mother had gone into the delivery room, to pace the hallways; to light a cigar and go tell the world of the news in some bar once the baby had arrived.

Only the elements, nature, had different ideas for us, there was a storm raging outside. The doctor and some of the nursing staff could not get through to the hospital that day. So I came to be carrying gas bottles and tubes into the delivery room as our first baby came into the world and, wrapped in a blanket, they gave her first to me. To me.

I had never held any baby before, not any child. What was I to do with this tiny precious bundle?

It was a girl; what did I know about baby girls? I had never been a very sensitive man but holding this newly born child in my arms, seeing her tiny hands and feet, perfectly formed, beautiful brown eyes and little lips; what a very special moment.

Thank god I was not pacing in the hallway outside; what I would have missed.

Our lack of planning, our lack of preparation, had been so complete that we had not even thought about any possible names for the baby but, after the name of the hurricane, we could now only call her one name, we had to call her Charlotte.

I had always told Louisa that I would never love anyone else but, with a new baby, all that changes, it changes in ways for which you just cannot prepare.

THE CRASH THAT SAVED HIM

She found him lying on the sofa, bare-chested, his shirt off lying on the floor, jeans half-off, still around his knees. The television was buzzing, a grey mess with no programmes, the remote control fallen from his hand.

The smell was awful, a sweet sickly smell of the pool of vomit on the tiled floor next to him. His eyes struggled to focus; his head hurt, his mouth, horribly dry. He looked terrible and he smelt terrible. He was embarrassed to be like this in front of her, it was not how he wanted her to think of him.

He snapped angrily, 'Leave me alone, go away.' Immediately, he knew it was wrong and he was at once ashamed but he could not stop himself.

He felt ill and now he felt guilty.

Louisa saw that the whiskey bottle bought just the morning before was now finished and lay on its side.

He stank, as the stale alcohol reeked from his every pore. It was the stagnant smell of drunks, a smell of which they are not even aware on themselves but their loved ones come to recognise only so well.

'It's disgusting,' she thought as she surveyed the scene in the living room of her beautiful home, fast now seeming to somehow lose some of its beauty. 'What was becoming of him? What was becoming of them?'

Louisa knew that Dan was surprised at how easily she took to being a new mum. He would say that it was almost as if someone had overnight reached inside her and turned on a maternal switch that she did not even know was there. It was true that she had never shown any maternal instincts before, not at any time when other people's children were near and not even during the nine months of her pregnancy. Yes she had worried how would she cope becoming a new mother when she had felt no particular motherly urges towards this little life growing inside her so, in truth, she was also surprised at the change in her caring for little Charlotte when she eventually came into this world, surprised and very relieved.

Because of this, because she knew how difficult the change must be, Louisa was also patient with him. Louisa knew it would be much slower with Dan, that he would have to take time to grow into fatherhood. Of all their contemporaries, of all their friends, no-one else had yet had any children and previously, she knew, he had always referred to children as noisy, a nuisance and to be avoided.

Louisa knew Dan was not really interested in having children, that he was not really ready, that he was certainly not prepared for the change. So, she knew it would be a slow process for Dan, to slowly change from what he knew, to slowly grow up and evolve into this new stage of their lives together.

At first, he had tried to make an effort but it was not really what he was interested in doing he came to seem preoccupied, as if his mind was elsewhere, preferring to be doing other things, and soon he had stopped trying, such that Louisa began to wonder what was happening to him, why he would seem so distant when she came home from working at the stables.

She knew this time must be difficult for him, that in Hong Kong he must have tasted a life so full and so exciting, so successful. She knew he would have enjoyed being involved with exciting things, meeting, creating, dealing, travelling far and wide and now, he just seemed uninterested in everything, always too tired to do anything. Now, he had come to not want to 'waste' the morning, as he called it, going with her to the village. He 'could not be bothered' to walk amongst the boats anymore or had 'no interest' to watch the local fishermen. He would not take her out in the evenings, saying he did not 'feel like it,' and, 'it was too much hassle anyway to get a babysitter'.

Most of the work on the house was now complete; the curtains and light fittings had been bought, the bathrooms finished, and a new kitchen installed. His project there was almost done.

She could see that, for Dan, the simple peaceful home-life had now become the mundane and the boring.

After the bustle of Hong Kong's full-on life, the pace of life in Ireland was so slow. Where was the buzz? Where was the excitement? Dan was bored.

Even though he was with them in body he was now distant, as if somewhere else, his mind clearly wandering in some other place, but this was not him, this physical presence surely resembled him, but the spirit was not his; this was no longer the soul destined to be forever entwined with hers; this was no longer the man who she had fallen in love with.

She had cried when she had seen the pictures on the screen of the first scan of their new baby inside her. She had been so happy that this new life seemed to her to cement the relationship, to wipe away all the heartache that had gone before, to finally say that yes, this was real.

Louisa was as fulfilled as she could ever be, her life was so completebut now she was so frustrated, they should have been having a wonderful life together. They had such high hopes, having found each other again, with a lovely house and now a beautiful, healthy new child. For her, it was more than she could have dared dream.

But she knew now for Dan it was not enough. She knew he was not happy and that he needed something more but that was part of him, that was who he was, intelligent, creative, driven – and here, in this wonderful place, in their quiet family life, he was like a caged animal. She also knew that he, himself, did not even know it. She knew it before he did.

The past few months had passed slowly and painfully. He had started to not sleep well, his mind whirring, working overtime. He became anxious, he worried 'What if this happened? Or that? What would we do?'

There were dark moments, dreams where he was alone in the room with him. Where he stood behind Michael in Hong Kong and placed the bag over his head, circling the tape around his neck, tighter and tighter, as Michael struggled, kicking and gasping for air, ignoring his screams, his pleas for mercy. The dream was so clear, so vivid, at times he even questioned what had actually happened, fiction now blurred into reality, the boundaries no longer distinct; had he indeed done this to his old friend? Or was it a sign that he had killed Michael, as surely as if he had in fact taped the bag around his head himself?

He started drinking earlier in the day now and drinking more heavily. He was eating more, putting on weight and becoming lethargic. Soon, he was not really doing anything, except drinking and eating, sitting on the sofa watching television and now he could hardly be bothered to leave the house. He was living in a wonderful house with a beautiful family. He was wealthy, he had it all!....or so he had thought, but he was bored, he was unfulfilled. *He had not made it at all!*

Louisa, secretly, wondered whether he may be slipping into a depression, perhaps?

She was concerned, but she knew better than to ask him about it.

He would, on occasion, accompany her to the supermarket, just so he could stock up on wine and beer but it was just the previous day that he had also bought the bottle of whiskey and she had started to challenge him.

'What do you need that for?' she had asked disapprovingly.

'I just thought it might make a nice change for a short cocktail before a meal. Lots of people drink it you know,' he replied defensively, 'I used to drink a lot of this before I met you. It's nothing new.'

But when they got home, he opened the bottle and poured himself a glass, neat with nothing to accompany it, not even ice.

'A bit early isn't it,' she started. It was only eleven in the morning.

'It's five in the evening somewhere in the world,' he said and turned to raise his glass to somewhere over and beyond the horizon in the southeast, and he slipped out onto the sunny terrace to sit and read the newspaper that he had just bought, leaving Louisa to pack away the rest of the shopping.

Over the course of that day, with wine at lunch followed by more wine and beer in the evening, he became very drunk, but not a party drunk, this was a surly drunk.

So, Louisa had left him alone and gone upstairs to bed before returning in the morning to find him like this, an incapable wretch, disgusting in his own pool of vomit.

At first Louisa thought that Dan's little experiment with the whiskey had finished as she did not see the bottles again, but his late nights of drinking continued. Almost daily now she would leave him alone in the living room and he would come to bed, much later, very drunk.

She could not know that he had now started to buy vodka which he kept out of sight, a bottle in the garage, a bottle in the shed, bottles in places she did not go.

But she knew him too well, she knew something was still not right. At times the tears would come, while she lay alone upstairs in her bed, tears for the life they almost had, a life tantalisingly out of reach, difficult to make out, obscured now by a hazy barrier of drink.

So, finally desperate now, she determined to confront him, unable to go on living with this impostor, wishing for the man she loved to return.

She found him, sat under the large oak tree that stood at the foot of their garden, a tree that had stood tall and strong through a hundred years or more. Slightly dozy, just coming back to consciousness following an afternoon of sleep induced by the bottle of lunchtime wine, he looked up at her slowly as she strolled over, 'I didn't see you there,' he mumbled with the surliness of the still tired.

'No, you don't appear to notice much anymore,' she replied.

'What do you mean by that?' he shot back, indignant, fast-angry as the ignorant or guilt-ridden often can be. He was certainly not ignorant or stupid but oh yes, he was full of guilt even if he was not aware of its extent somewhere, deep inside, his body at least knew he was doing wrong, that he was living a lie.

'Why aren't you happy, Dan?'

'What do you mean? I'm perfectly happy; or, at least, I would be if you didn't keep saying such stupid things. What did you say that for? That was a stupid thing to say.'

'I can't go on like this Dan,' she tried to fight the sobs away, determined to say what needed to be said, 'It's eating me up, watching you like this, all the drinking. I'm leaving'.

'Good! Go, what do I care!' words spat angrily, regretted before they had even left him, but as they reached their target she turned and fled up the stairs, shaken by his cruelty, leaving in such haste that just the sounds of her sobs remained behind. For good measure he shouted after her, 'But I'll save you the bother; I'm off out, and don't expect me to come back!'

Such frustration, he could feel his blood boiling up inside at the argument, he felt like he wanted to throw something, break something, hit her even, but he did not and he knew he never would that he would not, could not, ever do such a thing. It was not conscious; it was just a line he could never cross, an inner sense of right and wrong that would never permit him to ever do so.

Nastiness had filled the air but he could not find it within himself to go to clear it away, perhaps too proud, or perhaps not really bothered anymore. He knew it was not really her fault, he knew it was something else that made him like this, but he did not know what, he was no longer sure that he particularly cared enough to try to find out. Angry, he went out and slammed the door behind him, but he was shocked by what she had said, stunned.

As she cried herself to sleep that night, he drank alone in the small bar in the village. Yes, Louisa's comment had shocked him and it made him think. He knew she was right. He knew he was not happy. They were living a wonderful life but he was not enjoying it.

He did not know why he drank maybe, it was to forget things, to distract him from the realities of life maybe it was to escape, to avoid things? Maybe, he just drank?

The smell of the hard liquor in the glass before him also reminded him of something from many years before, something that repulsed him, but as quickly as his mind turned to memories of the past, he pulled his wandering thoughts back, not allowing them to go there. He could not allow himself to be dragged down, wasting energy on poisonous thoughts he could not change, and now he had come to see the world through eyes of alcohol. He knew he did not like what he was becoming but he failed to realise the vicious cycle he was already caught within, the liquor devil now deep inside taking a firm hold. He did not know it was his demons that made him drink, the anxieties of not knowing what he would do next, the depression of boredom, but he did not recognise these and he did not understand until he faced his demons; until he confronted them, he was lost.

His thoughts turned back to Hong Kong, maybe he should not have left. His thoughts then turned to Michael; somewhere inside he did still know it was not his fault, that he had merely done what was right, that Michael had indeed killed himself but that did not help the unoccupied mind from wandering, a mind out here in this sleepy town now isolated from the thrust and challenges of a daily vibrant life, which he was used to experiencing. It was Michael's choice, he did not have to do it, he reasoned. He saw Michael's face again, that night, when he confronted him with what he knew but now, for the first time, he did start to have empathy with his old friend. Dan still believed Michael was essentially a good person, just a man weak to temptation, turned by the lure of money, corrupted by the lust of greed, and, right now, if Michael was making him the offer to join him, he was not so sure he would have been strong enough to resist. Lines that had once seemed so clear and defined, right versus wrong, now seemed less so and perhaps he began to understand Michael a little more and be less harsh in his judgement.

It is funny how the devil of temptation's chances of success to trap even the most righteous can change, depending on the time he chooses to spring his trap and the extent of the assignment that temptation has for them. We each have good and bad within us, the ability to do both right and wrong, it is the choices we make that make us who we are. Michael was unable to resist his greed and chose to give in to it, others too weak to uphold their principles, to stand up for what they believed, to control their anger, to not hurt their most loved, to resist giving themselves over to the control of the juice. Who knows what any of us might do, who knows how desperate any of us may become?

Dan drank some more, not knowing he was in a battle he should be fighting.

He did not want to go home, how could he after such cruel words, after their little world had been broken so harshly?

A group of guys were laughing in the corner of the bar, drinking Irish whiskeys with their pints of Guinness and smoking hash. He had not touched the weed in years but, now, he was past caring; he could not care anymore about what he did. He looked over their way, maybe he should join them, 'Why not?' he decided and slipped down from his stool by the bar and strolled over to offer a round of drinks.

They were young, vibrant and full of passion, full of life. Their conversation was lively, fast and fun. It was just what he needed.

A band started up in the corner, playing traditional Irish folk songs in the main, it added to the joviality of the evening as drinkers would join in the occasional chorus or verse that they knew.

'Will you be travelling through?' they asked; he could not remember which of the group was speaking at any time, they seemed as one to him.

'No, no, I live here,' he explained, slurring his words, the drink having taken control, 'my wife works at the stables, Greenclover.'

'Ah, with the horses,' they all nodded wisely, 'that'd be a grand job.'

'I used to work in Hong Kong,' he offered, quick to contribute his own worth.

'Really,' they exclaimed in appreciation, 'that must be an exciting place to be.'

'Yes, it was certainly that.'

'So what are you doing in this backwater?' they asked together.

'You know, I really don't know what I'm doing anymore,' he replied.

He found himself dancing with a petite blonde girl with too much lipstick, her arms slung around his neck as she hung off him.

It was now much later, the intervening time had been a blur, a drink in one bar, another in the next, until eventually, they had arrived in this nightclub, dark and seedy, old red velvet seats encircled the dance floor.

Suddenly, it was as if he had just woken up and was only now realising what he was doing something was stopping him. This was not him, this was not what he wanted.

What was he doing here? Where was he even? How had he got here? There was so much confusion. How had he come to this point? The room was spinning. He had to leave, he needed air, he could not breathe. He went outside and threw up in the gutter of the road.

Across from the road he could make out the sea and as his eyes focussed some more he realised they were by the beach in some small old coastal town. He stumbled across the road and collapsed onto his knees on the sand, partly from the drink but mostly from the wave of emotion breaking over him at the state he was in, knowing it was not what he wanted but unable to stop it.

He turned and fell onto his back; the night was still dark, stars twinkled in the sky, he gazed up at them, memories stirring of youthful dreams to become an astronaut. Instead here he was like this, pathetic, a bum. Isolation, he felt the world was closing in on him, finding him out for who he really was, trapping him, but for what? Why? What was he doing to deserve this? Why was everyone after him? Paranoia and self-pity infiltrated deep inside of him.

'I don't understand,' he cried to the heavens, 'what more do you want from me?' As he started to sob into his hands now, he repeated more softly, 'What do you want from me?'

The next day was tense, the icy cold fall-out left by the storm of the argument before.

She had seen the dishevelled state he had come home in, the sand on his clothes and in his hair, the awful smell of drink and of sick, but he had made an attempt at an apology, of sorts.

A gentle thaw followed, slow at first, initiated by an empty promise not to drink so much. A thaw that meant he did not have to face up to the real issues, he did not have to confront his problems, and, for a time after, he became even more drawn into himself, even more quiet as confused thoughts tumbled around in his brain.

He struggled to try to work out what was wrong. Was he going mad? They say there is a fine line between genius and the mad, but the anxious contemplation that becomes depression is not the same as the unpredictable nature of madness, the erratic behaviour, unplanned, and there within lay the governing rule of Catch-22, that you could not be mad if you know you are. No, he was not mad, but he was lost.

It had been a bright sunny afternoon when they had set off.

Charlotte was playing noisily with her *Barbie* doll in the back of the car, flying her arms wide like a blonde supergirl, rising up in front of her before diving down again in whatever game her imagination was playing in her child seat in the back of the car.

'Can't you make her be more quiet,' he snapped irritably.

'She's alright, let her play,' Louisa murmured from the passenger seat where she was happily trying to doze off.

He wondered if life would be quite so difficult if they had no children yet; there was still so much he wanted to do, places to see, but he could not, he felt trapped. Oh, why was his life so miserable!

What an excruciating time it had been, lunch at Greenclover. Louisa had enjoyed it and in truth the McGowans' company was usually quite pleasant but today he was on edge, trying desperately not to have a drink, the inevitable talk, again, about horses started to grate, not helped by the impression Dan had that they knew all was not well between he and Louisa, probably been given chapter and verse in great detail about his miserable behaviour and night-time excursion of the weekend before.

Dan was glad to have now left there and, although he was not particularly looking forwards to the week ahead, another week with nothing in particular to do, he was at least looking forward to the next drink when they would soon arrive home.

The sunshine suddenly disappeared, to be replaced by torrential rain. At once, the car spun; there was no sound, no tyres screeching, no screaming. The car glided effortlessly down the motorway, then it hit the first crash barrier.

Dan did not recall any sound but there surely must have been some for he would later see that the metal sides of the car had been pulled open like a can opened by a penknife. He just remembered hoping the car would stop but after spending what seemed like an age pressing along against the Armco, the metal barriers, the car then seemed to accelerate away again as it continued to aquaplane down the road.

The car turned again and he was sure it was going to turn all the way round to face the wrong way down the carriageway when it hit the second barrier in the central reservation. Again, he did not remember any sound; again, he hoped the car would stop; again, it did not.

After another age sliding against another crumpled barrier, the car once more seemed to accelerate away, across the inside lane of the motorway, again to the other side to hit the barrier on the nearside once more.

Eventually, the car slowed and Dan was at last able to exercise some form of control to influence its slide. He realised the front tyres had burst but he was now just able to pull the car over onto the hard shoulder.

He immediately got Louisa and Charlotte out of the car and onto the embankment, despite the heavy rain coming down hard and the air having turned very cold, they had to be away from the traffic, he had to try to protect them. Dan rushed back to the car to fetch their coats, their hats, again to protect, and that's when he saw them, stood there together, his beautiful daughter, his wife, his family, stood on the bank by the motorway, stood very still, stood very quiet. He realised how lucky they had been, how close they had come to losing everything. How lucky he was to have them. His life did not flash before his eyes, he was not thinking about dying. He was just trying to survive, operating on instinct, trying to control the crash, trying to protect his family, but the aquaplane, that was unnerving, something that he could not control.

How lucky they were that, on a busy motorway, the accident had happened at a split moment in time when there had been no other traffic immediately around them. No cars where they would normally be in the outside lane next to them, or immediately in front, or behind; there were no lorries to hit.

How lucky they were not to have hit any other vehicle, how lucky not to have hurt anyone else. How lucky they were to be alive; in an instant their lives should have changed. They should have all been dead but, miraculously, they had survived. Was it luck? Did they have some guardian, an Angel, watching over them? Was it fate, part of some pre-determined path? Had some higher force intervened? A god perhaps had spared them?
Whatever god that may be; Christian, Jewish, Muslim; Hindu, Sikh, Buddhist; did some divine being save them that day? How different everything could have been; should have been, for each of them.

Dan remembered Louisa's look to him as the car first started to spin out of control. It was the desperate look from the waters of Thailand those years before, she was relying on him, but there had been little he could do. He had no control and they were firmly in the hands of the gods, in the hands of fate as the car continued its slide. Was this their karma, their destiny?

That night, Dan prayed. He thanked God they had survived, he thanked Allah, he thanked whichever Almighty was up there granting to them his protection that day, that his family, his wife, his child, were not hurt.

He could not sleep. He rose in the early hours of the morning; it was still very dark outside. The crash was replaying in his head, over and over, on a continuous loop.

But there was also something else in there. Something at the back of his mind, stuck in there, tumbling around, something that he could not quite work out, something that he had to resolve.

He did not go back to bed that morning but he did not turn to the bottle either as he may normally have done. No, instead he drove to the sea; why? He was not sure but he felt compelled, he was drawn to it. On the cliffs, high above the waves, he sat down and really tried to think. To think about what was happening to him, what was happening to his life.

He saw again the picture of them on the bank, his beautiful wife and child. It was in his head, as clear as if it were a newly taken photograph and his eyes filled with tears as he started to cry, as he sobbed, crying at the thought of nearly losing them that day. Of maybe still losing them as he came to understand the depths to which he had sunk. He sobbed as never before, the heavy tears of a mourning husband, of a grieving father. As he struggled to wipe the tears away, through his still watery eyes, he watched the twinkling lights of the village on the coast-road in the distance gradually fade as the black of night was first replaced by the deep indigo of the sky and the reds and pinks of the dawn, before eventually giving way to the burning yellow. As the sun began to appear from the sea in the east, he began to confront myself.

He finally accepted there was something wrong, that he could not ignore it any longer, that he was not happy, just as Louisa had told him before.

Now that he had accepted there was a problem, suddenly things began to become a little clearer and Dan could begin to understand about doing something about it and trying to think what it was that was making him so unhappy and, slowly, he began to realise something about himself that he had not appreciated before. Where was his challenge, his enjoyment, where was his fulfilment?

He knew he was not driven by the need to make money, sure, he enjoyed being successful and he enjoyed being able to buy nice things but he was not driven by greed. No, Dan came to realise that he was driven by the need to create things.

He had thought that in moving to be with Louisa, all would be as in paradise, that would be enough, but the reality was different, the reality was that he was bored.

He had gone from one of the most active, vibrant and exciting places in the world to one of the most slow-moving. And he had not formed any plans for what he would do next.

Where before he had made the decision just to be with Louisa, the two of them enjoying their life together, he now came to realise that being with her, just bringing her happiness was not enough. It could never be enough if it meant he was unfulfilled.

Then none of them could be happy. It is strange how our relationships can be affected by other things happening in our lives, outside influences, and ultimately, it is those closest to us that are affected most.

They were so lucky to have found each other so early in life and to have been able to have re-found each other to live this exciting journey together but as the page had turned to this new chapter in his life, he had not thought about what he would *need* to do.

His move from Hong Kong and the wealth he had made, they had bought him a freedom but with the freedom came choices and the choices he had made were not right for him. Louisa was happy; Dan was not. She was happy to be amongst her horses and her friends; she was happy to be with her child; she was happy to be with him. But Dan was not.

There needed to be something else; there needed to be something more for him; something more stimulating; and he was only just beginning to realise that. He needed to find the next challenge.

Sitting there, as that night became morning during that new dawn, a glint of light on the hedge next to him caught Dan's eye, a lacy veil, a web bearing the droplets of a heavy dew. Glistening in the now rising sun, the tracks of its veins shone like precious silver chords, the delicate intricate work of a master silversmith.

Intrigued, he stared at the wonder of it, this complicated network of slender strands, each weak and useless as an individual, yet strong and beautiful when combined.

A drop slowly ran from top to bottom, twisting this way and that, picking its way carefully, making its own path. Followed by another, shining bright as the sun's rays entered its translucent body, also carefully picking its way but pausing at the first intersection, as if in thought, deciding, before continuing on its way along a different strand to its predecessor. Many more followed, each taking a route different to the others, showing a hundred or more different permutations to reach the same end from the same beginning.

Maybe we do all have some predetermined karma, just as the farmer in Thailand had thought? Dan did not know.

Can we change our destiny? He decided he would like to think we could, for otherwise, what is the point in even trying in our daily lives. Perhaps, destiny shows us different opportunities and it was for us to choose, which route to follow. Dan hoped that our efforts could change the way we live; determine our different paths and maybe, just maybe, the harder we tried, the more opportunities would present themselves to us, the more choices we create, we are offered.

Whether any of this can be true or not, we cannot know but Dan knew at least he had to try to influence his path. That he could not continue to sit around waiting for life to happen for him. But what; what would he do; what could he do? Whatever it may be, he now knew he had to go out and make something happen, to take action, to take his life back into his own hands. Instantly, he felt better.

In the morning, Louisa saw the vodka bottles thrown out in the bin and she knew that he had come back; he had come back to her.

THE VENETIAN PROJECT

Richard was sitting on the terrace of his villa in the South of France looking out to the sea beyond, taking in the delicate perfume of the jasmine and the scent of the mimosa. The sun had long since started its journey, giving life to the flowers and drawing the colours from their petals, the white of the jasmine and the mimosa's, tiny, fragile balls of sunshine burning bright yellow; all set amongst the rusty reds of the terracotta tiles on his terrace and the intense blue water of the swimming pool, calm and still as a thick sheet of mirror. And the pillars of the house made from local light-coloured stone were covered in thick bougainvillea, the bright purple of its thin papery bracts that surrounded the small white flowers in its centre contrasting against the deep green of its shiny leaves.

A heat-haze shimmered in front of him, creating the illusion of a barrier of heat, seemingly rising up, a mirage of a translucent fence erected on the terrace wall before him.

There was not a sound save for the constant clicking of the cicadas.

Oh, it felt good to be away from the office for a break from the fast pace of his new life in New York to where he had moved the Knox head office last winter.

Surveying the scene before him, Richard took another sip from the small bottle of beer in his hand, admittedly it was still the morning but only just, it was almost midday and when on holiday he often had an aperitif before lunch; he was in France now after-all.

The sound of the phone ringing interrupted his peaceful contemplation.

'Hi Richard, meet me in Venice,' said Dan, 'there's something I want to show you.'

Richard smiled after he put the phone down. He loved Venice, so any excuse to visit was enough to get him on the next plane. But also, he liked Dan, he loved his energy and his enthusiasm. It would be good to see him again. And his call had left Richard intrigued.

'I wonder what he's up to now?' Richard said calling to his wife, Mandy who was just through the large open terrace doors in the kitchen preparing a light salad for their lunch.

'Who? Who's up to what?'

'Oh Dan. He just called. He wants me to go to Venice. To see something but he wouldn't say what.'

'You like him, don't you?'

'Yes, he's fun. And saved me a lot of money from that Michael character in Hong Kong remember.'

She smiled, he had told her this a hundred times or more over the intervening years, and coming out into the sunshine of the terrace now she gave him a fresh cold bottle of beer from the fridge and kissed him on the cheek, 'I remember. But it's more than that, isn't it? You can't fool me with your gruff business exterior, I know what a softie you are at heart. You're worried about him, aren't you?'

'I guess,' he trailed off, thinking ahead now, to their meeting, wondering what Dan had to show him. 'He's a good guy to have around. A good guy, very rare nowadays.'

Richard had kept in contact with Dan and he and Mandy had visited Dan and Louisa in Ireland to see their new daughter just a few months after Charlotte was born. But it was on that trip that he had started to become concerned for his young friend. Someone obviously so full of ideas, so full of passion, he somehow seemed to have lost some of his enthusiasm, he appeared like a wild animal now captive, and seemed almost to have given up.

'Someone like that needs to be doing something,' he called after Mandy as she returned inside to the kitchen with his empty bottle. He knew Dan had made a few property investments but they would not be enough to feed his active mind, but now Richard was encouraged, at least in this last call he sounded much like his old self.

In truth, Richard did not really enjoy holidays, he could never settle and quickly got bored, so he was pleased to have something new to occupy his mind. Filled with a fresh wave of optimism, he took another swig of the beer in his bottle, already feeling a little happier at the prospect of seeing his young friend again and impatient to find out what he was up to.

There are many things I love about Venice but it is not the obvious romantic over-touristed ones, I have never been in a Gondola and have no desire to do so. You cannot go there in the height of summer, it is just too hot and, being built on a swamp, too infested with mosquitoes for that.

But I do love the Venetian architecture, the narrow canals, the watery alleyways, where designer shops contrast with ancient stone buildings. Here, there is an instant feeling of history, of ancient civilisations and traders past.

Because of its nature, built years ago on stilts and islands in the middle of a swampy sea, it is so unspoilt by new buildings of a different style, unlike much of London where the flow of impressive buildings of a certain era is often interrupted by the haphazard imposition of more modern styles that can seem to be a clash of generations. To an extent, that style suits London and adds to its own character as a cosmopolitan, ever-changing, modern city, but, in Venice, the whole character is of history. The architecture conjures up images of times well past, of the founding forefathers who first built this strange place.

It is a city built on more than one hundred tiny islands along the Adriatic Sea, a marshy salt-water lagoon that protected the original Venetians against marauding invaders. The original founders were actually refugees from the north, on the Italian mainland, escaping successive waves of Germanic invasions and Attila the Hun during the first century AD. Fearing for their lives, the people fled and set up anew in this more protected place; and so, a City was born, but not just any city; these resourceful and resilient refugees refused to remain insular and took advantage of their position to become an increasingly important trading port between Western Europe and the rest of the world, particularly the Byzantine Empire and the Islamic World to the east.

Just like many of our other well-known cities, Venice has thrived over the centuries because of its geography, making it an important port and so, an important trade centre.

As London or New York Hong Kong, Sydney or Istanbul, Venice is also a natural harbour and through history its importance grew as the gateway from east to west, it became the main trading post for this new world. And with this trade came such money and investment that the famous Doges became fabulously wealthy.

Positioned at the western end of the famous Silk Road, the trade routes that connected Asia to the western Mediterranean world, the importance and prosperity of Venice grew even further when, in the thirteenth century, one of its most famous sons, Marco Polo, travelled further east than almost any European before him, into the then mostly unknown world of Cathay, of China, bringing back fascinating luxuries and tales of oriental cultures and customs.

Marco Polo traded through Turkey and Mongolia along his route to China and Hong Kong, through the steps of the Mongols, of Genghis and then later Kublai Khan; it must have been a wild and adventurous time, not one for the faint-hearted. Of course, for many the route was not something to be traversed in its entire extent but rather was a trading path along which various transactions and dealings were conducted.

The route derives its name from the lucrative trade built on the secrets of the Chinese silk worms, which had actually started to develop many years before, perhaps because of the earlier Roman desire for Chinese silk. But trade along the route also thrived in many things, especially luxuries, not just silk, but in spices, perfumes, medicines and jewels as well.

These trade routes also soon became important cultural paths for travellers, merchants and missionaries and so the development of Venice was influenced by many diverse civilisations from China to Egypt and to Persia.

By the late 13th century, Venice was the most prosperous city in all of Europe. At the peak of its power and wealth it dominated Mediterranean commerce with a huge merchant navy of thirty-six thousand sailors operating over three thousand ships and during this time, Venice's leading families vied with each other to build the grandest palaces and commission the work of the most talented artists.

The first ducal palace and the basilica of St Mark were built on the Rialto Island. And the Doges, local dukes and wealthy merchants, built ornate villas along the Grand Canal, some of which have now become famous hotels such as the Danieli, originally the palace built by the Doge

Dandolo family in the fourteenth century; and the Gritti Palace built as the residence of the Doge of Venice in 1525 and over the centuries, trade developed; the same trade that had first attracted me to Hong Kong, another staging post along the silk road, the same trade that had originated in Europe, here in Venice.

It strikes me that all we are doing now is an evolution of what has gone before. Yes, faster and yes, more efficiently. There has always been development to make trade faster, of steamboats to carry goods faster than by sail, of cars, trains, air-travel, typewriters, foreign exchange markets, banks, word-processors, fax machines, and now the internet and email but essentially, it's the same, trading goods made in the east and selling them in the markets of the west, bringing as well ever-more investment. At first it was to establish the factories to meet western demand and more recently now to also produce the same goods to meet the growing eastern appetite for designer clothes, watches, computers and mobile phones, as much in demand now in the shops of Shanghai and Beijing as in London and New York as the eastern consumer becomes ever-more wealthy.

Along the way, the west has had to change much from being a powerful manufacturer and producer to investing in manufacturing facilities in cheaper areas of the globe as the business world seeks to be ever more competitive. The consumer of course wants it all, the best, the cheapest and the newest. The stores want to buy at lower prices, to make more profit. So the manufacturer needs to produce more cheaply to compete whilst still making more money to feed its owners and invest in all the new technologies needed to keep ahead, but now these places like Venice have evolved, not reinvented, it has just occurred naturally as they changed from being places people visited to make their trades to instead become places of interest in themselves, to be visited now to see their history, to see how they used to trade, how they used to work, in days gone-by. So the tourism that followed has become increasingly important until, in some cases, they have now become the most important aspect of that city's trade, the sightseeing in the cathedrals, the shopping in the designer boutiques, the entertainment and of course the hotels.

I had arrived to the Gran Caffe Quadri in St Marks Square early to soak up the atmosphere. It was a bright spring day so I sat at one of their white metal tables outside in the main piazza admiring the light and shade of the rows of old columns and arches forming corridors outside the many boutiques and cafes surrounding the square.

Whenever I take coffee in the Square or on the waterfront of the Riva Schiavoni staring out south to Giudecca Island, I visibly imagine a time well past. The tourists milling around quickly become local merchants from an age gone by, rushing to markets, or I see them as foreign traders in town to buy the silks newly arrived from China perhaps. I envisage a group of cardinals striding across the square to attend an important mass in the Basilica.

The modern diesel boats of the construction companies taking wood to construct a new building become sailed luggers carrying a very similar cargo, for not much has changed in the fabric of the foundations of the venetian buildings or in the way materials have to be transported by water around the city.

I also love to get away from the tourist areas, to take a ferry or a water taxi around the backstreet canals. There you will see Venice still as a working City; working gondolas, bigger than the tourist variety, still paddle the shopkeepers to their stores and the university students across the canals;

at rush hour the people have to stand to attention, in a close line, facing forwards so they all may fit on these narrow black vessels whilst larger ferries plough their routes taking staff to the glass factories of Murano Island and workers to their offices.

I was dragged from my thoughts as I saw him; I recognised his familiar gait, waddling with a sideways motion to accommodate his growing paunch, coming through the crowds on the square towards me.

We had our usual initial greetings and Richard told me how much fatter I was looking.

'Too much of the good life having a wife to cook for me,' I said.

'Too much sitting around not doing anything,' he fired back and we both laughed.

'Well, in a way, that's what I wanted to talk to you about,' I started slowly.

'I guessed it might be,' he replied, serious now, encouraging me to continue.

'You know I've not been doing very much recently?' I said and he nodded. 'And you keep trying to offer me jobs with you, trying to persuade me to do something. Well, I've found something here.'

'Really, what is it?'

'I'll show you,' I said, getting up, 'It's just around the corner.'

'OK,' Richard replied slowly, realising that I wanted to show him personally and that now was not the time to press me for more, but he could see that I was excited, indeed, the excitement was contagious and he also wanted to see the surprise.

The building was not far from St Marks, just a short walk through the narrow alleys and across a small stone bridge that had once been white. As we came out of the shade of the building above, we soon reached the entrance to the source of my interest.

An old Venetian palazzo, red stone, contrasted by small white columns of marble lining the facing wall, then, through an old wooden revolving door set into the facade, we entered into a different world: a grand wide open space below a high atrium topped with a glass dome that flooded-in light. Coloured rays danced around the room as the light entered through a ring of coloured glass from the local Murano Island that encircled the bottom of the dome.

'Wow,' breathed Richard, 'It's incredible.'

I smiled, pleased at his reaction, 'Wait, come through here.'

At the end of the lobby, we went through a pair of floor-to-ceiling old double wooden doors leading into the most wonderful ballroom featuring frescoes painted on its ceiling, cherubs floating amongst the clouds but before Richard could comment, I marched purposefully through the room to open the old shutters wide, revealing the true magnificence of all the room as the colours of Venetian life flooded in, the bright blue of the sky, the pinks of the terracotta roofs opposite, the white tipped waves of the turquoise canal below and the varied colours of so many different boats running this way and that, going about their business.

We stepped through the tall glass doors, one of four that ran down the length of the room, and out onto the terrace overlooking the Grand Canal to be greeted by a symphony of differing sounds, excited chatter, the occasional horn, the wash of the boats, all accompanied by the background bass of the vessels' diesel engines.

'It's a real old gem isn't it,' I smiled. 'Obviously, it needs a lot of work but it could be sensational.'

'How did you find it?' he asked.

'It was bizarre really, a moment of serendipity,' I laughed. 'You know I was getting bored and looking for something to do, a new challenge, easy to say, a lot harder to actually do – to find something that actually has to work, puts meals on the table for the family, not just an idea that won't survive. But I knew I wanted to do something that could have the potential to grow into something bigger, grow into other areas, something with which I could establish a brand, a lifestyle. Well, last autumn Louisa and I decided to take a short break and never having been to Venice, here's where we decided to come and at the airport some guy was struggling with his cases so I gave him a hand. We got to talking and it turned out his cases were full of camera equipment as he was here on a photo-shoot for some fashion campaign in Elle magazine. By coincidence, we were also staying at the same hotel so transferred on a water taxi together and he invited me along to watch the shoot, which, as you may have guessed, was held here. It was derelict then but you could see these vast open spaces and the old features, the stone and the glass and it just occurred to me what a fantastic building it would be to renovate and bring back to its old glory; what an incredible place that would be to visit and come to stay as a hotel. Strange isn't it?'

'How so?' asked Richard.

'Well, how if I had not helped that guy with his cases I would never have had the chance to find this. A small act of kindness received a much bigger reward, the opportunity this traveller was searching for.'

I then went on to explain about the architect I was hoping to persuade to join us to bring us some of his magic to make this place truly fantastic. In the meantime, I had commissioned a few sketches to show Richard which I rolled out on a table before him.

I was pleased to see that Richard was impressed, that, as I had hoped, he could quickly understand and envisage what I was trying to achieve.

I then gave him a tour of the rest of the building and as we walked, I told him more of how I had managed to find it; the difficulty I had in tracking down the correct owners; the rumours that it was perhaps available for sale and the contrasting rumours that the family would never sell such a building; rumours partly because in a price negotiation it was always better for the owners to deny they ever really wanted to sell, but also to maintain the pride of the owning family, maintain their 'face'. Incredibly, in business, pride is still such an important factor, particularly where, such as this, the building had been owned by generations of the same family, emotions tend to run high.

I continued with how I had managed to put together a deal to buy the building and to obtain permission to change it into a hotel, persuading the local authorities what a great addition and attraction it would be for their wonderful city. And I recounted how it had taken such a long time, the frustrations of dealing with the local Italian bureaucrats.

It was to be called *La Vita*, the life! For the visiting guests in our future, the name would represent an enjoyment away from the stresses of their homes and their work; for me it represented the life that I had taken back; my life!

To the left would be the bar; a testament to Italian Venetian style, the length of the wall was adorned with vast panels of more coloured Murano glass providing the backlights which would bring to life the brightly coloured drinks bottles to be positioned below. I was hoping that the architect would help to completely open out the bar and the atrium of the lobby to make one open and vibrant space, full of life and energy, sparkling with light, puling people in, unable to resist being there, wanting to be part of what was going on here.

The restaurant would be situated to the right and guests would spill out onto another wonderful terrace running along the waterfront of the building, the twin of the one from the bar we had just stood upon. In between them, the hotel would have its own jetty to greet visitors transferred directly from the airport by its private motor launch.

I showed Richard through to where work had already started on the back of the house, the kitchens. I had not known much about hotel equipment before but I had quickly become an expert in the requirements of a modern hotel kitchen to ensure we could have lively restaurants offering the highest standards of cuisine.

It would not be the biggest hotel with eighty rooms and ten suites but it was certainly in a great position, a truly grand location.

We then returned to the bar. 'So, how much do you want then?' shot Richard, 'Presumably that's why you've asked me here?'

'Actually, no,' I smiled. 'But I knew you would think that. The money's already in place.'

'Really,' he exclaimed, raising an eyebrow, 'how, it must be costing a pretty penny or two?'

'Absolutely, and actually that's yet another bizarre moment of serendipity.'

'How so?'

'Well after I found the hotel, from my research I decided the most suitable finance company to approach would be a small niche fund that specialised in small boutique hotels like this rather than big chains. They're called Ventus Capital, very private, based in London, a young team with a reputation for being very dynamic. So I gave them a call and arranged to meet a guy called Dominic.'

As I began to recount the story to Richard, I recalled in my mind how a few days later, I had walked down Bruton Street and into Berkley Square. I was early, as was usual whenever I had an important meeting, so I could spend a few quiet moments gathering my thoughts to make sure I was always properly prepared.

I had popped into Starbucks and took my coffee to sit on one of the many benches in the middle of the green Square, to sit under the huge parasol of a plane tree, shaded by its vast canopy of green leaves.

I reflected awhile as I sipped my strong espresso. What was I thinking? Could I do this? People like me, from my background, a small town, not from the right school, we did not do things like this, did we? Why did I set myself these different challenges? Why not settle for the quiet life? What the hell was I doing here? But, from the depths to which I had previously been sinking, I now knew what the answer was; I needed to do this; I needed it. This was *me*.

Self-doubt, I always found was good, if you used it, positively, to analyse and rethink what you were doing, to ensure you never thought you knew it all, to always second-guess yourself, like the great actors who need the nerves flying around in the pit of their stomach, the butterflies to harness and use before they go on stage to fly to the heights of a great performance, if you did not have that concern, that care for what you did, whatever it may be, you were lost. You would not have the passion and you would never achieve levels of greatness. Levels you could only reach if you cared enough, if you had that passion.

But if you did not control it, self-doubt can become debilitating, like stage-fright, it can stop you from doing things; the fear that consumes an athlete, tightens them, stopping them from performing to their potential, freezing on the big stage.

The nerves I had eventually learnt helped me to make sure I prepared so all would go as well as I could make it. Without them I would surely fail, so I had learnt to use them positively, to harness their energy to help me and, although I always worried why I kept putting myself forwards into these positions, again, I had now learnt that, for some reason, I would always do so, that I, for some reason, did not seem to be able to sit by and watch for the sake of a quiet life, even if that did involve me in more work, in more effort, more planning, more doubt and more anxious moments like this.

The worry, the anxious moments, were my curse, my nerves to make sure I performed as well as I could, that I prepared as well as I could. That is what happens when you care about something, when you have a passion to do your best, to be the best that you can be, not to let yourself down.

I looked at the watch on my wrist. It was special, an old Rolex that Louisa had bought for me. The watch was from 1965, the same year I was born; she had searched it out for me as a special present when we got married. Inscribed on the back was the message *'For my Dragon, for our unique love'*. She knew how pleased I was that my Chinese zodiac was this, the most powerful of mythical creatures and the watch was special to me, not for its own outward beauty rather the thought and the love that had gone into it from her.

I wore it every day and each time that I looked at it I could not help but give a small smile as I was reminded of her and all that we had been through together; maybe there was something in this Chinese *feng-shui* after-all.

Strangely, this was now another year of the Dragon, twelve years since the last. Maybe it would be a good year?

'Who knows?' I breathed as I took another sip, finishing my coffee.

It was time, I put my empty coffee cup in the bin, passed the statue of a nymph which I touched for luck and strode as confidently as I could into the building where Ventus Capital had their offices. I took the lift to the twenty-fifth floor where the lift lobby emptied directly into their reception.

The pretty receptionist smiled at me and asked me to take a seat, Dominic would only be a few minutes.

I turned and sat in the single leather armchair, leaving the large sofa to my right free, my back slightly facing the lobby. I had a better view of the receptionist from here. Her head was down, fingers curling her hair, pen in hand, pretending not to look at me. I picked up a Country Life magazine and started flicking the pages, not really paying them too much attention.

While I was sitting waiting there, a man walked into the reception from the lift lobby.

The receptionist's demeanour immediately tightened, in the way that all employees across the world do when their boss is around.

'Good morning sir,' she smiled.

'Good morning Sophie,' he spoke confidently.

He was evidently originally from somewhere in the Middle East but spoke with a very posh English accent; he had been well-schooled.

He looked over at me and smiled, 'Good morning.'

'Morning,' I nodded and smiled back.

The man strode off to his office.

There was something familiar about him.

Dominic swept into reception, jacketless and no tie, the world of venture capital was an informal place.

He showed me into their large boardroom decorated with prestigious and expensive works of art and sculptures.

'Tell me,' I said, 'the Arabian looking gentleman I've just seen come through reception, what's his name?'

'Mohammed Al-Lubnani, he's one of the owners, why?'

'I've met him before,' I laughed, 'but I'm not sure I can tell you why.'

The door swung open and it was Mohammed.

'Mr Roberts,' he cried, 'this is indeed an honour to see you again.'

I smiled, a big, happy beam.

Dominic's face was a picture of pure bewilderment.

'I was just telling Dominic that I thought I knew you,' I laughed.

'Dominic, this man helped to save my daughter in the tsunami in Thailand those years before.'

I would swear later to Dominic that it is the only time I have ever seen first-hand someone's jaw drop to the ground, literally, in amazement as Dominic's bewilderment appeared.

I laughed again, 'It was nothing, instinctive, anyone would have done the same.'

'You are too humble, Dan,' he chided, continuing more softly, 'and no, I don't think anyone would have done the same. But Dominic, let me sit in with you. So what brings you here today Dan?'

It turned out that Ventus Capital, this bright young venture capital group was in fact funded and backed by investors from the Middle East, sovereign wealth funds of impossible rich Arab states which Mohammed personally represented. I outlined my plan; the hotel in Venice that was my first target and the plan to roll-out more hotels in different centres. I explained the detail of the research and background and I also showed them my plan for how to deal with the design element.

The presentation did not take long and Mohammed, like many wealthy men who have the power of lots of money to invest, or to withhold, obviously made decisions quickly and boldly.

'I have to tell you Dan,' he said slowly, 'it sounds very impressive, obviously we need to run the numbers to check they make sense but I am truly in your debt from our last meeting - you demonstrated then that you can obviously come up with solutions under pressure and that you are obviously a man of honour. There's an old saying in venture capital that you don't invest in the business, you invest in the people. Well, we would be very pleased to invest in you. Forgive me but I have to go as I'm now late for another appointment. Dominic, give Mr Roberts whatever he wants.' He smiled and stuck out his hand; I shook it firmly.

'Thank you,' I smiled back, 'that's fantastic news.'

'Don't mention it' he replied, 'now let's make ourselves some hotels.'

The next day Dominic called me; he said he had never seen anything like it the day before and later in the afternoon Mohammed had come back in to see him and told Dominic to reassure me that the money I needed was there, it was committed. So I could progress with my plans and negotiations without having to worry about having to find all the investment. It was incredible.

'You see,' I said to Richard, my mind coming back to the present now, 'what another bizarre moment of serendipity. What a coincidence that was, from a chance meeting in a foreign land, an instinctive act, he suddenly now trusted in me, perhaps you really do reap what you sow,' I tailed off.

'Well, he saw you when it really mattered, when there was nowhere to hide your true self, he saw what you are really like,' breathed Richard, ' Just as I have. I do know Dan, you do live your life by trying to do what is right, by your principles. I saw that with Michael in Hong Kong remember. So maybe sometimes you can be rewarded for living your life properly, for living it honourably. But you know as well as I do, what matters is what you see when you look in the mirror at the end of the day; you have to always be true to yourself.'

'Not sure I'm liking what I see as I get older!' I replied, laughing to break the serious tone of the preceding words. 'But isn't it strange, if I hadn't helped the photographer with the bags, would I never have found this building or would the fates have contrived for me to come across him elsewhere or to find the hotel some other way – or would there have been some other opportunity that I will now never know?'

'Who knows,' laughed Richard.

'Or when I had not helped Mohammed's little girl, would I still have ended up in the offices of Ventus Capital but without having ever known him and without his endorsement, or would we have met some other way?'

'Or was it already pre-determined that you would go to Thailand and help Mohammed, your destiny?' he laughed some more.

'Now I'm getting confused,' I joined his laughter.

'So, if it's not the money then,' he continued, 'why did you ask me here? Not just for the tour?'

'No, no; it's just that I need someone strong behind me; from the London City world of finance, particularly doing something I've never done before, I need to have someone behind me who the City financiers will respect but who I also know I can rely on, not someone who will doubt me. I need someone I can trust.'

Richard laughed, 'I know exactly what you mean. And Dan, you proved many years ago to me that you are someone I can trust, that is so important, and as for doing something you've never done before, you also proved to me that you can handle most anything.'

'It's going to be a lot of work,' he said eyeing me directly, gauging my reaction, Richard's final, most important test, to see if I really was prepared for this. 'Why didn't you just come to me for the money, that would have been much easier?'

'I'm not sure, I think that would have been too easy; the easiest is not always right, not necessarily best. Or, at least, not necessarily the best for me,' I smiled, knowing somehow instantly that I needed to do this the harder way, needing my independence but without really knowing why.

Richard had raised an eyebrow, knowing I meant something more by this and he knew it was something I was set on but he also knew that if my mind was set on this project, I was going to do everything possible to try to make it a success. 'OK, OK, let's do it, let's go make a hotel then, but I want to invest anyway, have some of the action,' he then laughed, 'But you better make me some money!'

I joined into his laughter, knowing he was serious; Richard was always serious about money, that was his way, it was in his blood.

'Welcome to the hotel business,' I said and we shook hands firmly, warmly, seriously.

On his flight back, Richard thought about his meeting with Dan. It would be difficult for him learning new ropes but he could manage people and he could manage construction projects; however, in some ways those factors were almost irrelevant. No, most importantly, Dan was passionate. He clearly had a vision but to also have the passion meant he would care deeply about what he was doing and that in turn would mean Dan would try his hardest to get it right. It's those people who do not particularly care about what they are doing who are the mediocre or who fail. Yes, he had no doubts about Dan's ability to make this a huge success.

'Well, we're in the hotel business now,' he whispered quietly looking into the bubbles of the pale champagne as he raised the glass slightly before him in salute to his partner, imagining him sat back below in his new Venetian hotel. He took a deep swallow of the sweet nectar, the tang of the taste and the fizz of the bubbles felt good, as did his re-joining with Dan.

Once I had learnt that the money from Ventus was in place, I had quickly arranged a meeting with the sellers of the building and negotiations began in earnest. It was obvious that they wanted to sell, the property still being owned by the original family that had first built the palazzo many centuries before. However, the new generation, split between so many, feuding factions of the family now spread far and wide across the globe, had stopped caring about the building and it had fallen into neglect.

I knew in deals like this, it often all came down to money, money and face. Face is the Chinese version of pride and in every transaction I had been involved with in the Far East we always had to work out how to massage the egos of the people we were negotiating with, never to openly criticise, always to give them face.

The past few months had been interesting for me, pulling myself from the low depths to which I had sunk under the wave of depression that I did not even realise was threatening to engulf me, dragging me down, drowning me, to now being bright and busy. Louisa had realised I had not been happy; she knew it before me, she knew I had to be involved in things, and now, I was happy. From the first phone call I made to see if this idiotic idea germinating from seeds sown by a chance meeting with a magazine's fashion shoot could actually now grow, could possibly take life and become real, I was happily putting together the business plan; I had enjoyed the dealings for the finance, dealing with bankers, the negotiations with the previous owners, with the authorities and now dealing with builders and suppliers.

I was enjoying being active; I was enjoying being part of something stylish. But taking a small seed of an idea and working at it, creating and nurturing it - to gradually see the embryonic vision grow, the dream begin to take shape, to become a possibility, become a reality, that was the real pleasure.

Strangely, I had learnt a lot about myself during this difficult time. I had been surprised at how quickly I had become bored and I now realised that, actually, I would always work, that I would always need some challenge to keep me occupied.

Projects were my opium and, as an addict needs his fix, so I needed my own project, a business, my own vehicle to drive, without them I would slip back into the clutches of a depression that would always be there, lurking underneath, ready to spread its evil tentacles once more on sensing any weakness or resolve.

Once I started to make the enquiries to try to initiate the project, I had instantly felt better. I had another project to consume me; I felt alive again. Louisa now said I looked to be at my happiest, and she knew me the best.

So here I was now building my own hotel in Venice. It seemed a neat circle – to follow from Hong Kong, a Territory whose own history was so intertwined with the merchants of this City, that barren rock's very existence was dependent upon the trade and voyages made by Marco Polo and others of its sons.

Whilst the building works were continuing, I had set myself up in a small office in an old red brick building that previously was a grain loft on Giudecca Island. Initially, it was just two empty rooms on the first floor. I put in a fax machine and had to install an extra telephone line as something called email, electronic messaging, was just starting and apparently, was going to change the way we all communicated and did business. So, now I was commuting between our home outside Dublin to my new project here in Italy. It was difficult to be away from Louisa and Charlotte but I knew I had to do this. I had to be true to myself and follow what I wanted to do, what I needed to do. Ultimately, they would also be happier that way and, hopefully, more proud of me and so, from here in these small rooms, my new venture had begun to start.

I felt a buzz, an excitement; it felt good to be back doing something but even though I now had the finance arranged and Richard on board, that was just the start, this fledgling hotel company was still just one person, just me, just as the China shipping company had been many years before. There was a lot of work to be done but I liked it that way it was up to me to make it work. Now I had to make it happen.

I had always thought how lucky people were who managed to be working with a product that they also loved. I enjoyed doing deals, structuring them and negotiating them, having a vision and creating things, making things happen but I did not exactly like the industries I had previously been working in. Hotels on the other hand, they were something different, something great, each one different; there was a style and there was a story. Hotels were sexy.

I knew Richard would not be able to resist this opportunity, most people love hotels no matter how wealthy or how successful or how powerful they are in their own fields, and Richard was no different, he loved the whole concept and was excited to be involved. Was it the style? The design? Maybe the fashion? Or the locations?

It was all of this and more. It was the sexiness, hotels were indeed sexy but sex with sophistication. They were usually sited in beautiful locations, cities with history, meaning different things to different people but always, they were symbols of dreams and an escape from their real world.

However, I also had an aim to build something bigger, to use the product we would create in the Venice hotel, not just to build a chain of hotels but to build something more enduring, greater. To build a brand but, importantly, a brand centred around the luxury lifestyle that we would create in the Venetian hotel that could move across into other areas, cosmetics, furniture design, lifestyle products. The success of our product would be design-led, not hotel-led. It would be fashionable. It would be stylish. That is why I called it the Venetian Project.

I was the happiest I had ever been in my work. It was exciting. I was creating a hotel and I was creating a business.

The site I had found for the hotel was truly a magnificent building, imposing architecture with big wide spaces and enormously high ceilings. It was in a fantastic location, on the Grand Canal with views across to the Isola di San

Giorgio Maggiore and its Basilica of the same name and from the higher floors stretching across the bay beyond to the shores of the Lido that protected the lagoon from the Adriatic.

I was convinced that we could make this a great destination, not just as somewhere to stay for visitors to Venice, business people and tourists but also somewhere for Venetians and local Italians themselves to come and party, to drink and to dine, somewhere to see and to be seen, a reason in itself, even, for a trip to Venice.

I still had to track down the architect to help me progress the design plan as I had outlined to Richard, to realise the vision. I knew that I needed someone with the expertise I lacked to help me make it happen but I did not actually yet have him onboard.

I had seen the work of a young interior designer, work that I really liked, an Italian. He was young, he had not had that many high profile projects but I had come across his work in some of my research and travels and I had seen some of his creations showcased in an issue of the famous Conde Nast Traveller magazine about a year or so before when the young designer had been an assistant on the refurbishment of an old famous hotel in Rome. It seemed he had taken the traditional Italian styling from a grand hotel such as that and then modernised it, almost with a refreshingly simple, sleek style, much as Armani had done in a similar way to Italian fashion.

Over the phone, I explained to the people at the Traveller magazine what I was looking for and promised them an exclusive on the hotel opening; they were very accommodating and so I flew to London where they permitted me to spend an afternoon in their offices looking through back issues to find the article I was looking for. In reality, I found the details I needed relatively quickly but I ended up taking the entire afternoon making notes and copies as I kept coming across inspiration after inspiration from all the wonderful destinations they had reviewed over the years.

I managed to track down the designer to his office in Siena, the scene of the annual *Palio* horse race in Tuscany. At first, he did not seem very enthusiastic, we were new and we did not have a grand, impressive name to work with but at least I persuaded him to meet and he agreed we could do so the next day - once I had an idea to do something, I always wanted to do it as soon as possible.

At the start of our meeting, the designer was indeed a little cool towards the project and I knew, as well as outlining a serious scheme, a wonderful opportunity for him, I would also have to play a little to his ego. I explained this was not just a project for one hotel, that it was the creation of a luxury lifestyle brand, to roll-out this idea in the major cities of the world, each location to be different to the others, not just rolling-out the same stale carbon-copy concept everywhere so the visitor never knew whether he was waking up in Milan or New York, Birmingham or Ohio. No, each hotel would possess its own truly unique style but always be incredibly luxurious, chic and cool - the places where everybody would want to stay.

It would need a designer with real genius to do this, to be able to constantly reinvent and evolve the concept in each new location whilst maintaining the core identity; the spirit. Yes, it would need somebody very clever, very gifted. We were only talking to him. He was the one we wanted.

The idea pandered enough to his ego so he agreed to come to Venice the following week to look over the first site.

When I showed him the site, I could see that the young designer was instantly impressed by the location. He clearly admired the old architecture of the building, by the volumes of the vast ceilings and the open spaces inside the lobby, flooded with the dancing lights of the Murano glass. It was when I showed him the Grand Ballroom that stretched to the terrace looking south over the Grand Canal, the ballroom that I wanted to transform into the most desirable bar and nightspot, it was then that the designer decided that here was a project he could really enjoy; here was a natural beauty born of good genes to which he could sprinkle his stardust, to dress with his haute-couture design to transform the neglected duckling into a fabulous, sensational swan.

I was pleased, it was important that he, too, was grabbed by the vision, that it was more than just an assignment to him, that he also was enthusiastic, that he was passionate.

Once I had secured the designer's services, the project started to gain momentum, but I also knew that one of the most important things in anything was people. Whether it be the people you are in business with, the staff you work with, or even those you choose to be around socially, your friends or your loved-ones, having good people around you is what is most important. It was vital to find the right staff. I had learnt over the years that to give good service, you had to have good people. That was true whatever business you were in, shipping, accountancy, or a shop; however, with a hotel it was particularly key.

I had a motto, that you should always avoid toxic people, those who, like bad apples, have a demoralising affect on others, the mean-spirited who sap and waste your energy unnecessarily when you could be using it on more positive things.

No, it was vital to find good people who understood the vision and would work tirelessly to see it come true, not accepting second best, people with passion.

Also service, I would continuously stress to all our new staff how important good service was. Once again, to give good service is important in any business but in a hotel it is key, we had to have the highest standards possible and then make them higher.

So, we set about finding the best people to work with, recruiting the best hotel manager, the best architects, the best building contractors. I knew that it was important for me to put a lot of effort into only engaging the best.

The back-of-house had to be first-class. The kitchens and its equipment had to be modern and efficient, and to suit the head chef's own individual preferences.

The chef! I was also convinced that it would be one thing to have a magnificent bar, the best in this part of Italy, a destination in itself for customers to want to come and visit but if we could also build a reputation for serving wonderful food, we would add another dimension to what we had to offer, another reason why we would become *the* place to be, *the* place to be seen.

It was not just about the entertainment, the food and the bars. We would also make the rooms chic and indulgent, small stylish worlds into which our guests would enter to feel cosy and pampered, wanting to return. The drapes and bedspreads would be luxurious in deep purples, plums and damson colours, rich and sensuous, exuding a sexiness, in the bedrooms.

The bathrooms would be opulent, also dark and rich in colour to continue the feeling of sensuality, not the usual light creams of most modern creations; they would be clad in beautiful smooth Italian black marbles ingrained with subtle veins of unusual colours, silvers and blues, with toiletries supplied from the leading designers, Clarins or Clinique perhaps.

Other, more hidden, concerns would be just as important, fundamental things like the bedding. So I became an expert on mattresses, on firmness, consistency and construction, and the sheets, they had to be made from fine Egyptian cotton with thread counts above 300.

As for televisions, they had to be flat screen and stylish, perhaps by Bang and Olufsen, hung on the wall, with DVD players and a truly extensive library of films available to view, old classics as well as the latest releases.

All rooms would offer simple things like free bottles of water in the room on arrival, plus even a free half bottle of wine as an added unexpected extra, accompanied by interesting information on other available wines, in the hope, of course, the guests would want more and order a bigger bottle from room service, more than recouping the original cost.

During this period, I also travelled and visited some prime hotels to see how they operated and to experience their atmosphere, to 'feel' the ambience, the worlds they had created. I thought about my other favourite hotels, I visited some more and I tried to take influences from them.

I looked to create a similar modern chic style to the Park Hyatt in Milan but mixed with the opulence and luxury of the Hotel de Crillon in Paris and the Peninsular in Hong Kong. The service of the Raffles in Singapore, impeccable, mixed with that of the Cristallo in Cortina, friendly and personal.

The reception and foyer would be dressed in highly polished, limestone tiles on the floor, large in size to create an impression of open space, contrasted with rougher, unpolished, tumbled versions of a similar stone on the walls, a theme continued throughout the whole of the ground floor. The effect would be magnificent.

The bar would be a modern, lively fusion of the famous Oak bar at the Plaza in New York, the open informality of the Palace in Gstaad with its deep, comfy sofas and armchairs in a large open inviting space, not intimidating, different to most of the dark bars that now existed and the buzz of the Captain's Bar of the Hong Kong Mandarin Oriental but all updated, modernised for the new generation with clean lines; to be chic, stylish.

And it was decided the chef would concentrate on creating one large informal brasserie, much like Langan's of London's Stratton Street. We would avoid stuffy dining and create a more relaxed ambience where diners could relax and enjoy themselves.

Although I looked for inspiration, I tweaked it; we improved it; we evolved it - to have our own new identity, to truly be *the* only place in a City to be seen.

I was excited.

Operationally, we also needed the best and our search had found an excellent General Manager who was also excited to join the project. He had been in the hotel trade for fifteen years so he had the experience of how to run and to operate a first class hotel but he was still young enough to want to evolve the traditional concept of service. He had not had the top job before so he still had the eagerness and enthusiasm to want to prove himself but I had many discussions with him prior to his appointment as I knew this would be the main person I would rely on to help me to implement my vision, to make it a daily reality. It was crucial he understood the vision, of what I was trying to achieve so, as well as having the technical ability to take it forwards, he had to also insist on the highest standards, he had to share my passion. Someone who did not also live and breathe the project with me, that just would not work.

We installed the best new IT booking systems for the rooms to work with what was then becoming a new phenomenon, websites which would revolutionise the way the world would market hotels and also enable visitors to reserve rooms instantly, in 'live' real-time.

Our small office had now grown to take over the first two floors of the old loft building.

Finally, *LaVita, 'the life,'* was ready to open its doors. It was my life; my new life. But first, before we could open, I wanted to show my creation to one person. To the one person who really mattered, to show it to my greatest supporter, just the two of us all alone, a private showing, in the quiet, with no fuss, without any glitz, in the calm before the bright lights of the opening.

I wanted to show Louisa.

I made her close her eyes as I led her into what had been the Grand Ballroom. Once there, quietly, slightly afraid now of whether she would like it, I asked her to open her eyes.

'Oh, it's fabulous darling,' she exclaimed enthusiastically. 'It's beautiful. Well done,' and she gave me a kiss.

I smiled, pleased that I could tell that her enthusiasm was genuine, that she really did like it.

The opening was planned for New Year's Eve, a perfect time it seemed to me to leave the darkness of the past behind and launch my new project, to launch the next chapter, my new life.

It was the morning of the opening, I walked over to the tall glass windows that stretched floor to ceiling and surveyed the City moving below, waking up; the red taillights of the cars snaking along the highway in the distance made patterns with the white headlights and yellow streetlamps. I liked this part of the day, before the sun had risen above the horizon, whilst the dawn was just starting, not yet in full swing, before the day would start and be lost to the phone-calls and demands of others. At this point I still felt like I had some control, to prepare, to fashion my destiny that day, to influence what the day would bring.

I had awoken early to prepare and after one last check that I had done all that I could possibly do I breathed, *'Que sera,'* and turned to leave for our offices, bracing myself for the inevitable madness that this day would bring. Finally, after months of hard work, we were ready. All that could be done had been done. I had prepared as well as I could, done the best that I could possibly do and that is all you can ever do, your best.

To arrange the opening party, we carefully selected a wide range of acts from circus style performers that would amaze the guests as they mingled amongst them gathered in the atrium, juggling, balancing, causing disbelief with their magical tricks, to the new generation of rock superstar who would entertain after midnight. I wanted to show that this hotel was not old-school, traditional or stuffy. It would epitomise the *'now'*, the vibrant cool of modern life.

We invited famous musicians and the real powerbrokers from the record labels that made them; supermodels would mix with film stars, of generations old and new and the unknown super-rich of old-money, conservative and secretive, would rub shoulders with the brash nouveau-riche.

Of course, just as I had promised, I personally invited my new friends from Conde Nast Traveller; it was vital that we received good exposure and reviews in magazines and newspapers to market and communicate our image and our lifestyle in the style we had planned.

The opening night was, indeed, an adrenaline fuelled rush, a huge success; the champagne flowed, the young songstress that was music's current hot property was received enthusiastically and, conveniently for us, a small scandal was brewing as one supermodel cuddled up close to a married Hollywood A-lister, which would occupy the front pages and gossip columns over the following days and weeks.

I was also introduced to another famous star, he wanted to know me, asking to be involved in our next site; there surely was something attractive about hotels.

From across the crowded room, I heard his unmistakable booming voice, Richard had arrived, with his lovely wife, Mandy.

'Well, you did it my friend,' he bellowed, 'congratulations.'

'Thank you,' I smiled my reply and tipped my glass of champagne towards him as I lent over to kiss Mandy in welcome. We were good friends, our involvement together in this project, if anything, bonding us closer; he had trusted, in me.

Everybody seemed to be happy.

I made my speech and thanked many people but mostly I thanked Louisa for many things, for being my foundation stone of support; she was embarrassed of course but she knew that I meant every word.

On the stroke of midnight, as the church bells tolled to ring in a new year, there was the accompanying crack of the first firework that burst forth into the sky, to be followed by another and many more, lighting up the dome of the Basilica opposite and the walls of the palazzos terraced together, standing on their stilts. The flashes of colour were reflected in the waters of the canal as booms echoed around, reverberating off the walls.

Later, I would come outside onto the balcony, alone.

It was New Year's Eve at the end of the year 2000, at the end of the first year of the new Millennium.

It was another year of the Dragon.

I had just looked at my watch and smiled again at the thought of the inscription on the back. It was strange how all this had finally come together in another year of the Dragon.

I had not considered what year it was, I had just pursued an opportunity I had seen, I would have followed it in whatever year it may have arisen. It was not something that had been predetermined by me, consciously deciding to try to carry out some challenge because of the year, but was it predetermined for me, by some higher authority, or just a bizarre coincidence, another example of the curious powers of serendipity? My karma?

I would still like to think my efforts had some influence on the achievements; I could not wait another twelve years before seeing what great thing might be possible next.

Standing on the balcony, watching the lights from the buildings on the bank of the Isola di San Giorgio Maggiore reflecting on the Grand Canal below, I sensed something and turned around. It was Louisa. I smiled.

'A penny for your thoughts?' she asked.

'I was just thinking,' I said, putting my arm around her shoulders, giving her a light cuddle. 'I was thinking, I really do have it all.'

Yes, I thought, all the hard times; the hardships of the past, they were all finished, over, done with; they were history. I had done it. *This time, finally, I really had made it!*

'I am the master of my fate; I am the captain of my soul,' – Nelson Mandela

181

SHADOWS OF THE PAST

The hotel opening had been a huge success and we were still basking in its glow. We were featured in all the major lifestyle magazines and travel supplements to national newspapers like *The Sunday Times* and Saturday's *Telegraph*; I was giving interviews everywhere. This was an exciting and fabulous time.

It was only a few weeks after the opening. 2:32pm. It was my birthday. I was still in the office and supposed to be coming home early but, as always, I had been delayed by matters that seemed like they could not wait.

The phone rang and I could see from the display that it was Louisa.

'Hello darling, before you complain, I'm coming, I'm coming. There's just so much to do after the opening. We're wanted in New York, we're wanted in Milan, hell, we're wanted everywhere,' I laughed excitedly.

'Dan,' she said quietly, 'your mother was here.'

'What?' I went cold, deathly cold and then, after a few seconds, 'I have no family,' I said icily.

'But she had photos, she said they were of you, as a boy. She said you're called Robert.' Louisa started to sob, 'Dan, what's going on?'

'Nothing,' I replied curtly and then, after catching myself, I continued more softly. 'Look I'm coming now and I'll explain. I'll explain everything.'

It was time to tell Louisa. It was time to face up to my past.

*****

Robert had just been on the receiving end of yet another beating from his father and enough was enough.

He looked around his room. What did he need?

A clean pair of jeans, a change of shirt, some pants, some socks. His mind was racing, his heart beating. Now the decision had been made, after all these years, he was at once excited and frantic but he knew what to do and amidst the excitement, there was also a certain sense of calm that comes with clarity.

A jumper, in case it got cold.

A note to write to his mum, a note telling her why, telling her not to worry, telling her he was fine but he could not stay any longer; he would not stay any longer; a note telling her that he was leaving; a note to tell her that he loved her.

He stuffed his clothes into a sports bag and went to the drawer where he kept the money he had earned from working over the summer.

His mum was taking a bath, she often enjoyed a long soak on a Sunday whilst his father was out as he always was at this time, drinking again at the working men's club. Here was a colourful, gregarious man, the life of the party, his company enjoyed by so many of his friends but here was an alcoholic, with a temper that would seemingly rise from nowhere, a man who could suddenly become a violent raging bull at home, behind closed doors.

He would probably be drunk and if he could remember the earlier beating, he would probably repeat it again, as a way to try and extinguish the guilt he would now be feeling, trying even now to wash it away with drink. In this vicious cycle of violence it was as if Robert had become a reminder of his guilt which the drink would fuel into resentment and eventually a determination that he had nothing to be guilty about at all, that it was Robert's fault and he should be punished, again.

Robert had three brothers; much older than him, they did not receive the same treatment; it was something reserved especially for him; as if Robert was his father's sole personal outlet for his grievances with the world, for when he could control his temper no longer, when he could no longer keep it calm inside, simmering below the surface and so he had to let it out, to let it rage.

When you are in the cycle, you think it is normal, you think it is usual, that all your friends are receiving the same treatment inside their homes, behind their closed doors. You start by thinking you deserve it. Because it is what you know, it is what you have been receiving for years.

Only as you grow older do you realise that it is not normal, that your friends are not receiving similar punishments in their loving homes. So you start to feel a hurt more painful, the sharp stab of realisation that it's only you, having previously thought beatings to be part and parcel of growing up, a father's privilege to dish out, before you come to understand that they are not, and as you realise that it is not usual, at first, you feel it must be your fault, that you are the bad one, until you eventually come to understand you are not;, that you do not deserve it; it is not your fault.

So, then follows the greatest hurt; the emotional pain which grows stronger and stronger, stabbing inside for you being the only one, the one singled out.

Robert left the note on his mother's side of her bed and descended quickly down the stairs before slipping quietly out of the front door. Then, he ran.

He felt liberated; he was invincible! Tall for his age, he looked older than his fourteen years and he knew what he was going to do, he had a plan. If they could be bothered, they would probably look for him at the train station and they would search for him walking along the main roads out of the town. He had to make it to the seafront before they realised he was gone.

Once around the corner of the top of his road, he slowed to a brisk walk so as not to alert suspicion, calming the exhilaration rising inside of him. He ducked down back roads and alleyways, away from where his family may look. He still had time, his mum would still be in the bath, his father still not home. He turned a corner to the left, then down to the right, more twists and turns, then across a playing field to some train tracks. He knew this was dangerous but it was the right thing to do, he had to get away; desperation breeds foolish chances.

His mind was now becoming scrambled; where before there had been clarity, it was now fast replaced with doubt and confusion, conflicting thoughts battling each other for space to be heard inside his head. Maybe his mum would have found the note by now; he should have left it somewhere else, downstairs; he should have bought himself more time; no, he had to give his mum some time to read the news herself without his father around. His father; he would kill Robert if he ever found him.

He climbed the fence, crossed the train tracks, over the fence on the other side and across a ditch into a housing estate. Through the uniform maze of red brick houses, he finally came to the seafront. He rushed across the road and down the steps onto the beach below to make sure he could not be seen as he walked along under cover of the promenade above.

The beach was made up of large pebbles, the sort that hurt your bare feet when you swim and are hard and knobbly to lie on under your towel when you are sunbathing. They do not hurt to walk on in your running shoes but they move underfoot and make for heavy going.

He knew it would be quicker to go back up onto the promenade but to do that would risk exposure. And now, out of sight from the roads above, he felt safe, a sense of calm beginning to return. He really did not want to get caught; he was free and it felt good, his new life was starting.

So he carried on. He was out of the town now, the promenade had finished but there was no longer any road next to the beach. Here he was below a small cliff edge, a cliff made of white chalk, like a miniature version of the famous white cliffs of Dover further to the east of where he was; they gave him extra cover. It was now six o'clock, two hours since he had left. The sun was still high at the end of what had been a wonderfully hot summer. He had made good progress and soon came into the small town of Bexhill, a sleepy seaside town called 'god's waiting room' as it was said that people only came here to die. Certainly, it had, then, an extremely high proportion of old age pensioners who once retired from their jobs elsewhere in the country would come to seek the relative warmth of England's southern coast.

He walked into the train station and bought a single one-way ticket to Brighton a few miles more up the coast.

The doors slammed shut and the train pulled out of the station, slowly at first and then gradually gathering speed. The train was old and very quiet on a Sunday evening. Most families would be sitting down to Sunday dinner; the traditional English dinner with roast beef, potatoes and gravy. He had managed to grab some fish and chips for himself before he had boarded the train. This was a time before the fast food explosion, before McDonalds had made its way out of America and begun its global domination. It was another time. It was also a time before mobile phones existed; he knew he should really find a phonebox and call someone just so they could let his mother know he was fine.

Brighton was bigger than Hastings, livelier. It seemed the land of opportunity. The train station was built in the Victorian era, built in yet another time, when the whole country was fast being connected by train, connected by steam; the industrial revolution of the 1800's. As he walked out of the main entrance to the station, the road ahead, Queen's Road led down to a clock tower and straight to the seafront beyond; it invited him, like a wide boulevard. The sky was beginning to turn dark now so he walked briskly down towards the sea.

In those days, there were then two piers in Brighton, old iron structures also built in the Victorian age at the end of the nineteenth century for holidaymakers to walk along to enjoy the seaside, to take tea and sit in the sunshine; some also housed dancehalls where many local boys and girls would have met on a Saturday night and enjoyed their first kiss, perhaps even his parents had met in a similar way on the pier back in Hastings.

Now they were full of cheap amusement arcades, fish and chip shops and tacky tourist shops selling the famous sticks of rock and hats with silly quotes like 'kiss me quick'. Later in life the west pier would fall into decay and neglect and be ravaged by fire, sitting for years as just a twisted skeleton of metal; a sculpture to a bygone age.

At the intersection where Queens Road met the seafront, Robert turned left and walked along the promenade towards Brighton's other pier; he was thirsty but the pier was open. He knew he had to be careful and conserve his money until he could find some work but that would not be a problem, he figured, now he could do what he wanted; he could work full time, on a building site or in an office. He had done jobs like that before in the school holidays so he knew that would not be a problem, would it?

He tried his luck in one of the slot machines and pulled the big chrome handle to the side. The wheels turned and he was in luck; he won fifty pence. It felt great; everything was going to be fine. He went and bought a bottle of coke and treated himself to another bag of chips which he covered in vinegar.

Eating his chips out of the wrapped newspaper, he walked back along the promenade and down a ramp onto the beach. He had never actually been on Brighton beach before but he had seen what he was looking for in the movies and sure enough, there they were, built back into the retaining wall, holding up the promenade above, were large arches. In later years these arches would become nightclubs and restaurants as Brighton reinvented itself as a trendy destination to visit but this was in the early 1980's when the British seaside resorts were neglected and seedy. He guessed they had been built to house machinery and now they were used to store the striped deckchairs that would be put out to line the promenade during the summer days for holidaymakers to sit on for twenty pence a day.

He was in luck, one arch was empty and open, it had no doors. He laid out his towel on the cement floor and lay down.

It was the end of summer, early September, so the evening was now much chillier than just a few weeks before. Luckily, he had a thick leather biker's jacket to wear; he did not ride a motorbike but he liked the heavy rock music and this was their uniform.

Robert slept well and awoke to see the sun had just risen to his left and was now sitting above the sea. It was a dark yellow ball, not yet so bright that you could not look at it. The sea was as flat as a millpond; it was going to be a beautiful day.

He looked at his watch; it was only half past six in the morning. He was not used to getting up this early; normally he would lie in bed and wait for as long as possible as most teenagers do before his mother would come up for the third or fourth time and ended up pulling the covers off the bed with him hanging grimly onto them.

'Mum,' he knew that he really should let her know that he was fine. He knew he should call someone today.

As he walked out of the arch and onto the beach, his kit stuffed back inside his bag, he knew he could not stay sleeping where he was. He would be sure to be found and asked awkward questions, maybe even by the police. He had an idea and smiled to himself. He was enjoying this.

The telephone call could come later.

He walked east, along the promenade, his sports bag slung over his shoulder looking just like any other young man. As the piers diminished in size behind him and the main road curved away from the beach, the wide promenade gave way to a narrower stretch of pavement until it became a small path, a path once again protected from prying eyes by small white chalk cliffs and here he found what he was looking for. Just as in any English seaside resort, there were always beach-huts, brightly coloured and under-used, standing to attention in a long row, as infantrymen on a military display ground awaiting inspection, there must have been about twenty of them, all different colours, yellows, reds, greens, pinks, not one in the same shade as any other, all painted differently by different owners over the years and all in differing states of repair, mostly shabby and tatty, neglected soldiers of a bygone age before the coming of cheap package holidays that lured their masters to more exotic locations.

He inspected them closely and saw that those furthest away to the east, furthest away from the town, looked to be in the worst state of repair and the least visited. He reckoned that these huts would probably be mostly owned by people living out of town who probably only visited once or twice a year, coming down from London only on the hottest weekends, and with this being the end of the season, no-one would probably visit until next year.

The hut second from the end was only secured with a padlock on a small bolt: it was easy to unscrew one side of the bolt and it fell down leaving the door free to swing open. He looked inside. It smelt of damp and was very dusty; it probably had not been used that year. He brushed aside some cobwebs and placed his bag down to one side. To his delight, he found a small camping stove, still with a small blue gas canister attached through the rubber pipe, a kettle, some saucepans, a few cans of baked beans and up, above him, he could even see a mattress for a sun lounger which he could put on the floor to sleep.

Robert found some matches in a drawer and tried to light one of the small hobs on the camping stove. He could hear the rush of gas as it came out of the ring and once lit, the blue flames burnt strongly. He opened a can of beans and made a note to himself that he must replace it for the people who owned the hut. He would also have to screw back the bolt whenever he left and he thought he could even clean up the place a little for them as a sort of payment for his unknown rental of their holiday home. He smiled to himself as he imagined their amazement when they next visited and found their hut so tidy and organised.

Looking into the blue flames, he found himself staring intently. A negative thought popped into his head, quickly pushed out again.

'I'm not going back,' he breathed defiantly.

The hut even had a small wooden veranda deck just large enough for him to pull a deckchair out from inside and he sat there enjoying the sunshine on his face as he finished the beans which he ate straight from the pan. He brushed aside some cobwebs and placed his bag down to one side.

There was no running water in the hut but behind were some public toilets. He could wash the pans there but he could see some people beginning their day in the distance to his right, a couple walking their dog on the sand below the shingle as the tide was out, a few people cycling to work going into central Brighton and some fishermen preparing their boats and drying their nets from last night's catch.

Robert knew he should be careful and to sit there much longer may raise a few enquiring glances. He pulled the deckchair back inside and decided to leave his bag. He turned his back to the west where all the activity was going on, so as to shield what he was doing as he screwed the lock back on to keep the door shut and to avoid any passers-by noticing another hut that had apparently been broken into, and then he set off for the day.

The morning was not a very encouraging one. His plan had been to find a small building site and ask if they had any work. He figured they would be only too happy to pay cash and avoid any unnecessary social security and tax charges for some cheap labour and he could not go to a job centre and register without having to give his real name. For the same reason, applying for an office job may be difficult, but after a couple of hours of walking the backstreets of Brighton, he had only come across two building sites; the first was too big, an operation by the homebuilders Wimpey and all job applications had to be made via head-office; the second was a small family operation, a father and two sons renovating a house and although the sons said they could do with the extra help, the father said they could not afford it and, anyway, they would just use an extra pair of hands as an excuse to slack off.

Plus he knew he needed to make that phone call; he really should not put it off any longer. He found the phone box, in these days the famous English red phone boxes were still very much in daily use and not just a novelty. He lifted the big black plastic handset, inserted the coins and twirled the dial round with his forefinger.

'Hello,' answered Steve. He was one of Robert's oldest friends; a few years older than him, Steve was already independent, out working in the wider world.

'Christ, you've caused a lot of trouble,' exclaimed Steve at the other end of the line. 'Where are you?'

'London,' Robert lied.

'Well, how are you? Are you OK?' his questions came blurting out.

'Look, I'm fine. I'm great. Can you just tell mum that there's nothing to worry about.'

'You haven't half caused a stink you know. Can we meet?' asked Steve. 'I'm often in London on work. I'll be there later this week.'

The beeps started, signalling only seconds were left, 'Look, I've got to go, can you just let my mum know, let her know I'm OK. I'll call again, I promise.'

'Reverse the charges next time,' shouted Steve after him, a hint of desperation in his voice as he rushed the words out before the line went dead. 'Take care,' he whispered to no-one in particular as he replaced the handset, fearful for his young friend out there somewhere on his own.

By the end of the day Robert had not had any luck with finding a job, but not to worry, it was only Monday; he would try again tomorrow, he thought, as he walked back to his beach-hut.

On the pier that night he had no luck with the fruit machine either; he pulled the arm, the reels spun, nothing this time. He tried again and again, no luck. He put in some more money and pulled the arm again, still nothing. He tried five more times and had now wasted eighty pence.

'Stupid,' he thought as he left the pier and walked back along the beach. A breeze was beginning to pick up. It was cold, coming from the north, it would start to bring the cold air from the arctic down as summer gave way to autumn, winter would not be far behind. Luckily, he had his big leather jacket to zip up and keep him warm.

That night he slept fitfully. Despite the relative comfort of a thin mattress, the four walls and a door compared with the previous night sleeping under the arch, he could not sleep well. The night before where his dreams had been warm on the back of his elation at his freedom, full of hope and plans for the future, in contrast this night his thoughts were full of dark thoughts, of anxiety and trouble.

Eventually, the morning was starting to arrive. He woke early, still tired from the lack of sleep and in the still half dark he walked up on to the top of the chalky Sussex cliffs over-looking the sea.

The phonecall of the day before had made him a bit depressed. He had done it and got it out of the way but rather than making him feel better, it made him think again about the reality of what he had done, the trouble he had caused and the upset his mother would now be going through, but he could not go back; he would not go back.

Robert could not really remember when the beatings had started. In fact, he could not remember a time when they did not happen. He supposed there must have been that time but he could not be sure.

He had always had a slight limp from when his leg was broken when he was much younger, probably only about five years old, he thought. He could not remember the incident very clearly. In truth, he did not want to. He remembered that he was already crying before his father hit him, crying, just as many young children do, because he was being forced to eat the remainder of his dinner.

After his father's first smack across the face, Robert fell onto the hard kitchen floor but it was the following kick that must have broken his leg. His father demanded that Robert be left in his room and it was days before his mother, eventually, secretly took him to the hospital, explaining that he had fallen over a step rushing to eat sweets. Following the delay, the leg could not then be set quite properly, the resulting limp probably only heightening his father's resentment towards this unwanted child, serving as a reminder of any shame he may possibly have felt.

Robert remembered his mother trying to explain that it was not his father's fault. He had been drinking that day and he had just lost another job; it was not his fault.

Robert could remember, clearly, the reasoning of his younger self over the following years, that if it was not his father's fault, then it must have been his own; it must have been Robert's fault.

Of course, there were also his much older brothers; the bullying, the fights; but that seemed explicable, natural, the law of the jungle, with the older, stronger preying on the weak, the young; primal instincts encouraged and left unchecked by the example of their master, the leader of their pack.

Increasing in frequency, the beatings now were mostly conducted behind closed doors, executed in a fashion to leave no visible scars.

Maybe there were reasons for what his father did, excuses even - perhaps he needed to exert his power, his will, enforce his control, or maybe Robert had just become an outlet for him to vent the frustrations of his inadequacies compared to his wealthier friends with better jobs and Robert was now a constant reminder sat before him, taunting him.

Perhaps it was because they were poor, his life not having turned out as he would have dreamt, moving sporadically from job to job with local factories that did not pay well; maybe that made his embarrassment more acute. Or perhaps he resented the extra mouth to feed that had arrived unexpectedly but there were poorer families than them, it was no excuse.

If there was any redemptive element for his father, it was not because he was stupid, rather it was that he was uneducated and illiterate with primeval emotions that, when mixed with drink, would run out of control. And with no governors on his emotions, as the pressure red-lined, his temper would explode the release-valve, screaming and hitting were his means of expression. He knew no better, with no capacity to imagine the consequences of his actions.

To Robert, he just now supposed it was because he was an inconvenience, extra hassle, extra work, extra grief he did not need, an embarrassment to have around, he was an unwanted child after the three elder boys; he was a mistake.

Whatever the reasons, it was still his father's fist that hit his child, ultimately his responsibility, his choice.

But if the beatings were designed to make Robert submit, to make him comply, they had the opposite effect. They made him fight, a fight inside, within himself, of defiance. He fought for his independence and he grew to be his own man. The beatings did not defeat his passion, it only grew stronger.

He formed his own sense of what was right and what was wrong; he formed strong principles, his honour. He always did nothing in retaliation to his father, he just took the beating. His silence became his victory, his defiance. It probably only served to annoy his father even more, increasing his sense of guilt and so feeding the cycle that continued, aways taking the moral high ground; a child showing a man what was the right thing to do.

Not knowing when the next time would come but invariably expecting it when his father returned late from drinking, on a Friday after eventually coming home from work via the club or a Saturday after a late night at a local bar, coming home surrounded by that smell which Robert had come to know well, the stagnant smell of a drunk. These were times he tried to avoid being around, or still awake. First, hiding under the covers, quiet as can be, breath held in tight, not daring to make a sound. Then, as he got older, just staying out, wary not to come home too early; no, definitely do not come home too early.

And so he got to enjoy the early morning, the pre-dawns, with street sweepers and birds gathering for the dawn chorus, timing his return home after his father would have finally gone to bed and before his late morning angry, heavy-headed rise.

But what really upset Robert most was not the physical pain of the beatings, the sudden crack of the elbow to the nose or the harsh smash of the head slammed against the coarse hard wall of concrete, no, it was more the emotional attack that penetrated deep inside of him, to constantly be told, 'You're no good. You're useless. Get out of my sight.'

To reason that he must be some form of unwanted mistake, for that to be why he was not loved like the others. It was not the physical pain, it was the emotional, the realisation that you were not wanted, that was what really hurt. That his father must have really hated him to do what he did.

He was a mistake, an embarrassment, he was not wanted. *He did not belong.*

The latest beating surely confirmed this. Well, if he was not wanted, he would leave and that would solve their problem for them. That must be the best thing for all, and with each of those last swings of his father's elbow to his face, his resolve inside grew stronger, with each bash, his determination became more powerful and with the final blow the decision, to leave, was finalised.

Sat up atop of the windswept cliff, the vast expanse of sea stretching far away beyond the horizon, he was very aware of being alone, completely all alone in the world. However, strangely he felt empowered by this thought as he imagined himself unbeholden to anyone, now free. He noticed for the first time the seagulls that flew there, gliding, swooping low to the sea and occasionally seeming to miraculously somehow stay stationary, hovering almost, suspended in time and place, at all times completely effortless, as they used the natural forces of the wind and the thermals. Not permitting all these forces to batter them, they soaked them up, harnessing them to work to their own advantage.

Robert must have watched the birds for an hour or more as the sun rose to start its daily journey across the sky and their flight seemed to give life to an inner strength inside of him, a sense that he was doing the right thing. A sign sent from the skies? Maybe, maybe not, but he found it incredibly positive and empowering to watch them fly. He had soaked up everything that had been thrown at him; it had made him stronger; it had made him a better person and now he was going to use it. He was not going to be a victim, he would not let it beat him; he was going to make it work for him. There would definitely be no going back.

Sitting there, he swore to himself that was the last time he would think about them. He now had no family.

Eventually, he made his way back down the path to the beach. The sun was now bright but with a few light clouds high in the sky, the breeze remained, as it did coming from the north, from the shore, making the sea appear relatively calm but also bringing with it a cold freshness. It certainly did now seem like the lingering end of summer; it seemed very final.

It was only then that he noticed a man in the beach-hut at the other end of the row, at the end nearer to the path, one of the better kept huts that Robert had purposely ignored for being too well kept, too often frequented. Still, the presence of someone-else at the end of the summer during the week surprised him. He chided himself for not having noticed the man earlier, lost in his thoughts as he had been, returning from the cliff-top. He would have to be more careful, he warned himself.

The man was sorting out his fishing rods and had them leaning on the banister of his veranda. He had already seen Robert, too late to try to quickly duck back inside but he just carried on untangling his lines, he did not seem too concerned about the boy at the other end of the row.

However, Robert still decided it was best not to hang around any longer that morning, lest the man came over to be neighbourly and ask any awkward questions - no time for any beans this morning then, he quickly dressed and left.

Robert had to walk past the man's hut at the end of the row as he followed the path out to the town but as he passed him the man seemed engrossed in his fishing tackle and just raised his head as Robert passed and gave him a slight nod of the head in acknowledgement of a fellow beach-hut owner, which Robert returned with his own nod and slight smile.

The day in town was turning out to be another disaster. It also started to rain, meaning he took refuge in a small café where he tried to make his cup of tea last as long as he could. Nursing his second cup, Robert thought about the possibilities for work. There did not seem to be as many building sites as he had hoped to find. He had only come across two that morning and again, they were both unhelpful. He had picked up one of the free local papers and was scanning the job ads in there. Maybe he could get a job in an office, after all, it was not as if he had to be at school, he was allowed to work and maybe the police were not even looking for him. Even if they were, if he had a job, what could they do? Could they force him to go home? He ringed a couple of possibilities with his pen and decided to give them a call the next day. It had stopped raining and if that old man had gone, he could go back to the hut with some soup to heat on the camping stove for his tea.

As he walked back from the café, he came to a large supermarket, Sainsbury's, one of a new type of store that was beginning to arrive in every high street in England at that time; previously the preserve of corner shops and small grocery stores, these new supermarkets were now just beginning to take over. He went inside, he had heard that their prices were usually cheaper than the corner shops and he needed to conserve his little money. This store had obviously not been there long and there were notices up recruiting for new staff - just fill out an application and hand it in to the store manager. He felt a shiver of excitement, this could be it; this could be the start he was looking for. He paid for his cans of soup and the girl on the checkout found him an application form and, uninterestedly, called the manager.

He barely looked at Robert. They needed people; he could have a job stacking shelves and help sort out the stock in the back of the store. 'What's this he said looking at the national insurance card proffered under his nose, 'Daniel, eh.'

'Yes,' he replied quickly, taking advantage of the manager's carelessness, 'Daniel Roberts, Sir.' So by virtue of this stranger's inattentiveness, he gave a gift, as when his mistake made it to his first payslip, Robert Daniels became, forever more, Daniel Roberts.

In good spirits, Dan then returned to the beach-hut, first having stopped to check from a distance that his near neighbour was no longer there. The soup tasted great and that evening he went back to the pier deciding he deserved another treat of more fish and chips and a coke now that he had a job and his life could start properly.

He lost again on the slot machine but even that could not dampen his spirits; as he turned away, however, suddenly, he felt a hard shove from behind. There was some laughing and he turned to see a large lad, a bit older than him, somehow he looked vaguely familiar.

'Watch it,' the larger boy sneered down at Dan.

'It wasn't me,' Dan replied, protesting. 'You backed into me.'

He had never learnt to keep quiet and take the easy way out, he always had to try and stick up for what he believed in.

The larger boy was with a few other boys and some girls who were now laughing and jeering some more.

'What did you say?' the larger boy was quickly riled and clearly, in front of his gang of friends, he could not be belittled by this younger kid; he could not lose face.

He came over and grabbed one of the lapels to Dan's jacket.

'Fuck off,' Dan defied him.

'You little shit,' he snarled and he lent back to take a swing with his free hand. It did not connect well and Dan had been ready for it. As he swung, Dan smacked him hard on the side of the face. He knew it was a suicide punch; his one and only opportunity to land a blow before the inevitability of the grabbing hands from the boy's crowd behind. He felt a fist to the stomach that knocked out all his breath, followed by a kick as he dropped to the floor.

He could hear their laughter as they moved away. There was blood in his mouth but he only tasted it later; that was not his first sensation. No, it was not of physical pain, his first thoughts were of their voices, the familiar emotions of the pain from the nasty sounds of their jeering and laughter belittling him.

'Nice one Danny,' he heard one of them say to the large boy and looking up from the ground he could see the boy's friend clapping him on the back as they walked away.

'Danny,' he thought, 'that would be an easy name to remember now.' He still managed a small smile in spite of the fresh blood he could now taste as he licked his lip to soothe its newly-formed cut.

The next day after he had finished his first day in the stock room of the supermarket, his first day of proper work, he changed his route back home and instead made a detour that would take him past the second building site he had visited a few days before. Standing out front, shovelling cement into a mixer, was the father with his two sons.

'Hey, Danny,' called out Dan, 'going to fight me now you don't have your gang?'

The three of them looked up at the same time.

'What's this?' asked the father.

'Your son likes to get others to help him fight,' said Dan.

'Did you give him this then?' laughed his older brother. 'It does pretty him up a bit.'

Dan had not noticed at first but could now see that Danny's lip was swollen where his punch had got him. Dan smiled.

'Don't tell me,' said the father turning to his son, 'young Harry and Clive got involved as well to help you out?'

'So what?' replied Danny scornfully. 'What you here for? Going to press charges?'

'You know, that's an idea,' Dan answered, 'but what I really want is a job.'

He had taken a chance, but a chance with nothing to lose. Fate had delivered up an opportunity, a painful meeting that maybe he could now use to his advantage. He could only but try and the worst that could happen was that they could say, 'No'. As it was, they agreed and Dan now had a better job.

Life was not easy in those first few weeks but he soon had enough money to move into some lodgings with a few of Danny's friends from the pier.

As Dan left the beach-hut for the final time, he took two cans of beans from his bag and placed them on the shelf above the cooker.

'Just returning something that didn't belong to me,' he thought and although he had little money and even though he doubted if the owners would come back for many years and remember what the contents of their hut had been, he smiled to himself, a smile of approval, for doing the right thing.

As he went to shut the door to the hut, he breathed, 'Good bye Robert,' and he turned away as Daniel, leaving Robert and his past life behind him, turned to a new start, to a new act in his story, *to another life*.

Life in his new housing was bohemian and colourful; it was really little more than a squalid squat, too many of them crammed into a small run-down house in a bad area.

Their life was not easy; they were a strange mix, always one step away from the fates that awaited so many runaways who would surely fall into lives of despair, prostitution and drugs. There was always the inevitability of drugs, hash, cannabis, at first, later followed by harder stuff, speed supplied from strangers his housemates had found in the park. There were endless comings and goings of different waifs and strays who came to somehow fill the house like lost souls. The drugs seemed to attract people of that nature, lethargic, with no inclination to do anything but to rely on others, wasting their lives away, or perhaps it was the drugs that made their disciples become like this.

But working with Danny and his father and brother began to feel a little like some strange form of new family, like some form of belonging, and Dan loved his new found independence which, hard-fought, he had come to crave so much, having had to grow up, in some ways, quicker than most boys his age. He needed the freedom. Ironically, it was probably his early need to fight for his own independence that saved him from the downward spiral that life in this house was becoming.

He was always trying to think of some options, for what was next, not because he wanted to somehow *'better'* himself but because it just seemed natural to be planning, driving towards something new, something more than this wasting existence that they were falling into, that he was now, also, falling into.

The others seemed happy to just live like this, many of them just drawing benefits and sitting around all day in a wasted state. But he knew he wanted more.

He needed more.

At school he had always been bright, a clever boy, top of his class. He would sometimes wonder if he was somehow wasting it, whether he should be carrying on with his studies, going to university, training to be a doctor, a lawyer or an accountant, perhaps. He knew that most people did not have such opportunities and here he was throwing them away, not taking advantage of what he could do.

Dan was trying to save a bit of money, put a little aside so he could get somewhere of his own, so he could move on from this place, but it was still not enough, besides he had friends here and he was not sure what he wanted to do, the excuses could be varied and extensive. Then, one day, Dan received the wake-up call he needed, the final push, the realisation that he needed to do something more with his life, to take control before it was too late.

He came home one afternoon to find his occasional girlfriend, Ella, in bed. She was with a guy Dan recognised vaguely as one of the suppliers who would occasionally be hanging around.

'Hey baby,' she slurred slowly as he came into the room.

'What's going on?' demanded Dan.

'Nothing special,' she answered, 'Carl's just sorting me out with some blow. I didn't have any money.'

'What's up,' said Carl in greeting as he sat up, 'yeah, we're cool.' His response was casual, acknowledging nothing particularly strange with their behaviour.

Dan was not really upset that Ella was sleeping with someone else; they had made no commitments to each other, they were not even boyfriend and girlfriend, they just sometimes slept together when it was convenient and he knew sometimes she would make some extra money by turning tricks around the local parks where her midnight customers would assemble, the guys leaving the nearby pubs, local young lads having a drunken fumble or the Irish navvies away from home, over here to work the tar on the roads, but now, somehow seeing her selling her body in exchange for drugs seemed so seedy, dirty, desperate.

This made him think even more, was this really what their lives were becoming? He could suddenly see, as clear as crystal, where they were headed. What had started as a few innocent puffs of weed had quickly disintegrated as they tumbled down the slippery slope of a life dictated by drugs. He knew the time to move on had arrived. In fact, it had already passed, it was time.

That evening he slipped quietly out of the large black front door, stopping on the top step briefly to look up at the sky, he permitted himself a small smile as he whispered, 'Time to go.'

Dan's destination was London; arriving late at night, he found a doorway in which to seek shelter from the harsh breeze. The hard stone floor did not help sleep to come to him easily but sleep he must have done for he was suddenly awoken rudely by a person kicking at his feet. 'Get out of the way, go on, bugger off!' a man shouted, spitting in Dan's face as he passed to open up the door to the shop that had been Dan's sanctuary.

Humbled and cold, Dan moved off feeling very alone now, his destination was to find a youth hostel he had heard of in Camden Town, and there, indeed, life with Camden's famous lock and market was eclectic and exciting; it was a world frequented by musicians and artists. Life was also hard, drugs were still prevalent and, at times, it was difficult to keep himself from giving in to the temptations all around him and from stopping working for something more but Dan was determined and he knew to do so would be weak and he would have lost, to whom he was not sure but that is how it seemed, as if he would have let someone else or something else win, to have beaten him.

With his friendly nature, Dan quickly made friends in an environment like this and soon managed to find odd jobs, working in bars, cleaning and even modelling as a nude for local art students and, soon, he had managed to gather enough money to move into a small bedsit and enrolled into a college on a business studies course. It was here that Dan's lecturer, recognising something in him, encouraged him to apply for the Knox management trainee programme and, having previously worked there himself, he made a call to persuade the company to give Dan an interview, to give him a chance.

Dan supposed the people interviewing him at Knox were impressed enough with his perseverance to offer him the job with their prestigious firm, which he only accepted on the basis that they kept his background confidential so that he did not stand out from the other recruits, obviously not one of them, obviously not belonging.

*****

'That was tough,' my eyes were wet and only now, when I had finished the story, did I turn to look at Louisa for the first time since I had started to recount the past, my past. 'I didn't realise I felt like this. I haven't let myself think about these things since they happened.'

Truly, these things had been buried deep; it was now as if it had been a completely different life; a life belonging to somebody else.

A mist clouded her eyes; Louisa had sat and listened to his story in complete silence. She was crying now but whereas hours earlier, after his mother's visit and before Dan had come home to tell her his story, her tears had been of worry, for maybe a man she did not know, who had kept this secret from her, tears of fear that her life may be built on a web of lies; now the tears were different. Tears of a complicated nature, indescribable, a mixture of both sorrow but also happiness, tears of pity for what the man she loved had endured as a child, tears of pride for what he had been through before he met her, to achieve what he had.

She felt an overwhelming wave of happiness and relief that the man she loved was not someone different.

'I suppose I never really did find out where you were from,' she sobbed; he also remembered the question and his reply on their first meeting at the concert those many years before. 'I told you, you would have to find out. Well you've stuck around long enough and you have your answer,' he looked up at her. 'I told you that you never know what goes on behind closed-doors; well that was our story.' He smiled and she remembered their people-watching game from Green Park.

It was a strange coincidence, she thought, that they were both the youngest child from their families; maybe that was one reason why they had such a close affinity with each other, an instant understanding from the very beginning when they met all those years before. And she remembered the stories he had told her during their first memorable summer together about the young princess prevailing over her wicked family, perhaps, this is why he had understood how she felt.

Maybe that was why these two fiercely independent people had so quickly come together, without knowing, without thinking to become as one, still independent but as one, now relying on each other. She had built her cold wall to protect her built from the bricks of the teasing of her elder sisters, now she saw that he too had his own mask.

He had built a quiet strength, developed a keen sense of justice, of right from wrong and forged a determination of steel, hard and uncompromising and, unbeknown even to himself, he had taken a decision, never to compromise, always to do everything as well as he could, and she began to understand some more.

Perhaps that was why he had acquired a keen edge of cynicism, despising hypocrites and finding so many people to be frauds, unable himself to find pleasure in a life where he was driven to wander, searching, looking to be accepted, trying to find where he belonged. Perhaps that was why he was unable to be happy.

'So,' she started slowly, 'Robert's your real name?'

'No,' I replied, 'I am Dan. I am the same man that you know. It's still me.'

Indeed, he was still the same man she had always known him to be but now, through her upset, Louisa could begin to see some of the pieces that had been missing from the jigsaw of her life with him come, slowly, into view. And she admired him and loved him anew.

She could understand now why she knew so little of his past and she could see why he had not wanted to talk about it, the hurt buried so deep down inside him that even he no longer knew it was there.

Mixed with her tears was also relief. Relief that after all these years she could see now even better what had helped make this man. Relief that the holes that had existed in his past had not made him into a fraud. This was still the same man she had fallen in love with.

So, he had not been an orphan after-all, at least not in the literal sense, but he had chosen to become one and it did go some way, she thought, to explain why he was driven to succeed, always wanting to prove himself to people, always wanting to please, not knowing that he did not have to, that he could just be himself, just be happy.

She wondered about the fates that had brought them together. Without this experience that he had been through, would they ever have met? Would they not have understood each other so well, not been attracted to each other so strongly, never have become soul-mates, never had their children together?

She also wondered why Dan had only changed his name slightly. Why not change it to something totally dissimilar so he would never be found. Was that on purpose, even subconsciously, had he wanted to be found? For this day to one day come?

'Why won't you see your mother?' she asked. 'She seems desperate to see you, to see her grandchildren.'

'I can't, Louisa,' I replied softly. 'I swore to myself I would never allow myself to be dragged back again, to be a victim. It's too long ago.'

'But…' she started.

'No,' I shouted angrily, 'I never want to think of those days again. They don't exist. That's the end of it.'

I could see that Louisa was upset and, trying hard to stop herself from bursting into tears again, she turned and went upstairs, stopping herself from running as she wanted to.

I stomped into the kitchen and threw my coffee cup into the sink to the crashing sound of fragile china; the sound of a life breaking into a few pieces.

I did not care.

I went to the cabinet above my head and took out the bottle and poured myself a glass of whiskey.

Shit, I thought. Why did this have to happen? Why now? Just when things had seemingly come together, just when I thought I had finally made it, life keeps throwing up something different.

Then I was shocked. I did not realise I felt like this. I was shocked at all the feelings I had buried deep, so very, very deep that I did not even know they existed down there, buried away from over thirty years before, feelings that I had tried to forget, so that I could get on with my life, my new life away from all of that, away from all of that hurt.

So many emotions were forcing their way to the surface inside me, conflicting emotions. The thoughts I had buried long ago resurfaced, raw, angry, confused with new guilt that Louisa was now upset and confused also with doubts, doubts for my mother, was I being too harsh to exclude her from my new family?

I knew I should not be taking it out on Louisa; I knew it was not her fault. I went upstairs to see her. She was sitting on the edge of the bath, her hands in the running water, her face wet where she had tried to wash away all the tears.

'I'm sorry that I shouted,' I whispered, 'it's just its difficult to think about these things. In fact, I haven't even thought about them for so many years, I buried them, and I just don't understand them. How can you explain something like that?'

I paused before carrying on, 'Look, I can't help growing more in love with my children every day. It's incredible, a love of great wonder, without boundaries, just when you think it cannot possibly be any stronger, it deepens some more. They constantly amaze me, surprise me, with the things they do and say, their thoughts, their skills, their jokes, their cuddles. I could never raise a fist to them, but not because I have to stop myself, just because it's natural. So, I don't understand how he could have been like that?'

There was silence and then I went on, 'He must have really hated me. I was a mistake they didn't want, a mistake to be blamed for all his mistakes, to take out all his frustrations on. To see her again would just remind me; it's better apart.'

I went back downstairs. The smell of the whiskey was repugnant now, and reminded me of him. I poured it down the sink; I knew I did not really want it.

I started to think, alone, about those times, for the first time in some thirty years. It was a different time; it felt like a different life, somebody else's life. It was an earlier chapter, hazy now but still, unavoidably, the story was mine. Incredible, even, for me to believe that I had really been through this to get to where I was now, incredible that I had survived. I could picture the innocent fresh-faced Robert, fourteen, invincible; the mistaken invincibility of youth that is really a heady cocktail of naivety and hope.

I knew, now, that I had been lucky to have survived, many runaways do not; I was lucky to have survived the temptations that could have overwhelmed me, lucky not to have suffered real evil cross my path on those streets, lucky to have got out. I had fought, but I was also lucky.

I thought of how Michael had disowned his family in Hong Kong, embarrassed by his humble origins and how, conversely, my family had not wanted me, and with a similar opposite reflection, how I had somehow managed to resist the temptations set before me but to those set before him, he had succumbed.

Yes, no matter how much I tried to forget, it was still a chapter from the story of my life. Was this why I always wanted more from life? Was this what drove me? Ambition did not drive me; but I was driven by the need for independence. Was this why? Was this why I always needed to be working, creating? Was this why I became infected with the urge to keep moving that had taken me to Hong Kong and all the other places I had been? Was this why I was always moving? Was I still running away?

'No,' I breathed, I was always moving forwards, always moving towards something. I was not running away from the familiar; I was running towards the *'new'*, towards excitement, to always feel alive, not to stagnate, to look for the new challenge. It was not wanderlust, it was a desire for the bright lights, for the big city and, then, I realised, I had done all I had done because of a desire to really experience life. 'To live life!' I said out loud, managing to bring half a smile across my face.

Upstairs, through her tears Louisa realised how far he had come, not just from this different past, an earlier life, a prologue before their own but also how far he had grown since even their own more recent chapters, since the birth of their first child joined now by a sister and younger brother, how he had grown-up, matured now, evolved, how much he did indeed love and care for their children, for their family. But it was a natural evolution, not one that had to be worked at, or consciously programmed, it was just what had come to pass, naturally, what had come to be. No, this past did not define him; it did not own him, but yes, it had helped to fashion him, to form his principles embedded within, his integrity, his honour, his sense of always having to do what was right, no matter how much more difficult that made life for him. It was not a choice for him; it was part of his DNA, fashioned from such injustice. It *was* him.

It was strange, Louisa thought, what are the motivations living within us all that may have shaped us, that may drive us in so many different ways? Some are driven by ambition and, as with too many politicians, the lust for power, others by integrity, the wish to do good, to help others. Some are driven by competition, the desire to win, perhaps by the wish for adulation, to be worshipped, others by the converse, the fear of failure, not wanting to let anyone down. Some have no inclination to do much at all, to offer no contribution, to rely on others, and some, the lucky ones, are truly happy. Some are driven by the struggle to find their place in this world, to establish their own reality, some fight to be heard, but most, above all else.....most are driven by the need to be loved.

'The world breaks everyone. And after, many are strong in the broken places.' – Hemingway.

TIMING

A summer had passed since the Venetian hotel opening and Richard had asked me to come to New York, he lived there now and he thought he may have found an interesting site for a second *La Vita*. I was genuinely excited, not only for the opportunity to expand our fledgling business, but also because I always liked any chance to visit that City, it was so vibrant and full of life; I always enjoyed my time there.

It was September 2001.

I landed at JFK airport in New York on the 10th of September, and as I came out from behind the doors that enclosed the baggage carousels and into the buzz of the arrivals hall, I saw a young man of Arabian descent holding up a board bearing my name.

'Hello,' I said, introducing myself, 'I'm Dan Roberts and you must be Mohammed's nephew.'

'Yes, that's right,' the young man replied enthusiastically, the eagerness of youth, keen to please, 'my name is Ahmed.'

'Well, Ahmed, it is very kind of you to come out all this way to meet me but as I told Mohammed, it is really unnecessary, I would be quite alright catching a cab into town.'

'I am sure Mr Roberts,' he smiled, 'but once my uncle had told me what you had done to save my cousin, there was really no argument and I so much wanted to meet you.'

'Oh, it was a long time ago and, in any case, it was nothing anyone else would not have done in the same situation,' I replied, a little embarrased by the attention, and, please, call me Dan.'

We had soon reached his car and were on our way to to my hotel, another Hilton, on Avenue of the Americas, in the heart of the City, at the centre of Manhattan Island, a lively bustling metropolis. It is essentially a grid system of roads, making it very uniform but very easy to get around. The architecture is mostly art deco, I guess because much of it was built in that period in the first part of the 1900s. You will know the iconic pictures of men sitting on iron girders having their lunch suspended high up in the air without any safety harnesses as they built the City, the Empire State Building, the Chrysler Building, the Rockefeller Centre.

The hotel was also next door to the vast Central Park, which seems to carve out an expanse for itself amongst the buildings in the middle of the upper part of town. It is strange how the mind plays tricks and from the air it appears as the opposite to reality, the buildings seeming to be the natural vegetation, sprouting up reaching for the light, out from under the sides of the cover of the park's green blanket laid over top of the buildings' roots beneath.

'My plane was delayed, sorry, I'm pretty tired so I'll probably check-in and get some rest tonight,' I called to my friend from Ahmed's black town car ferrying me from the airport.

'No problem, buddy,' Richard drawled excitedly; I loved how enthusiastic he was, his energy was infectious and it made me smile. 'We'll meet for breakfast tomorrow, buddy.'

'OK, where should I meet you?'

'You should go to the top of the World Trade Centre,' chimed in Ahmed, 'I work there, it's going to be a beautiful day tomorrow.'

'Did you get that Richard,' I asked down the phone, 'Mohammed's nephew says it's going to be a beautiful day tomorrow.'

'That it is, buddy, that it is!' declared Richard.

'God, you even sound like a local New Yorker now,' I teased him, 'I'll see you tomorrow.'

And so I came to wake on 11th September 2001 in New York. The day the Towers came down, the day they say the world changed.

Although I had been tired last night from the trip, I was still pretty much on British time which was five hours ahead of the East coast of America. I had slept well but it was only 4am.

I dressed in my running kit and pulled on my training shoes. I took the lift downstairs, walked through the quiet lobby, deserted at this time of the morning save for one solitary soul behind the reception desk who returned my nod of the head in greeting and I ran into the darkness. I crossed the road and jogged into Central Park. Night was giving way to day quickly now and it was, indeed, going to be a beautiful sunny day.

After I returned and showered, feeling good with the world and excited at the prospect of seeing my old friend again, I took the metro subway train to the World Trade Centre. I preferred New York's system to London's outdated underground trains from the Victorian era. Neither was as clean nor as efficient as the MTR in Hong Kong, the mass transit railway system that links underground across that island and beneath the harbour to Kowloon but New York's system had an immense character, perhaps it had something to do with all the different movies I had seen it appear in, subconsciously making it seem more romantic, or I fancy it was more to do with the wide variety of life that hustled and bustled down here, the businessmen and women, the young students, the families, the lovers, the prostitutes and the vagrants, all together in one great lively colony living under the artificial strip lamps, a different race living beneath the human cousins above.

I got out a few stops early to walk through the West Village and watch New York as it was preparing itself for the day. I was purposely early so I could take in some atmosphere of this place that I loved so much before I met him, as then I knew the rest of the day would become lost to our discussions.

I came out from underground and blinked as my eyes adjusted to the brightness from the sky above.

Across the street in front of the building opposite, I saw the street vendor behind his stand selling pretzels to a chubby guy in a suit who looked like he had probably had too many of these each morning already, the young mother who stopped her push-chair to pick up the soft toy which her young daughter had just dropped and then.....

I heard a roar and, suddenly, I caught a fleeting glimpse of shining metal before it passed behind the dense wall of buildings above, a large silver bird set against a glorious blue sky, making a strangely beautiful sight, a mask of the true horror of its purpose about to unfold.

I stopped, 'That was low,' I said out loud, the words sucked out from within by my surprise, for I hardly had time to take in all these impressions before an enormous wall of sound unlike anything ever heard, the explosion of a thousand sins and the wailing protests of the gods in whose name the murderous act was supposedly made.

Only later would I see those now infamous pictures on television as the plane banked over the Hudson River in those beautiful clear blue, early morning skies before the first plane ploughed into the tower.

I thanked god and fate that the terrorists did not choose to attack later that morning when I would have been up there, up at the very top, in the restaurant with no escape.

My first reaction was to run towards it, to run to see what was happening, but as I started to get nearer, there was panic, everywhere, people running towards me, running away from the disaster. It soon became clear that I would not be able to go closer and, even if I could, that was probably not such a good idea so I turned and started to make my way, quickly, back to the hotel.

The subway had stopped so I would have to walk. I tried to call Richard but I could not get through. All the mobile phone networks were down, crashed in the confusion of a million simultaneous attempted calls.

I hoped he was alright, that he had not arrived early for our meeting. I hoped he was not already up there. I tried to call his wife; the phones would not work.

On my way back to my hotel, I could intermittently just make out the tops of the towers and could see smoke plumes rising into the clear blue air.

I reached the hotel and entered the lobby; the same lobby that earlier was empty and peaceful as I went for my run; the same lobby that later would become full of people seeking cover like refugees covered in a sandy dust.

Now, the scene was of people rushing from all over to cram into the bar to watch the televisions to see the pictures and hear the messages of the news channels. The images on the screens were of both towers smashed and burning after they, by now, had each been hit by different aircraft. Planes full of innocent passengers. Buildings with innocent workers, innocent tourists, young and old, enjoying the beautiful new morning, not knowing it would be their last - people of all races, faiths, religions, creeds and colours.

We saw people hanging out of windows waving for the miraculous rescue of an action movie, flames lapping around the steel framework, seeking them out, coming ever-closer; we saw the flutter of white papers fluttering on the breeze, free now, escaped from the inferno within and we saw dark black objects falling faster, the bodies of people jumping with no chance of any escape for themselves.

My initial feeling was one of anger, it was one of war.

My initial reaction was to fight, to find these people who had committed this wicked act, whoever they may be, these murderous people, to fight them and to fight those who helped them, those who harboured them and those who funded them.

But then.....then, the towers collapsed.

A gasp went up from all in the bar, an uncontrolled, reflex action to what we had all just witnessed and, for a brief moment, all went quiet. A shockwave, enormous in its magnitude and silence, rolled through us all standing there in the hotel lobby as we all struggled to comprehend what had just happened, to believe that what we thought we had just seen had, indeed, truly happened, a horror that never before could have been imagined.

It was early afternoon in England and Louisa, thousands of miles away, watched as the towers fell, screaming at the television. She knew Dan was meeting Richard there that morning; he had told her the night before.

His phone would not work but she knew he would be there. Why would his phone not work? It must be buried, with him. Her thoughts were not of war or of retribution; or revenge, they were only of grief, of anguish so great it hurt, as it punched its way inside her and ripped her insides apart but merciless as it was, leaving her still alive just so it could send another wave to rip her open again each time her consciousness returned to think of the realities of the day, to think of what must have become of her Dan.

For her, this was true horror at its worst, her mind imaging the most terrible things whilst witnessing the images in her living room, not knowing, unable to do anything.

At the time the first plane struck, Ahmed was standing at the window of his office on the twentieth floor of Tower One, looking out over the Hudson River, admiring the bright blue sky, enjoying the warmth of the sunshine in the knowledge that summer must soon end.

Suddenly, a deathly shadow appeared over his world, accompanied by a terrible roar. His heart stopped and he jumped to the floor in an instinctive reaction, the apparent speed of an airliner hurtling towards you being far more intense than the gentle glide seen by those watching on television. The plane smashed but ten floors above him, exploding, shaking the building as if in an almighty earthquake.

Ahmed picked himself up from the floor and opened the door to his office to go out to the main area; all around people were screaming, shouting, panic was moving in the air. Fear was not his overriding impression, his main thoughts were of confusion.

'We have to get out,' he heard someone shout rushing to the lobby.

'Don't take the lifts,' shouted Ahmed instinctively, 'take the stairs.'

He looked around him. 'Quick,' he gestured to his fellow workers, 'come on. We should get out, then we can find out what's going on.'

His PA filed past him plus his friend Luke and his secretary and their boss. 'Is that everybody?' demanded Ahmed.

'I don't know. I'm not sure,' was his boss's reply.

'I'll go check, you make sure everyone goes down the stairs. I'll catch up,' stated Ahmed and he headed off round the corner to ensure everyone had left. Sure enough, the girl from accounts was still, conscientiously, trying to gather together items of work she may need.

'Leave them,' demanded Ahmed. 'Quick! We've got to go now.'

Thankfully, she heeded his call as the natural impulse of flight took over with a fright growing with every new thunderous sound of an explosion and tremble of the building. It had become clear that this event was not yet at an end.

They quickly ran to the stairwell and were surprised by the scene that greeted them, of the wounded and those in shock, of the people shouting and those sobbing, of a war zone.

A man collapsed as he came round the corner of the stairs above him, crying in pain as he fell down holding his leg, bloodied and broken.

'Here let me help you,' shouted Ahmed, going back up the stairs to him he lifted him up and put his arm around his slender shoulders. They made their way, slowly, shuffling down the stairs.

The man was from an office five floors above Ahmed's own. When the plane hit apparently the ceilings had burst open, debris flying everywhere as shrapnel had scattered its way around the room like a cluster bomb, finding targets everywhere. People were still up there, hurt, unable to move unaided. They needed help, a fire had started, from the ceiling. They needed help.

'Medic, medic,' Ahmed shouted as he emerged from the stairwell into the foyer of the building with the man. There was some fire officers. 'This guy's hurt, he needs help and he says there are others still up there, hurt, unable to move. Quick, we've got to help them.' Turning around Ahmed rushed back up into the stairwell to see who else he could help.

He would not come out.

By the time I saw the second tower collapse, the loud protest and shouts of rage that had preceded the first tower's fall had now been replaced by speechless astonishment, by sobbing, by a deep shock that come over us all. Some people left to try to find their way back to homes in the suburbs, others left just to find a way off Manhattan, off the Island, unable to watch the events unfolding on the screens any further, trying to protect themselves from what surely could not be happening if they were not watching, from this dream worse than any nightmare could possibly be.

In deep reflection now, my thoughts had turned; how could things have become this bad, so bad that humans would exterminate their own brothers and sisters, so indiscriminately, not even knowing the identities of their victims?

I could not understand. How could things have become like this? How could man plan such an horrendous crime against man? Over and over I struggled with it, my mind in shock, in turmoil, continually asking myself that same question, and, I saw the vision of the future, an apocalyptic sight but not the dark alien horsemen of the apocalypse pictured in Hollywood films, nor some plague of locusts or the earth shattering apart no, my premonition was for a future of man in a continual fight against himself, a battle set against a sky fire-red, of an earth ablaze with man's rage, his blood-lust in his thirst for a vengeance that could never be quenched and with no chance now of the fire ever being put out man was caught in a spiral, never-ending, battling his fellow man; man was destroying mankind.

Through my incomprehension, from my vision of what the apocalypse was, how the end of the world would arrive, how we would destroy ourselves, through this incomprehension, a clarity came over me that we could not carry on like this, that it had to stop.

We had to be brave enough to stand up for what we believe in the face of aggression, so that the aggressor's crimes are revealed for all to see for the evil they truly are when contrasted against the outstretched unarmed arms of his victims, rather than to be given some corroboration by retaliatory violence that somehow dilutes the original evil. Surely, we needed reconciliation, not confrontation. We had to wage kindness, not war; we had to wage love.

We should try to reason, to persuade; you do not win debates with fists.

Perhaps, if mankind were to reach out in peace, not revenge, all would come to understand that the terrorists' acts were not heroic; they were indiscriminate, they killed people of all faiths and of all races, mothers, brothers, daughters, sons.

Ahmed was a devout Muslim but the terrorists did not worry about who they would kill that day, even if they were of their own faith, and Ahmed did not worry that day that the man he carried down so many flights of stairs to safety was not a Muslim, or what religion or race would be the people he rushed back into the building to also try and save. He did not even think to look at such criteria; he just tried to save his fellow man, brothers, sisters. He did what came instinctively to him, without thinking, he followed what his natural urges demanded of him, he acted with the natural urges of humanity.

So who was the true standard bearer for their faith that day, Ahmed or the terrorists, who was the best example of all that is good in their religion's values? This was not protest, it was not religious, it was not war, even. It was criminal, an act against all humanity, regardless of colour, creed or religion.

Why are so many cruel acts perpetrated in the name of religion? It has ever been thus but why should it be so, do not all religions essentially preach the same message of love and peace towards our fellow man? Does love preach the demolition of buildings, the waging of wars across continents? Are all religions essentially love, essentially the same? Are all gods, if any even exist, essentially the same?

This was, indeed, an horrific atrocity, one that shook the world, but did it justify dropping a bomb that might kill even one innocent child, an innocent man or woman, another human being. They are not soldiers; they had not chosen the path of terrorism anymore than you or I.

Close your eyes a moment, imagine a woman, standing at her window, looking out at the trees. Her young child is sitting at the table in the shade, drawing a picture, of her and his father, of their family. Maybe she waves as the father turns to go on his way to his work, just going about his daily business, as usual. Suddenly, with no warning, the blast of an explosion, as a bomb rips through the apartment, rips through their lives, leaving the father without a wife, without his son. Now open your eyes and imagine this scene is in New York's Greenwich Village, or London's Kensington, or in your neighbourhood, your building.

The family were not to know that a terrorist hid in their building, in one of the apartments on the floors above. The family was not to blame.

Would the western leaders sanction such an indiscriminate tool for surgery in their own lands, just because a terrorist hid there?

Then why should that become acceptable overseas? Do we now execute the children for the sins of their fathers? Was that justice?

How could it ever lead to any resolution, breeding more anger and hatred, an anger which could never be satisfied, a bloodlust that could never be sated?

Helping the terrorists recruit more poor young men rushing to them, to fight for the cause, to be martyrs because of the murders of their sleeping babies by an unseen missile from far away.

Now, imagine the new-born hatred of the recently widowed father grieving for his lost wife and son and the newly-found hatred of his dead wife's father and her brothers, a hatred, not of the terrorists but a hatred of those who sent the murderous bombs, a hatred so raw so fierce, a wish for revenge, to last a thousand years or more. The revenge of a perpetual cycle to end mankind forever.....

Unless any were strong enough to stand up and say, 'Stop! Enough. This is wrong.' Unless, any were strong enough not to escalate the violence but instead to reach out to their foreign cousins, to reach out with help and understanding, to reach out with love.

Show them there can be a better way, better for all, a world without terrorism. Then no-one would want to harbour these criminals, no-one would want to join them to be martyrs to such a murderous cause and the world, maybe, would have a chance to unite behind this great atrocity and the world would have a chance for peace.

225

Just as with the parable of how the sun beats the strong wind to persuade the man to take off his coat, with warmth rather than by force, that was the approach this huge problem demanded.

The western leaders took their countries into a war in which all would lose but the terrorists, with more poor young souls becoming disciples to their cause. If only those leaders had more vision.

I did not know it then, of course, but a few months later, over two million people would come out to march in London in response to the folly of the war in Iraq upon which their leaders were about to embark.

A staggering amount of people voted without any ballot papers. They voted with their feet, hundreds of thousands of them, factory workers, businessmen, musicians, salesmen, shop workers, farmers, football fans, truckers, people from all walks of life, here they all stood side by side, individuals each mobilised by their own conscience. They came together as one great voice but their voice was not heard by their leaders. Or, perhaps, it was heard but ignored. They chose not to listen. Is that what democracy is?

As I got back into the safety of my hotel bed that night of 11th September 2001, I thought about timing and of choices, the choices we make and what fate has in store for us, our karma.

But for another thirty minutes or so, my friend and I could have been at the top of the World Trade Centre when the planes struck and I would probably not be here anymore.

Much as with our honeymoon in Thailand where but for a few minutes, if that wave had arrived just before, when Louisa and I had been swimming, we surely would have perished, caught beneath its unrelenting advance, unable to escape in time.

In the context of the age of our universe, the vast amount of time, millions of years since earth's creation, the margin of our escape from such a prehistoric event was so negligible but also so great, it was everything, the difference between life and death, the difference between our children's very existence, their very being. Once again, a small space in the erratic vagaries of time had saved me from a different fate.

'The waging of peace is the hardest form of leadership of all.' - HRH Queen Elizabeth II, UN address, July 2010.

FAITH

Fate, karma, is it real? Can it possibly be so? There is nothing to prove it exists but the idea, surely, is too difficult to ignore. It knows no boundaries, prevalent in disparate cultures and ancient civilisations, present in the minds of men in distant places spread across different sides of the globe. The idea that some events were destined, meant to be, their fate, their karma.

There are echoes in conflicting religions; believers in divine gods, whatever god that may be, say all things happen as part of their god's will, all part of a bigger plan. Religious faiths urge their followers not to doubt just because some people suffer, to keep their faith, as their god has a reason behind these events.

Or is there really no fate but of that we make ourselves? If so, what of the events beyond our control; we cannot control everything - the illnesses, the actions of others, how do we explain these? Are they predetermined, destined to happen?

More and more, I had come now to contemplate my faith; what was it, did I even have any, what did I believe in?

I know not whether any religion can be real, Islam, Christian, Hindu, which is correct. But their faith is real, faiths that often share at least a common theme, one of love.

Is it not strange that in a world where men go to war in the name of peace; go to war in the name of religion or money or power and in a world where men argue over politics and human rights, in this world there is one thing that man can agree on – and that is the feeling of love.

I do sometimes look up at the sky, at the clouds, at the stars and offer some words, perhaps asking for advice, seeking answers, or perhaps offering thanks, whether to a person real or not, to a god maybe or to someone now lost, a granddad or uncle, it does not really matter for always, the words are with love.

I suppose we all come to consider what our beliefs may be at some point, as we begin to consider our own mortality. I know Louisa's mother would often say, just like Louisa's grandfather before, that she did not believe in any god but growing up in a catholic school I suppose she must have believed at some point as a little girl, maybe, as a young nurse starting out in a life of caring for others or perhaps as a new parent. She surely had some faith then, before the cruelness of the harsh world infected the pureness of her young innocence.

She never said why she no longer believed, why she had lost her faith but I do know she lost her sister early, too early, so unfair a young mother leaving behind two young children, too young to have no mother.

I do not know if that is why she had no faith but Louisa's mother would simply say that there could not be any god if bad things happen to the good and the evil are left to do their harm, and so, for every child that was taken or molested by someone evil, for every earthquake that caused death and destruction, as far as Louisa's mother was concerned, it was just yet more proof of the lack of any god. There cannot be any god, she reasoned, because her god would not let that happen.

Later, we would find that Louisa's sister, Lucy, was also diagnosed as having breast cancer. Starting as small pains in her arm, innocuous twinges you may neglect, being caused by this invisible killer. She had two young children, also too young to have no mother.

All her mother's worst fears returned. The disease thirty years before had taken her sister but left her behind. The part of her where their love had been, replaced with an irrational guilt for being the one spared. Now the killer had returned to try to take something even more precious, her daughter. How could she stop it? How could she get it to take her instead? But she had no control over it. There was nothing she could do, nothing, except pray. So she prayed, every day and almost every hour of every day, her anxiety never leaving her. She made pacts with God, 'Save my daughter and take me, I'm old.' 'Save my daughter and I will never doubt you again.' This time there was a happy ending; her daughter survived.

So did she now have some faith? I do not know but I know she must still believe in something; she loved her children, she most certainly did believe in love. She still had some faith, her faith was *love*.

NATURE'S WAY

Following the success of the Venetian hotel, we had just opened a second *La Vita* in London. Mohammed and our investors were very happy and keen to expand the roll-out of the brand across the world. It was all very exciting and becoming very glamorous but I decided I needed to take some time to spend with the family.

So to escape the grey Irish weather, we had decided to pass Christmas in the snow on a skiing holiday with the children. It was just following our return that Louisa first started to get the headaches.

What a wonderful time we had spent, simply enjoying the opportunity of free time alone with our children over the holidays, away from the small trials and tribulations of daily life which seem so vitally important when they are upon you that they cannot wait.

I have always loved the mountains, unusual it may seem for someone who mostly leads his life rushing from one project to the next, driving, flying, hurtling around the world, it is only when I am in the mountains that I seem to be able to stop and take a while, to take some extra time.

I love snow; it is a mythical, magical substance, particularly when its falling in big fluffy flakes that seem too impossibly dry and light. When the sun shines in the early morning on newly fallen snow, it positively sparkles like a carpet of twinkling crystals laid out invitingly and the air full of diamond dust, sparkling and dancing before you.

Mostly, you ski above the tree-line but, occasionally, you come across a group of pine trees, standing tall on a ridge, like sentinels guarding the precious valley beyond, a beautiful backcountry so peaceful if you did venture off, away from the crowds, only with a guide, of course.

One of the things I enjoy about winter holidays is that I do not have to just lie in the sun all day, bored, doing nothing; or restless, wondering, 'what am I going to do now?' No, in the mountains, I am up straight away and out onto the slopes for the first tracks and with the children we have something that we can do together, enjoying each other's company, sharing experiences; no doubt there would come a time when they will be too quick and want to do too much for us, leaving Louisa and I to simply lunch long in the strong mountain sunshine.

Louisa loved the sun and she liked to stop for coffee, often!

We had taken to visiting Gstaad in Switzerland, a place as pretty as a picture as you could ever imagine, relaxed and refined.

The family's accommodation to me was to rise to be up with the first lifts after nine in the morning and our accommodation to Louisa was to stop by ten at the Eggli bar. A beautiful wooden chalet, the Eggli was full of typical rustic Swiss style and Louisa would always be the first into their sunloungers in the most exposed sunny part. The prices for drinks were expensive but a small price to pay to ensure that our Louisa was happy and settled in the best seat in the Alps.

From that base, the children and I would set off to ski the mountainside and return to check if she felt like coming out with us or wanted to remain in her sunbed; it was often the latter.

The weather was kind to us, not too cold and with much sunshine to keep Louisa happy. She still skied a little more than maybe she would have liked, trying that little bit harder than usual, otherwise the children were going to improve way beyond her abilities; Charlotte, now thirteen, her sister Jade, eleven, were already faster and better than their mum and even their brother, Jensen, at ten was almost on a par in ability and, with the daredevil nature of boys that age, he was never the slowest.

This break seemed so wonderfully perfect, so relaxing. Towards the end of the week Louisa and I were sat in the sun loungers outside the Eggli, taking in the warmth of brilliant mountain sunshine watching the children play in the snow that bordered the terrace. I turned my head to one side to look at her.

'You know, since we first met, I've been all around the world, eaten in the best restaurants, had the finest wines.....'

'And girls,' she interrupted, laughing.

'Built exciting businesses,' I went on, ignoring her, 'lived in beautiful homes, shopped in the nicest stores but sitting here now, like this, outside with you and the children, I'm beginning to realise that I don't really need very much to be happy.'

'You're happy now are you, managing to relax?' she asked knowing it was unusual for me to do so.

'Yes, I believe I am,' I replied. 'Just like our first summer, I was so happy back then, walking in the hills, sitting in the parks; it takes something like this to make you realise it's the simple things that are the best.'

'Good,' she smiled, her eyes closing as she soaked up the sunshine, she added laughing, 'But don't think you can stop buying me jewellery though!'

She then continued, 'So what's next? What are you going to do now the London hotel's going well?' she asked. 'Milan, Paris, look again at New York, I suppose?'

I turned again and surprised her, 'I thought maybe I'd spend some more time with you, perhaps finally get to grips with some of the things in our garden.' I went on, 'I thought we could take some more time for ourselves, go on that safari maybe, do some of the things that we keep putting off.'

Louisa was excited, sceptical, of course, that I would get distracted, consumed by some other new project, another hotel opening but excited and happy nonetheless.

'I love you,' I said and leaned over and kissed her. She looked beautiful with her long dark hair falling down, framing her face glowing with a slight suntan of the mountains, the sun being very strong up here in the rarefied atmosphere and with so much reflective white of the snow.

'I've never loved you more,' she whispered.

So after seven fun-filled days we regretfully returned to our home in Ireland, ready to start another New Year.

I know Louisa had sometimes struggled to keep up with us skiing on the trip but there was nothing particularly unusual about that and we were all so exhausted from the day's exertions and the mountain air that Louisa and I regularly fell asleep early each evening while watching a movie and left the children to put themselves to bed.

I remember that Louisa did sometimes say she felt a little out of breath but again, there was nothing particularly unusual about that when pushing yourself to race around a mountainside which you only did for seven days each year.

Once or twice she mentioned she was getting the onset of a headache, innocuous, the occasional migraine-type headache was also nothing particularly new.

It was only when we returned to England that things became a little strange.

Initially, the headaches seemed to become more frequent, but what is a migraine anyway? It is just an annoying headache that will pass, right?

I was not even aware at first as, mostly, Louisa would put herself to bed in a dark room whilst I was at work and the children at school.

Yes, she sometimes seemed more irritable than normal and 'short' with the children in the evening but that was just the end of a tiring day, wasn't it?

It was only one Saturday afternoon, in late January, pulling out weeds in the garden that things changed for the worst when, for no apparent reason, Louisa started to be violently ill, vomiting profusely and complaining of feeling very faint and very cold.

She confessed that a similar thing had happened to her the previous day and thought it must have been due to something she had eaten. We had been to a seafood restaurant with some friends earlier during the week so maybe that was the reason. Come Monday, she was still being ill so that was not the answer after-all.

I took her to the doctors and they asked if she was pregnant? But they gave her some antibiotics, in case it was food poisoning.

She improved during that week but a week later, it started again. Only, if possible, somehow it was worse. Again, it was a week-end, again, we waited to see the doctor on the Monday. 'Are you sure you're not pregnant?' 'Yes, I'm sure.' 'Well, then it must be due to last week's food poisoning, the bug must still be inside you.' More antibiotics.

The third time it happened, we insisted she be sent to hospital for more checks.

'Well, if you insist' said the GP, somewhat terse at the time being wasted by this fussy woman and her oversensitive husband.

By the time Louisa had her scan at the hospital, she had already slipped into a coma. There was no time for the doctors to usher me into some office and to tell me as they do on the television; 'We have found a lump. It's in her head. It's attached to her brain. We will have to operate. Don't worry, we have a fantastic surgeon. It's amazing what they can do these days.'

No, there was no time for any of that, Louisa was already in a coma from what I did not know.

'Your wife has a brain tumour. We have to rush her now to a different hospital,' they saw my face, the disbelief clearly evident. 'They have a specialist neurological unit there. Quick, jump in the ambulance with her.'

'Now? But I don't understand. What's wrong with her? Is she going to be alright?'

'They'll tell you more when you get there.'

As a young boy, even as an older boy, you always imagine the thrill of speeding along, sirens wailing, blue lights flashing, that is the dream; that may be fun in a police car chasing the bad guys, or in a fire engine racing to save lives and to put out a fire, but the reality, sat in the back of an ambulance with someone you love, rushing to save their life with nothing you can do, except hold her hand, limp now in this unusual sleep, this unwanted sleep. The reality is that you want that siren to stop, you wish with everything you have that you could arrive immediately. Every ounce of blood pulses, every sinew strains, but you cannot move, you cannot do anything to make it any quicker. You tell yourself, 'Everything's going to be alright. It has to be. It's amazing what they can do these days.'

They operated immediately; the surgeon said she would not have made it through the night otherwise, if there had been any more delay. The tumour and the cyst were the size of a fist but he was confident he had got it all.

It was now March. We should be seeing the bright colours signalling the start of Spring with the return of the sun's warmth but it felt very cold.

I told the girls first and asked them to be strong when we later told Jensen.

'So, is she going to die?' asked Jade, slowly.

Charlotte said nothing, the first drops of tears started and she buried her head into my shoulder.

'Don't worry, mummy's going to be just fine,' I said. I tried to sound convincing for them, absolute.

I wished I knew that for sure, 'She has to be alright,' I pleaded to myself. The surgeon said he had got it all. I had promised the children. She had to be alright.

I was scared, a strange emotion to have when it was not my life in danger. If I was scared, Louisa must have been very frightened, even though she did not show it. I tried to push my fear away for her sake and for the children, I tried to appear strong, but, all the while, I felt helpless.

I could not control this, just like gliding down the motorway those years before, if only I had some control, if only I could drive the cancer away to a different place, out from her body. But unlike our experience in the car, where the loss of control was transient, this feeling would not leave, it would not pass.

If only I could do something to help. But what could I do? How could I help?

We researched the internet, searching for a miracle cure that the amazingly intelligent and gifted surgeons may have somehow missed. It felt better to be doing something, anything to try and gain some control over this thing. Where had it come from? Why did no-one know what it was? But if our doctors were not sure what this type of cancer was, how could we do any meaningful research?

So, I prayed. I prayed for Louisa to be alright; I prayed for the surgeons to save her. I prayed to a god; to which god, I did not know. I prayed to all gods, to the almighty, whatever his true name may be, God, Allah, to the divine, for the help of a Buddha. I prayed to any god that would help me. I prayed for everything to go back to the way it had been; I prayed, 'Take me. Take me instead.'

In the days after the operation it was amazing how quickly Louisa seemed to get back to her old self, smiling and laughing and , incredibly, she was back home with us inside a week.

But then came the radiotherapy. First, Louisa had her long hair cut short in anticipation of the hair loss but even so, when it did, inevitably, fall out she was, of course, still upset, just as any girl would be.

And now she became very tired with the combined effect of the strong drugs they were giving her and the doses of radiation. She struggled to do anything without feeling out of breath and tired. After the elation and euphoria of the brightness that was the post-op Louisa, we were not ready for this setback, we were not prepared for this. This did not seem like our Louisa., but despite the struggle, she was happy, happy to be with us, happy to be with her children, happy to be living life.

After the end of the radiotherapy course, Louisa had an MRI scan to check and the doctors told us that they could see no trace of the tumour; they were happy with their patient. The surgeon had cut out all of the lump; she had been shot at with radiation and they would check that it had not come back with a scan every 3 months. She would be in remission for five years and then, she would have the all-clear; she would be a survivor.

Louisa's hair was growing back and now she had stopped taking some of the drugs, she was no longer so tired. Everything was going well.

Almost exactly a year since the ambulance ride that rushed her, in her coma, to the operating theatre, we returned, happy and smiling, to see the consultant oncologist for the results of her latest routine scan.

'The tumour is back.' A dark freight train crashed into our world. No-one was prepared for that.

You do not always remember well what is said in circumstances such as this. It is all a bit hazy and afterwards you wish you had asked more questions, questions you had rehearsed but disappear as your mind goes blank and you do not react in the way you expect.

Nobody said out loud how aggressive the cancer must have been to have returned. Nobody said it; but we all thought it.

'We will operate again.'

'In two weeks.'

We had not been ready for this. All had been going so well. This could not be right. There must be some mistake. For me, the feeling of helplessness returned, sliding once again down a cancerous motorway, nothing to do but to once more make my pacts with god. But which god? Any god that will listen.

Where previously all had happened so quickly, the operation coming whilst she was asleep in her coma, this time Louisa did have the chance to reflect, time to think about the people she would leave behind, about her children. This time she did have that opportunity, time to worry.

Once more, the operation went well, the tumour was removed and this time she would undergo a course of intensive chemotherapy in conjunction with the radiotherapy which she would have to endure again, stronger this time.

But, this time, Louisa did not recover so quickly; this time, she did not come home within a week. She seemed always to be so weak, always so tired and, with difficulty eating, she was slow to gain strength; she seemed to be making little progress.

It was frustrating, specialists operating out of different hospitals and often, no-one seemed to know what to do, how to care for our beloved Louisa.

Three weeks later she was still in hospital and supposed to have started her course of chemotherapy; the poison to kill the killer, a poison they needed to put in her but that in itself would make her violently sick. Was she ready for this? Was she strong enough? There was now no choice, she could not wait while the evil killer inside her marched onwards, unrelenting.

I looked at her in the bed. She was now so small, so frail, but, despite it being so difficult, her spirit burned bright, still the spark shone inside.

My mind drifted to the summer we had first met. I pictured her laughing as we walked along the seafront, still laughing after I had pushed the ice cream into her face.

'I knew,' she whispered, a faint breath reaching up to me slowly from the bed below.

'Knew what?'

'When I first met you, I knew I would be with you for the rest of my life. In the bar I knew our love had met before, somewhere. Perhaps, it will do again, somewhere, someday. Nothing loved is ever really lost.' Her voice was hoarse, it was difficult for her to speak now or even to move she had so little strength but she seemed determined to let me know this.

'I knew too,' I lent down and kissed the top of her head, tenderly, as I gently stroked her hair.

'Take my hand, you asked me once,' she whispered, 'in your poem at our wedding. Now, please, take my hand again,' she asked, lifting it slightly towards me. I knew this must have taken her a lot of effort and I grasped her hand tight, massaging it with my other, I bent down to kiss it gently. As she fell asleep she murmured, so quietly I could barely make it out, 'When were you most happy Dan? Please do it, for me, please be happy.'

I awoke with a chill. It was cold. I looked at my watch and again gave a brief smile as I remembered how she had given it to me. It was just past five in the morning. Through the window I could see the sun rising, a beautiful fireball just emerging above the horizon.

I still had on my shoes from the night before; I had clambered on top of the small single hospital bed to cuddle her, still holding her hand as she had asked.

Groggily, waking up, I recalled how she had silently nuzzled her head onto my tummy and I had stroked her hair, just as we had done at the end of *our* summer on the top of a cliff many years before. There she was, with her beautiful face still snuggled into me, the sweet smile remaining still on her pink lips; she was my *Aphrodite*.

I stroked her hair again, in the way I had done many times before, and I knew; I knew, instinctively, that she had gone away. I did not call the nurse; I did not cry; I just lay with her, stroking her hair, enjoying her embrace and I gripped her hand ever more tightly.

And so, my beautiful Louisa was taken from me, taken by some invisible, unrelenting enemy that I could not confront. My wonderful wife; the mother of my beautiful children. My best friend. This hurts; Love hurts. So, now I know love surely exists, yes, just a word; but love is a yell for it is the connection, the emotion we feel to it.

Now, I know love is real.

It is so difficult, impossible even, to try to make any sense of a tragic loss, the unfairness of a life lost too soon, of the unanswerable question, 'Why?'

It is so difficult to fight past the grief; I do try instead to see the joy they had brought, I do try to remember all the good they had done, all the people they touched, the people to whom they brought a smile, those to whom they brought joy, the joy of love.

For, surely, is the value of a life best measured not by the time spent on earth, by the length of that life but rather by the influence, the contribution, the guidance and the happiness they have brought. Surely, with some people's presence, a whisper can indeed be more enduring than a shout.

I try to take comfort in the thought that, perhaps, some people are sent to show us how precious life is. Of course, we will still say that it makes no sense; we will still ask why? What is the reason?

But what if their influence had been enough? We being the better for having had them, even briefly, in our lives than not at all, to help us, to guide us. What if they are as our Angels?

Ours had been a wonderful love story, a long enduring journey together. By their very nature, all love stories must, eventually, come to an end but, perhaps, love survives, love endures and, maybe, love truly can conquer all.

So, this was our ending. Even though, increasingly over the past few weeks, I had known this day would come, nothing could still prepare me for it.

How fragile is life and what we do. One moment all can be fantastic, the next as bad as it can be. What a wonderful holiday we had been having, what a great time with the children, skiing the Christmas before she became ill. We had all been so happy and I was so at peace at last with my life. Only a few days later that world to be turned completely upside down by something unforeseen, completely out of our control. Yes, it was sad. Yes, there was a great hole in my life after my ever-present companion was suddenly gone, my confidante; my sounding-board, the constant in my forever changing world.

What would I do without her? She made me.

But I had to keep myself together. I had to for the children, our beautiful children. They were her legacy, her contribution to this world, to this life and I had to for Louisa; that is what she would have wanted. To let it all fall apart would be a failing, a failing of all she had done for us, all she had given us. I had to go on.

At the beginning of each day I see the pictures of her in the house and I have been thinking should I move on and get rid of all the things that remind me of her, painful memories? Should I sell the house; throw away all the photos of Louisa and I together? Or maybe I should do the opposite; surround the house with pictures of her from the past? Embrace the change?

I find her still in the garden she loved so, in the shadows of the bushes as I remember things she had said or done in different parts of our garden, the argument in the orchard, her joy at the marrows she had grown that took over the greenhouse. I see her in the blooms of the roses she pruned and trained every year and I try not to be too sad when the petals fall, their time, also, now at an end.

But most of all, I see her in the eyes of our children.

Perhaps her spirit, and maybe mine, would continue and endure within them and even in their children, nature's circle of life. As surely as one day dies, another is born, also to be enjoyed.

Yes, there would be pain when I thought of her, but also much joy. Yes, it would be tough, and, yes, I would miss her, but, I would remember all that she had done and I knew I was better for having met her, for having had her in my life, to help me, to guide me. She was doing it still, maybe now even more than ever. Louisa had, surely, been our Angel.

She was my Angel.

I picked up the phone.

It was time.

I dialled the number my mother had left Louisa those months before.

THE WONDERFUL JOURNEY

Recently, I returned to Paris; a black limousine brought me into the drive outside of the Ritz Hotel in Place Vendome. It was early evening, the fairy lights surrounding the white entrance canopies bearing the hotel's famous name were sparkling in the twilight.

It reminded me of that night, so many years before when we had pulled into the Hilton in Hong Kong.

I had not arrived then as I had thought.

I was just beginning!

Life – bold, dark, rich, always an experience, offering up opportunities, chances, choices. Life is a constant journey, always arriving, forever travelling.

I had not made it all those times before; that first night I arrived in Hong Kong or when we married in Ireland, not even when we opened the new hotels in Venice and then London. You never really do make it; you never win; I realised that now. No, the trick was to enjoy life; Louisa had taught me that.

When we were married, I felt I was as happy as I could ever be, that I had everything I could ever want, but that of course was only the beginning of our lives together, the beginning of that chapter of my life. Of course, the journey of love is not so simple, or clear, or straightforward, that is why it is a journey to be enjoyed, to be cherished for what it may bring.

I sometimes feel like I have lived five or six different lives already.

Maybe, like a cat, I still have three or four more chapters to live before it will be my time to have a long sleep.

I just need to make sure the remaining acts of my play are as exciting as the first few and I will be able to go to my rest content that I have truly enjoyed life.

The girls are growing up to be young ladies now. Their brother is full of joy, kicking a ball or running around the garden with his beaming smile. They never cease to surprise me with the things they do. I do not know what the future has in store for my children and I do not know how I can help them, how I can protect them. I know I cannot control it and I know I should not try too hard to do so. All I know is that I have to let them live it, and encourage them, whatever they choose to do, to do it with a passion. To live life, to experience it, to enjoy being themselves, to enjoy the wonderful journey.

The next day I walked once more into the *Jardin des Tuileries*, where I had been all those years before with Louisa. Much was just as I remembered it, rows of plane trees standing in uniform lines stretching from the front of the Louvre.

Early morning in the autumn, this place has an eerie beauty, not the dramatic show of burning colours, of a forest afire, as you may see in the spectacular bright reds and yellows of New England in the fall. No, here, in Paris, the show is less dramatic, more a gentle fade from the greens of summer to pale yellows, browns and burnt oranges, perhaps more in keeping with my own melancholy mood.

I sat on a bench, all alone with my thoughts, the low-light of the late autumn afternoon throwing shadows long across the ground. Like Louisa, the Ferris wheel where I almost proposed has now gone but the trees remain and, like my memories, they endure, everlasting.

High above, a shaft of light burst through the clouds and, incredibly, a flock of swallows swooped down low over my head, giving me a brief display as they fed on the wing.

As I sat staring in my wonder, smiling with the enjoyment of the moment, I thought how birds seemed to have played a significant part in my life, perhaps they are my angels, watching over me, helping me, guiding me. Maybe Louisa was up there with them now. Perhaps she was showing me she remembered the good times.

I smiled as I watched them go and I whispered to them a quiet, *'Thank you, my Angel.'*

****

Thanks

To Vanessa Louise and all my family, Jessica, Gabriella and Leo - I did not know love could be like this and I am learning still its depths, so great they know no limits as it continues to grow every day with a power so exponential to the wonder of some small detail seen, a drawing, a song, a smile, a kiss, a hug; I love you all so very much.

To my parents, sister and brother, my uncle Gordon, a huge inspiration ever-present still and cousins Tim and Nick – brothers in all but title.

I would not change anything for the world, I have been so very lucky.

With special thanks to all those who read the first drafts and encouraged me to keep on writing, in particular, Emma, Matthew, Kirstie, Foster, Rosemary, and, above all, Sarah: without your encouragement for my writing, this story would never have been completed.

With thanks to Paul, Matt, Andy and all those at i-ride.co.uk whose help has enabled this work to happen.

This story is a work of fiction and all characters and events are either the product of the author's imagination or used fictitiously. Any similarity to any person or event is unintended and entirely coincidental.

However, the tragic ending is inspired by a very brave colleague of the author and all readers are urged to donate and support cancer charities to assist in the battle against this terrible disease. If the telling of this story can help in any small way to contribute to the fight, the work will have been very worthwhile.

I would not wish anyone to mistake Ahmed for any of the poor innocent souls who lost their lives in the disaster of the World Trade Centre in September 2001; his story is not real but his fictional character was introduced to demonstrate the indiscriminate nature of the killing that day, contrasted with the overwhelming good that is within human nature.

www.danfox.ch

Jardin des Tuileries

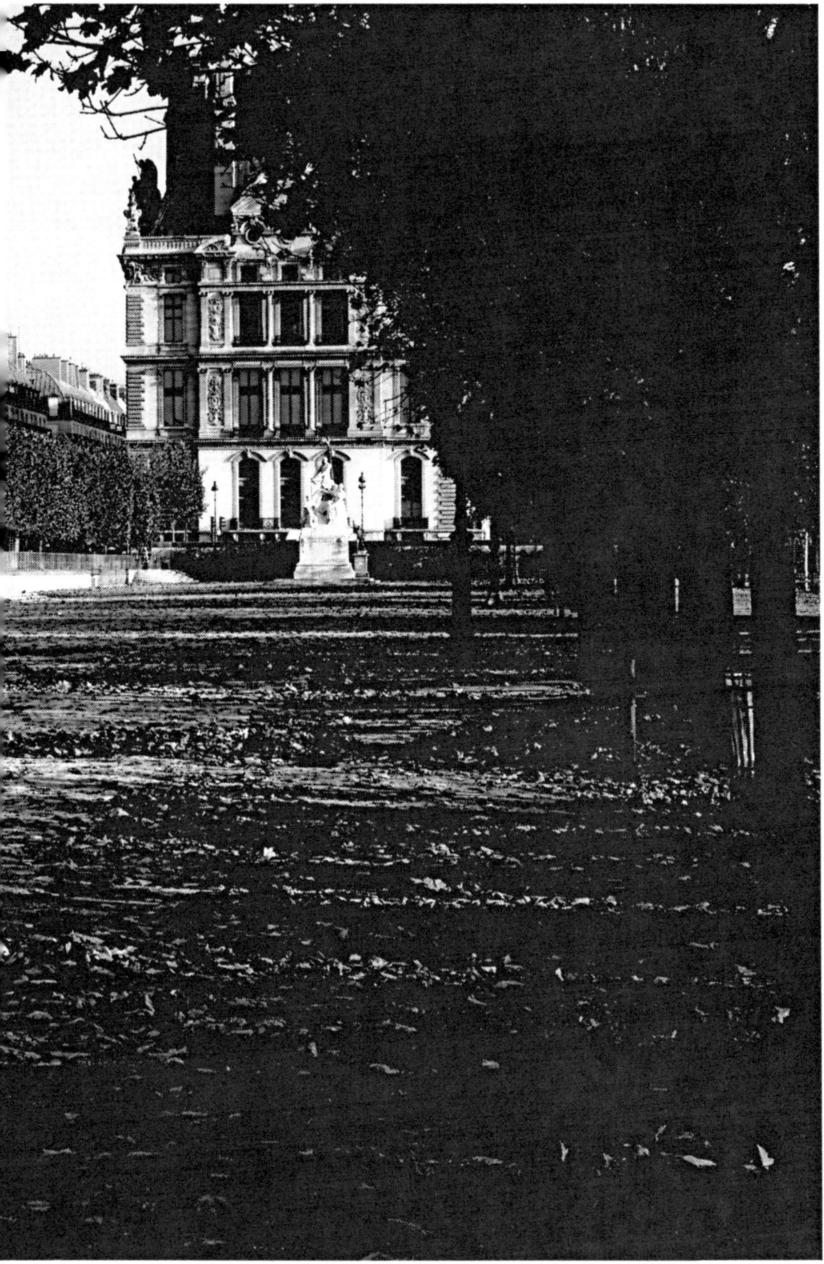

Dan Fox

Nine Lives is the first novel from the author, Dan Fox. The author writes about life, asking questions and provoking thoughts about emotions and feelings that touch us all. He has a distinctive voice, a unique style of writing which flows and is somewhat poetic. With an incredibly honest approach and a certain rawness, his writing gives a deep and meaningful insight into love and life.

Painting pictures with words, his writing takes the reader on an emotional journey containing many reflections on life, so purposely provoking discussion in the reader's mind, a quiet contemplation; but without seeking to give a view - indeed, it is as if the reader is joining the author on a journey of discovery as he finds these different thoughts arriving within him.

Dan Fox is the *nom de plume* of Ian Wilson, a father of three who was born into the typical middle classes of an old English seaside town, Ian left for the bright lights of London as soon as he could and after studying law at King's College London, he spent 8 years in Hong Kong where he soon left behind a legal career as 'too boring' and has since built successful business interests that have taken him all over the globe. He now lives in the mountains of Switzerland.

Nine Lives is his first finished novel, with more projects currently under creation.

Further information can be found at www.danfox,ch

Lightning Source UK Ltd.
Milton Keynes UK
26 March 2011

169854UK00001B/24/P